THE HALFADAY CREEK SERIES BY
JAMES B. HENDRYX

Skullduggery on Halfaday Creek
The Saga of Halfaday Creek
Adventures on Halfaday Creek

Visit www.jamesbhendryx.com for more information on
forthcoming installments in the Halfaday Creek
uniform matching series.

THE SAGA OF HALFADAY CREEK

James B Hendryx

THE SAGA OF HALFADAY CREEK

JAMES B. HENDRYX

ILLUSTRATIONS BY
PETE KUHLHOFF

ALTUS PRESS • 2013

© 2013 Altus Press • First Edition—2013

EDITED AND DESIGNED BY
Matthew Moring

SERIES EXECUTIVE CONSULTANT
Richard Hall

PUBLISHING HISTORY
"Finger Prints" originally appeared in the March 25, 1946 issue of *Short Stories* magazine (vol. 194, no. 6). Reprinted by arrangement with the Estate of James B. Hendryx.

"Black John Advises" originally appeared in the August 10, 1936 issue of *Short Stories* magazine (vol. 155, no. 1). Reprinted by arrangement with the Estate of James B. Hendryx.

"Black John Finds a Missing Heir" originally appeared in the November 10, 1938 issue of *Short Stories* magazine (vol. 165, no. 3). Reprinted by arrangement with the Estate of James B. Hendryx.

"The Law Visits Halfaday Creek" originally appeared in the May 21, 1938 issue of *Argosy* magazine (vol. 281, no. 6). Reprinted by arrangement with the Estate of James B. Hendryx. Cover and interior artwork from *Argosy* magazine courtesy of Argosy Communications, Inc. Copyright © 1938 by The Frank A. Munsey Company. Copyright renewed © 1966 and assigned to Argosy Communications, Inc. All Rights Reserved.

"Dead Man's Nugget" originally appeared in the August 25, 1941 issue of *Short Stories* magazine (vol. 175, no. 2). Reprinted by arrangement with the Estate of James B. Hendryx.

"Thunder on Halfaday" originally appeared in the January 10, 1942 issue of *Short Stories* magazine (vol. 178, no. 1). Reprinted by arrangement with the Estate of James B. Hendryx.

"Black John Solves a Crime" originally appeared in the November 25, 1943 issue of *Short Stories* magazine (vol. 185, no. 4). Reprinted by arrangement with the Estate of James B. Hendryx.

"Lost" originally appeared in Bulletin no. 13 of *"Lost" and Other Campfire Stories* (series 3, 1928). Reprinted by arrangement with the Estate of James B. Hendryx.

THANKS TO
Theresa Burau Baehr, Deborah Fellows, Joel Frieman, Robert Loomis, Richard Moore, Rick Ollerman, Julie Rhodes, Garyn Roberts, Cynthia Whyte, & the Leelanau Historical Society

TABLE OF CONTENTS

FINGER PRINTS

OLD CUSH, PROPRIETOR of Cushing's Fort, the combined trading post and saloon that served the little community of outlawed men that had sprung up on Halfaday Creek, close against the Yukon-Alaska border, carefully folded the newspaper he had been reading, placed it on the back bar, shoved the square-framed, steel-rimmed spectacles from nose to forehead, and reached for a bottle, two glasses, and a leather dice box as Black John Smith crossed the floor and elevated a foot to the battered brass rail.

Black John picked up the box, rattled the dice, banged it on the bar a time or two and rolled out the little cubes. "I'll leave them three sixes in one, seein' as I feel kind of lucky, this mornin'," he said.

Cush gathered the dice, and rolled them out onto the bar. "There's three aces that says yer sixes ain't worth a damn. How does yer luck feel, now?"

"It would feel a damn sight better if you'd rattle them dice around a little instead of slidin' 'em out the same way you put 'em in."

"I rolled 'em fair an' square, an' you know it," Cush retorted, as he returned the dice to the box, shook them, and rolled them out onto the bar. "That's a horse on you, an' if you don't beat them four deuces in one, it'll be two horses an' the drinks on you."

Black John failed to beat the four deuces. As he filled his

glass, Cush made the proper entry in his day book, and filled his own. He indicated the folded newspaper with a jerk of the thumb. "I seen a piece in the paper there where it tells about some fella down to Chicago which he got somethin' the matter with some bone in his leg that laid him up, an' three, four different doctors fooled around with it an' didn't do him no good, an' finally they figgered the best way was to cut off the leg an' be done with it. But the fella wouldn't let 'em, an' he hired some doctor to come clean from Noo York. An' this here Noo York doctor he went down to the slaughter house an' got the leg bone out of a sheep they killed down there, an' sawed out part of this here fella's leg bone, an' spliced the sheep bone onto it, an' by God, the fella got all right! Now what do you know about that?"

"Not a hell of a lot, except I would want no part of a sheep spliced on to me—'fraid I might start growin' wool instead of hair, er mebbe I'd jest stand here an' blat when I wanted a drink."

Both turned at the sound of a chuckle, and eyed the stranger who had stepped into the room and was approaching the bar. "What's this about blatting when you want a drink?" the man asked.

Cush reached for a glass and slid it across the bar as the newcomer lined up besides Black John. "Fill up," he said. "The house is buyin' one. The blattin' was jest some fool notion of John's, there. I was tellin' about a piece I seen in the paper where some doctor splices a sheep's leg bone onto a fella on account somethin' ailed the fella's leg, an' the fella gits all right again, an' John he claimed he wouldn't want no part of a sheep spliced to him er he might start growin' wool an' blattin'. By God, what I claim—if splicin' on a sheep's bone would put two good legs in under me, I wouldn't give a damn if I would grow a little wool, here an' there—er blat a little when I talked!"

THE STRANGER laughed, and swung, a light packsack to the floor at his feet. "I guess there wouldn't be much danger of that. The fact is I was very much interested in the newspaper account of that operation, myself. Bone grafting is ticklish business, at best. I'll look forward to seeing the technical account in the medical journal."

"You a doctor?" Black John asked.

"Yes. A doctor turned prospector. I saw that general practice in a small town wasn't getting me anywhere, so when the papers began printing glowing accounts of the gold country, up here, I decided to take a shot at it."

"The accounts was ondoubtless a damn sight more glowin' than the country," the big man observed. "Ever do any prospectin'?"

"No," the man replied, filling his glass from the bottle Cush shoved toward him. "But neither have most of the others I've talked with since leaving Seattle. I figure my chance of making a strike ought to be as good as the next man's."

Black John nodded. "Yeah, just about. There ain't but damn few chechakos goin' to make a strike. Most of 'em'll be lucky to make wages. Where'd you hear about Halfaday Crick?"

The stranger picked up his glass. "Here's how," he said, nodding at Cush. He swallowed the liquor at a gulp, returned the glass to the bar, and glanced at Black John.

"Halfaday Creek? I never—er—heard of Halfaday Creek."

"Jest happened in on us, eh?"

"That's right. I drifted down the Yukon in a canoe I picked up at Whitehorse, and happened to camp at the mouth of the fiver, into which this creek flows. After I'd eaten my supper I sat there and watched the boats drift past—dozens of them, all heading down the Yukon. And I got to thinking that with all these people crowding into the Dawson area, besides those who are already there, a man would have a much better chance of finding gold if he explored a river not so thickly populated. So in the morning I headed up this river, and eventually came to the mouth of this creek. At various spots along the Yukon I had heard men say that gold was more likely to be found on small creeks than upon the larger rivers, so I left the river and pushed on up this creek. I was much surprised to find that it is already occupied."

"You was, eh? Yer name ain't by any chance John Smith, is it?"

"Why—no. It's Jones—Franklin K. Jones, M.D. And—may

I ask your name?"

"That's Lyme Cushing, there behind the bar. Cush, he's the proprietor of this emporium. An' I'm John Smith—better known as Black John, owin' to my whiskers bein' tinged with that color."

"Oh—you're Black John!" the man exclaimed, then hastened to add, "Seems to me I heard the name mentioned—Whitehorse, or possibly Lake Bennett."

"Nothin' detrimental to my character, I trust?"

"No, no! Certainly not! In fact I don't remember anything except that the name struck me as odd, that's all."

"Yeah, John Smith is a kind of an odd name, at that—when you come to think about it. An' now yer here, do you figure to tarry amongst us—er shove on."

"Well, I don't want to intrude on anyone. That is, I mean that if this creek has already been prospected to the extent that a man wouldn't stand much chance of locating a claim that would be worth while, there wouldn't be any point in staying here. On the other hand, if there is a chance of making good, it would be mighty convenient to be located near a trading post. It would no doubt be quite a trip to Dawson for supplies."

"Yeah, it's quite a trip, all right. Halfaday Crick ain't what you'd call over-populated. None of us has ever made what you could call a hell of a strike. But plenty of us is takin' out better than wages. An' there's a hell of a lot of likely ground that ain't be'n staked yet."

"In that case, if it's all right with you men, I believe I'll locate here. I have a tent, and I can pitch it somewhere in the vicinity till I can find a likely location."

"You won't need to bother about settin' up yer tent," Black John said. "Jest throw yer stuff into One Eyed John's cabin. It's handier'n a tent."

"But—this One Eyed John? Won't he object?"

"He ain't apt to. We hung him a while back."

"Hung him! What for?"

"Damn if I remember. Ondoubtless it was fer somethin' he done."

"You mean, you lynched him!"

"Hell—no! Lynchin' is one form of amusement that wouldn't be tolerated on Halfaday fer a minute. He was hung by due process of a miners' meetin'. You see, Doc, layin' clost to the Alaska line, like we do, quite a few of the boys that inhabits the crick is miscreants of one sort or another, it bein' handy fer 'em to step acrost into Alaska if he's a Yukon wanted—an' vicy vercy, if he's a U.S. wanted. What a man done before he come to Halfaday is his own business. After he gets here, though, he's got to live moral as hell. I don't mean he's got to obey all of the ten commandments to the letter—but he's got to refrain from murder, larceny in any form, claim jumpin', an' all forms of skullduggery."

"How do you define skullduggery?"

"It's a flexible term, its definition dependin' entirely on circumstances." The big man paused, his glance resting on the light pack at the doctor's feet. "Is that all the outfit you fetched in with you?"

"Oh, no. I left the rest of my stuff in my canoe, at the landing. This bag contains merely a few personal items. Where is this cabin you mentioned?"

"It sets back from the crick a piece, about forty rod down from here. I've got a few minutes to spare. If you'd like, I'll help you pack yer stuff down there. After you get settled you better come on back to the fort, here, an' meet the boys. They generally come driftin' in of an evenin', for a few drinks er a session of stud. They'll be glad to know we've got a doctor on the crick—in case someone got sick."

"I'll be glad to do whatever I can. My supply of drugs is of necessity extremely limited. And beyond a scalpel or two, and an assortment of forceps and retractors, I brought no instruments."

"That's ondoubtless enough. I cut off a fella's leg once with a meat saw an' a huntin' knife."

"Did the man live?"

"Shore he did! What the hell d'you think I cut his leg off for? He'd died of blood p'izen if I hadn't."

AFTER HELPING the newcomer with his outfit, Black John returned to the saloon.

"It ain't no bad idee—havin' a doctor amongst us," Cush opined, as he set out the bottle and glasses. "I mean, like if he really is one."

"If he ain't a doctor, he's a damn good imitation of one," the big man replied. "He opened up one of his packs an' took out a little black leather bag like doctors carry their stuff around in."

"Seems kinda funny a doctor would quit his business an' pull out like he done, fer to try somethin' he don't know nothin' about—like prospectin'. Do you figger he's on the up-an'-up?"

"It's my candid an' onequivocal opinion that he's ondubtless one of the most onmittigated prevaricators who ever foisted himself into our midst."

"Yeah—an' on top of all that, I figger he's a damn liar—him claimin' he hadn't never heer'd of Halfaday Crick, an' then speakin' out, kinda s'prised like, when you says you was Black John. An' when you says did he hear nothin' dentermetal to yer character, he says 'no, certainly not!' Anyone would know he's a damn liar."

Black John scowled. "What do you mean by that?"

"What I mean—it's a cinch he'd heard of Halfaday, an' you, too. An' if he'd heard of you, he'd heard you was an outlaw—an' what I claim, if that ain't dentermetal, er whatever you call it, to yer character—what the hell is? Besides that, if he hadn't heer'd about Halfaday Crick, why the hell would he show up here? You know damn well there ain't no chechako goin' to go kihootin' alone up some river like the White into a country he don't know nothin' about, to do somethin' he don't know how to do when he gits there.

"You know as well as I do that chechakos is like salmons an' snowbirds, an' sech as that—they go in flocks. Who ever seen one snowbird in a flock by hisself? An' who ever seen one salmon head up a river alone?"

Black John grinned. "Yer reasonin' seems sound, even if yer exposition of it is a bit abstruse."

"When they make bigger words, you'll say 'em," Cush replied, wearily, "but they won't mean nothin' to me. I seen you had yer eye on that there little pack he fetched in an' set on the floor by his feet when you told him he could move into One Eyed John's cabin. I don't s'pose you managed to git a squint inside of it, to find out what them there 'personal items' was that he claimed was in it?"

Black John frowned. "You know damn well that pack didn't thump the floor hard enough to have had much dust in it. Personal items means things like a man's comb, an' toothbrush, an' mebbe an' extry shirt, er a pair of socks."

"Yeah," Cush replied dryly, "an' if them there items was mixed in with a few packages of big bills, they wouldn't thump the floor very hard, neither. Jest you remember, John—when we hang that damn cuss, I git cut in on the proceeds."

II

THE STRANGER FITTED himself into the life of Halfaday Creek. His evenings were spent at Cush's saloon where the men of the creek were wont to foregather. He played a good game of stud, drank drink for drink with the best of them, and held his liquor well. During the daytime he wandered up and down the creek, taking much interest in the sluicing operations, lending a helping hand here and there, asking innumerable questions about the business of prospecting for gold. When a flume support gave way and caught Red John beneath it, he deftly set and splinted the broken arm. And when, one evening, Short John complained of a persistent pain in his belly, he performed a neat appendectomy, on a makeshift operating table, with Black John as assistant, while the men of Halfaday looked on in wide-eyed approval.

Thus three weeks passed when he showed up in the saloon one morning with pan, shovel and blankets, and interrupted a dice game between Cush and Black John. He tossed an empty packsack onto the bar.

"Fill that up with grub enough for a three or four weeks' trip into the hills. I've got a fish line and some hooks, so you don't need to go very heavy on the meat."

"Goin' to do a little prospectin'?" Black John asked.

"Yes. I've been looking on, and bothering the boys with questions till I guess I've got the hang of it. They most of them agree with you, that there are plenty of good locations left here on Halfaday. But I've got a hunch that maybe, on some creek that hasn't been prospected, I might strike something really big. If I don't hit it, there'll be plenty of time to come back and play a sure thing, later."

"Oh, shore," the big man agreed. "Gold's where you find it, an' you might be the one to hit the jackpot. But there's a hell of a lot of country back there in the hills. Look out you don't get lost."

"I've got a compass. Guess I can find my way back, all right."

When the man had departed with his pack, Cush eyed Black John. "Y'know, I kinda hate to see him go. I've sort of felt safer, after seein' them jobs he done on Red John an' Short John. By God, if he hadn't of be'n here, Red John might of got his arm set wrong, an' Short John might of died of that there append-eetus he had in his guts. He's all right—Doc is. An' when you come to think about it, he might not be no crook, at that. He never claimed his name was John Smith."

Black John scowled. "Why, you damn fool—everyone whose name happens to be John Smith ain't a crook!"

"Not mebbe if that's their reg'lar name. But if they claim their name's that, they're damn apt to be. All a man's got to do is look around him to know that. We're so used to havin' damn liars show up here, that when he first come I didn't even believe he was no doctor."

"Oh, he's a doctor, all right—an' a pretty damn good one. But I've got a hunch that he's also somethin' else."

"How do you mean—somethin' else?"

"How old would you figure he is?"

"Well, I'd say somewheres around thirty-five, forty."

"Do you rec'lect what he said when he first got here, about seein' that general practice in a small town wasn't gettin' him anywheres."

"Yeah. That's what he claimed."

"Um-hum. An' what I claim, if general practice in a small town would net a man eighty thousan' dollars in cold cash by the time he's forty, he wouldn't figure it wasn't gettin' him anywheres. An' he wouldn't pull up an' hit out for the Klondike, or anywhere else—not if he had all his buttons, he wouldn't."

"Eighty thousan' in cash!" Cush exclaimed. "How do you know he's got eighty thousan'?"

"It's in that there little pack of 'personal items' he fetched in with him, that first mornin' he showed up. I mistrusted there was more in it than a few socks an' an extra shirt or two, or he'd have left it in his canoe at the landin' with his other stuff. So one evenin' durin' a stud game in which he was ridin' a winnin' streak, I slipped over to One Eye's cabin, an' sort of looked around a little. Most everyone that moves in there finds that secret cache behind that loose log in the wall, an' he's no exception. I deem it expedient, for the good of the crick, to sort of get a line on the various characters that shows up amongst us, so I give his cache the once-over."

"I figgered the same way," Cush said. "An' don't you fergit, when you come to divide that there eighty thousan' up, you divide it between the two of us—an' not jest you! I seen that pack as quick as you did!"

The big man grinned. "What do you mean—divide? Listen, Cush, as long as Doc stays amongst us, an' refrains from committin' any crime on the crick, that eighty thousan' is as safe in his cache as it would be in the Bank of England. On Halfaday, we respect property rights. That eighty thousan' is his property an' it's none of our business how it was come by."

"Yeah, but you know damn well he never saved up no eighty thousan' dollars doctorin' folks in no little town, an' him not no older'n what he is. He got that eighty thousan' crooked—an' you know it. What I claim, onct a crook allus a crook. An' anyways, we got a right to hope, ain't we?"

NEARLY A month passed before the doctor returned to Halfaday. He reported having no luck in the hills, prospected here and there along the creek, and was a nightly visitor at the saloon.

A week after his return Corporal Downey appeared at Cush's, accompanied by another. "Any strangers showed up here within the last week, or two?" he asked as he lined up beside Black John at the bar.

The big man shook his head. "Nope. Has some specific crime be'n committed? Or you jest makin' a general roundup of the sinful?"

"The Yukon Dredge Company's thirty thousan' dollar pay-roll that the bank was sendin' out to Ophir was knocked off about six miles out of Dawson. This man here is the guard that was sent out with the messenger."

"Cash pay-roll, I s'pose?" Black John asked.

The guard answered. "Yes, the messenger he carried it in a satchel. He was walkin' ahead along the trail an' I was behind him with a rifle. When we come to a place where the trail bends around a big rock, I hear a noise like a thump, an' the messenger goes down an' the satchel rolls into the bresh. Then before I kin swing the gun on him, a guy jumps out in front of me an' swings at me with an iron bar—an' that's the last thing I know'd till I woke up in the horspital. But before the damn cuss hit me, I got a good look at him—an' you bet, I'd know him if I seen him in hell!"

"An' besides that," Downey added, "I got the best bunch of finger prints I ever seen. I got 'em off the iron bar he killed the messenger with, an' off an empty tin an' an empty whiskey bottle the robber left there beside the trail. He evidently knew about the pay-roll an' laid in wait fer the messenger. While he was waitin' he et a tin of peaches an' finished off a bottle of liquor. He must have got his hands sticky from the peaches, an' then handled the bottle, an' the tin, an' the bar. I fetched photographs of the prints along with me, an' sent photos of 'em down to Ottawa to be checked up with prints they've got there of known crooks.

"This finger printin' has got to be quite a thing, the way they're workin' it. They're havin' us send in the finger prints of the different crooks we pick up, an' they're classified an' filed away together with the crook's name an' record.

"It's like if some burglar left his finger prints on a safe he cracked in Montreal, an' mebbe got caught an' done time fer it, an' after he was turned loose a set of prints comes in off'n a safe, say, in Vancouver. The expert in charge of the finger prints in Ottawa, could tell at a glance, by the whorls, an' islands, an' curves of the prints, that the same guy done both jobs. They've even figured out a way with numbers an' letters, wrote above an' below a line, so one finger print man can describe a set of prints to another by mail.

"It wouldn't take much of an expert to spot these prints, though, because besides the whorls, an' islands, an' things, this guy's got a scar on the index finger of his right hand. A lot of times you might run acrost two men that look alike—but they ain't never yet found two guys with the same finger prints. A witness might be mistaken. Or he might even try to lie someone into trouble—but finger prints ain't never mistaken—an' they don't lie."

BLACK JOHN nodded approvingly. "It looks like a swell set-up if it works good as you figure it does. I'm tellin' you, Downey, a few more systems like that, an' the damn crooks won't have a chanct."

"They ain't got much of a chanct, as it is—if they leave their finger prints around," Downey replied, as he tossed off the drink that stood before him.

A man entered the room, and the next instant a loud cry from the guard riveted all eyes on the newcomer. "There he is now! That's the coot that knocked off the messenger an' clouted me over the head with that iron bar! Grab him, Corporal! There's yer man!"

The newcomer paused for a moment, meeting the blazing eyes of the guard with a smile. "What's all this?" he asked, advancing to the bar. "My good man, what in the world are you driving at?"

"You know damn well what I'm drivin' at! Where's that there satchel with the Yukon Dredge's pay-roll in it that you grabbed off'n that messenger there on the trail."

The man turned to Downey, who had stepped to his side. "What does he mean, officer? Or is he some lunatic you've taken in tow? He mentioned having been clouted over the head with an iron bar. May have suffered some injury to the brain."

"I guess his brain's all right," Downey replied dryly. "At least, the doctors at the hospital said it was, when they let him go. On his identification, I'm arrestin' you for murder an' robbery—the murder of a messenger, seven miles out of Dawson, on the Ophir trail, an' the robbery of the thirty-thousan' dollar pay-roll he was carryin' at the time."

The prisoner laughed. "The idea is preposterous. Murder and robbery, indeed! If this poor fellow is identifying me in good faith, he's mistaken—that's all."

"We'll know damn quick whether he's mistaken, or not," Downey replied, and shot a reproachful look at Black John. "I thought you said no strangers had showed up on the crick in the last week or two?"

The big man nodded. "That's right. None that I've seen or heard of. Doc, here—he's be'n livin' amongst us fer a couple of months. You fellas has be'n doin' so much talkin' I ain't had a chanct to introduce you. Corporal Downey, meet Doc Jones."

The doctor grinned affably. "You're a little late, John," he said, glancing down at the handcuffs Downey had slipped onto his wrists. "Corporal Downey has met me already."

Downey eyed the man sharply. "Be'n right here on the crick all the time? Every day, fer the last couple of months?"

"Well, no. I've been on a prospecting trip out in the hills."

"Yeah? An' how long was you gone on that?"

"About three weeks."

"Didn't go down nowheres near Dawson, I s'pose?"

"I did not."

"The hell an' you didn't!" blurted the guard. "By God, you was within seven miles of Dawson when you knocked off that payroll!"

"If that man's not demented, he's sadly mistaken," the doctor said glancing into Downey's eyes. "And you are making a serious mistake in arresting me for a crime I had nothing whatever to do with."

Corporal Downey smiled grimly. "It won't take long to find out how much of a mistake I'm makin'," he said. "Hold out yer hands."

As the man thrust his manacled hands forward, Downey took the right one in his hand and examined the index finger. His brow clouded. He dropped the hand, and opening his pack, withdrew a packet from which he produced an ink-pad and a sheet of paper. Pressing the man's fingers onto the pad, he carefully transferred his prints to the paper. Picking up a magnifying glass, he studied the prints minutely, then with the glass scrutinized a set of finger print photos he took from the packet. Very deliberately, he returned the items to their place, and replaced the packet in his pack. Then he unlocked the cuffs from the man's wrists.

"Sorry, Doctor," he said. My mistake. Or that man's, rather."
He indicated the guard with a jerk of the thumb. "He seemed
so damn shore you was the one he seen there on the trail, that
I thought he must be right."

"Hey—what comes off here?" cried the guard. "By God, he's
the fella, all right! What you turnin' him loose fer? I got a good
look at him—an' I'd never fergit that face to the longest day I
lived!"

DOWNEY SHOOK his head. "It was someone else you seen.
Someone that prob'ly looked like the doctor, here. But it wasn't
him. It couldn't of be'n. He ain't got no scar on his index finger—
an' his prints ain't nothin' like the ones the robber left on the
bar, an' the tin, an' the bottle."

"I don't give a damn about no finger prints!" the outraged
guard cried. "By God, if I git a good look at a man, an' then he
whams me over the head with a chunk of iron—I ain't fergittin'
him none! Not by a damn sight, I ain't!"

"I don't claim yer forgettin'," Downey said. "But I do know
yer mistaken. Like I said, the robber prob'ly looks like this man.

"An eyewitness can be mistaken. That's be'n proved in courts
hundreds of times. But finger prints can't be mistaken. An' in
the face of them prints, I'd be makin' a damn fool of myself if
I was to take this man in."

"You'll be makin' a damn fool of yerself if you don't," the
guard retorted angrily. "He's the one that done it, all right. I'd
swear to it on a stack of Bibles a mile high!"

"An' that jest goes to show that a lot of innocent folks has
prob'ly be'n swore into prison on jest such evidence," Downey
replied, and turned to the doctor. "You're lucky that crook left
them finger prints around. On this man's evidence, you'd be'n
convicted shore as hell."

The doctor smiled. "I'm lucky that an intelligent officer is
handling this case. A man with less acumen and experience
might well have overlooked those prints, or ignored them."

"We don't send out rookies on murder cases when we can help it," Downey said. "Fill 'em up. I'm buyin' a drink."

"No, no! The drinks are on me!" the doctor exclaimed, and motioned the guard to the bar. "And you, too. Step up and join us, my good man. I believe you are honest in your identification, and I—"

"You know damned well I am!" the man interrupted.

"As I was going on to say," the doctor replied evenly, meeting the glaring eyes squarely, "I bear you no ill will. Come on—have a drink with me."

"You go to hell!" the man blurted. "There ain't no man livin' kin wham me over the head one week, an' buy me a drink the next! Not by a damn sight, there ain't!"

III

A FEW DAYS after Downey's departure the doctor outfitted for another prospecting trip, and disappeared into the hills. The spring clean-up progressed apace, and some three weeks later, as Black John stepped into the saloon, one morning, Cush jerked his thumb in the direction of the huge iron safe.

"Guess you've got to make a trip down to Dawson," he said. "The boys has be'n fetchin' in dust every night till the safe's gittin' all clogged up."

The big man frowned. "Why the hell can't someone else take the dust down, for a change? It's a hell of a chore—makin' that trip. Why pick on me, every time?"

Cush set out bottle and glasses. "You know damn well the boys wouldn't trust that dust with no one but you. Trouble is, John, they know yer honest."

Black John laughed. "The reputation for honesty shore is a draw-back, at times."

"Huh. There ain't no danger of yourn ever hurtin' you none. Hell, everyone knows yer an outlaw. But the boys all knows, the same as Downey does—there's a damn sight of difference in outlaws."

One Armed John stepped into the saloon, crossed to the bar and ranged himself beside the big man, as Cush slid a glass toward him.

"They's a fella camped in Olson's old shack," he announced, reaching for the bottle. "Claims his name's John Jones. Looks like some damn chechako."

"Jones, eh? We seem to be threatened with an influx of Joneses," Black John said. "We circumvented the plethora of John Smiths by the adoption of the name can. Can it be that styles in names change the same as in clothin'? Or is someone in Whitehorse tippin' off the unholy that the name of Smith is *de trop* on Halfaday?"

Cush scowled. "Does that mean we got to invent another name can, same as we done fer Smiths? By God, if it does, you better fetch in another book when you go to Dawson to copy names out of! We used up all the names in that there history book. An' there ain't only three more books on the crick—that there statue book you stole off'n that lawyer down to Dawson, that time, most likely ain't got no names in it. I got a hymn book an' a Bible that my fourth wife had. Them Bible names—there ain't no one but you could say most of 'em after we'd got 'em wrote down."

The big man grinned. "Let us hope that the invasion of Joneses may be met without recourse to another name can. Go ahead an' make up that pack of dust. If I've got to take it down I might's well get goin'.

AT OLSON'S old shack, some few miles down the creek, he paused to chat with a hard-eyed man who was dipping a pail of water from the spring. "Figure on locatin' here?" he asked.

"Yeah, anyways till I kin look around a little. Looks like the place is abandoned."

"That's right."

"What's the matter? Wasn't the claim no good?"

"Well, fact is, no one ever worked it long enough to find out. Lots of 'em's moved in here from time to time—but damn few's ever moved out."

"How do you mean by that?"

"Meanin' that the former tenants, almost to a man, has either died, or got murdered, or hung—one of the three."

"Hung? What was they hung fer?"

"Oh, different things they done—er mebbe, didn't do. On Halfaday, under our skullduggery law, a sin of ommission may be fully as hangable as one of commission."

"You must be Black John Smith, ain't you?"

"That's right."

"Heard about you up to Whitehorse. Feller there tipped me off you boys up here is all outlaws. My name's Jones—John Jones," he added with a wink. "This feller says how the name of John Smith don't go no more up here. The Law got to crowdin' me too clost, back in the States, so I lammed out on 'em. S'all right if I hole up here fer a while, ain't it?"

"Oh, shore. What a man done before he come to Halfaday ain't no one's business but his own. After he gits here, though, he's got to refrain from crime in any form—or get hung. Onct a man gets that principle firmly grounded an' lives up to it, he can stay here as long as he likes. If I was you, though, an' had any considerable amount of cash er dust on hand I'd deposit it in Cush's safe instead of cachin' it. Most of the boys wouldn't bother a cache—but there's no tellin' when some damn cache robber might show up."

"Oh, I ain't got nothin' anyone would bother about. I'm damn near broke."

"Okay. So long. I've got to be goin'. See you later."

UPON REACHING Dawson, Black John deposited the dust in the bank, strolled over to police headquarters, drew up a chair, hoisted his heels onto the edge of Downey's desk, and filled his pipe. "How they comin'?" he asked. "Did you pick up that robber—the one you was huntin' on Halfaday?"

Corporal Downey scowled. "No. An' what's more, we've got another pay-roll robbery on top of that one—an' the same set of finger prints. The Amalgamated started a twenty-five-thousan'-dollar pay-roll to Squaw Crick. Thought they'd play smart, an' instead of sendin' the messenger out in the daytime with a guard, they slipped him out at night, alone. Couple of fellas found him next day, dead on the trail with his head stove in. I hustled out there—an' found jest exactly what I found on the Dredge Company job—an' empty peach tin, an' empty whiskey bottle, an' an iron bar—all with finger prints on 'em that jump right out at you—the same prints, with the scarred index finger. Seems like the damn cuss leaves 'em there a-purpose."

"Hum. That's fifty-five thousan' he's got away with, ain't it? The sum is worth contemplatin'. Looks like he goes in fer cash instead of dust, eh?"

"Yup. So far, the messengers comin' in with dust from the workin's haven't be'n bothered."

"Bills is easier to pack, at that. He must be a pretty slick article. Either that, or a damn dumb one—leavin' them finger prints around. An' if he was that dumb, he'd made other miscues that you'd have picked him up on, before this. Maybe he's someone that feels sure you'd never suspect him. After all, you can't go around takin' everyone's finger prints. You might keep an eye out for scarred index fingers. You could do that without folks knowin' it. It would take time, though."

"Too damn much time—at the rate he's workin'. But you don't know the half of it. Here's a headache—if there ever was one! Ottawa says the man whose finger prints these are is dead!"

"Dead!" Black John exclaimed. Then threw back his head and roared with laughter. "Hell, Downey, that simplifies yer case immensely. It eliminates the livin'. All you got to do, now, is hunt for a ghost—an' there's damn few ghosts."

"Laugh if you want to," Downey replied glumly. "I can't get no laugh out of it."

"Mebbe there's some mistake—like their gettin' them prints mixed up, back there in Ottawa."

"No chanct. They've checked, an' re-checked. The man is dead, all right. He died in prison. There's no question about that. An' here's one fer the book—take this glass an' look at them prints. See that scar on the index finger? There ain't no mistake about that scar. But Ottawa says the guy didn't have any scarred finger. Their set of prints are identical, except fer that scar."

"Looks like yer case is gettin' easier an' easier," the big man grinned. "The ghost hurt his finger after his demise—so now you can eliminate all ghosts with sound fingers. There can't be no hell of a lot of sore-fingered ghosts runnin' around."

"Have all the fun you want," Downey growled. "An' then chaw on this one—this bird, Jack Brower, was a lifer who died suddenly in prison of a coronary thrombosis. He was finger-printed when he was admitted to the prison, an' the prints show no scar. An' there's no record of any injury to his finger while he was there, although the prison doctor is supposed to record all injuries, sickness, an' such.

"His body was claimed by a brother, an' buried in a lot bought fer the purpose in a local cemetery. They've got the affidavit of the undertaker that the man was dead, an' affidavits of several witnesses to the burial. But the prison doctor who signed the death certificate can't be located, an' investigation uncovered the fact that Brower had no brothers, an' the guy that claimed the body has disappeared. An' on top of all that, they got a court order to dig up the body to check that scar with his finger—an' when they done it, all they got was an empty coffin! Can you tie that?"

"Jest crawled out of his grave, lock, stock an' barrel, eh? An' then hit out fer Dawson an' begun gatherin' in pay-rolls? Did Ottawa say what his specialty was, durin' his earthly sojourn?"

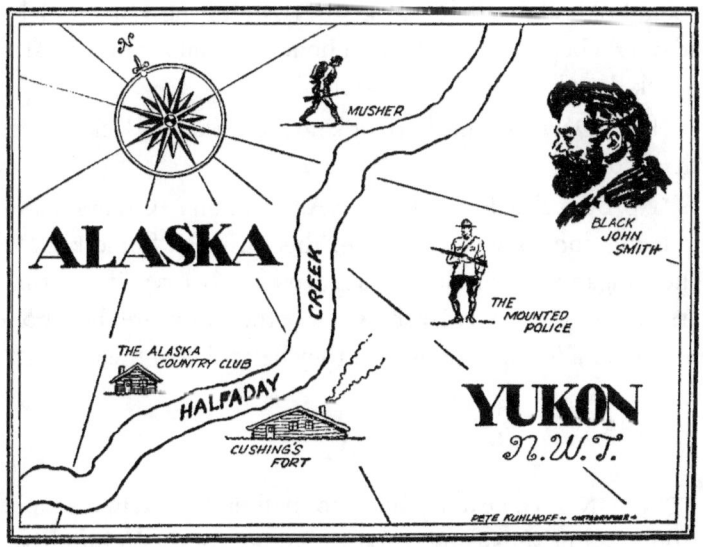

"Yeah, they sent us his record—robbery, armed—express an' bank jobs, mostly. Got sent up fer a robbery in Windsor where an express messenger got knocked off."

"What did he look like? Did they describe him?"

"Yeah—here's all the dope. Jack Brower—six foot two, black hair, V-shaped scar on his chin, thirty-two, liked the women—but never touched booze. Hawk-bill nose. Slight squint in the left eye. No one like that showed up on Halfaday, has there?"

"Nope. If he does I'll shore as hell keep an eye on him. We don't want no damn skunk on the crick that's liable to bash our heads in with a crowbar. Well, good luck to you. I'll be trottin' along an' see if I can't stir up a stud game. Pullin' out in the mornin'. I'm shore glad I ain't a policeman."

"By the way, Downey—if you should happen to grab off this here ghost—what you goin' to keep him in? If a coffin an' six foot of dirt won't hold him, he'll filter out through them cell bars of yours like water through a sieve."

"Get to hell out of here! I've got to catch him before I worry about holdin' him. An' don't be surprised if I show up on Half-aday agin before long. I've got a hunch it wouldn't do no harm to ask that doctor a few questions."

"Hell, Downey—he don't look no more like this Jack Brower than I do!"

"No. But he's a doctor, ain't he? An' accordin' to Ottawa there's a doctor somehow mixed up in this business. Some kind of shenanigan went on down there, you can bet yer life on that. An' any stray doctors that shows up in the Yukon are shore goin' to answer a few questions—an' they better know the answers!"

IV

AT NOON THE next day Black John disembarked in his canoe from the upriver steamboat at the mouth of the White River and began the laborious upstream grind. After supper that evening he filled his pipe and sat staring into the glowing embers of his dying fire as he strove to make sense out of the facts Downey had given him. He spoke half aloud, as is the wont of lone men. "Doc is guilty as hell, all right. After he pulled out on that second prospectin' trip I looked in his cache agin, an' that thirty thousan' the Yukon Dredge lost was in there, along with the eighty thousan' he had when he come. An' I'm bettin' when I look in it next time, I'll find the Amalgamated's twen-ty-five thousan' there too. An finger prints, er no finger prints, that guard shore knew what he was talkin' about when he identified him.

"Doc's got plenty of guts, all right—the way he defied that guard to his face without battin' an eye. He's a damned cold-blooded murderer. But how the hell does he get away with them finger prints? An' where does this Jones that's holed up in Olson's old shack fit into the picture? I've got a hunch his showin' up on Halfaday so close on the heels of Doc, ain't no coincidence— by a damn sight.

"Yet, neither one of 'em answers the description of this Jack

Brower, either. An' where does Brower fit in? It's a cinch he ain't dead, or he couldn't be leavin' his finger prints around on peach tins an' crowbars an' whiskey bottles fer Downey to find. That undertaker an' them witnesses was ondoubtless greased plenty to swear to them affidavits. No wonder they've got Downey runnin' around in circles."

Suddenly he jerked the pipe from his mouth and slapped his thigh with his palm. "By God, I've got it! Or part of it, anyhow. Doc signs a fake death certificate an' gets Brower out of the pen. Then they hit out for the Yukon, an' Doc shows up on Halfaday—but Brower don't. Doc's got him hidout somewheres. When they pull off a job, Doc does the work, while Brower lays back, an' when it's over, he slips in an' gets his hand sticky with peach juice, an' then handles the tin, an' the bottle an' the crowbar. That accounts for the finger prints that knock hell out of any eye-witness identification—an' the reason his new prints show a scar is because he's hurt a finger since he got out of the pen. That don't account for John Jones—but we can ondoubtless 'tend to his case later. Doc's got to be put out of circulation before he murders some other pore devil. But the hell of it is, Downey can't never convict him until he locates Brower so he can account for them finger prints. An', after him fixin' up Red John an' Short John the way he did, I'd have a hell of a time tryin' to convict him in miner's meetin' on some kind of skull-duggery charge because the boys wouldn't never vote to hang him.

"Of course, if worse comes to worst, when Downey comes along I could show him Doc's cache, an' he'd have him dead to rights. In that case I'd have to forego any profit on the venture—but by God, I'll do it before I'll leave him runnin' loose to murder another pay-roll messenger, profit er no profit! In the meantime I'll lay back an' let nature take her course. Mebbe I can locate this Brower, myself."

EARLY ONE morning several days later as he shoved up Halfaday Creek, Black John beached his canoe at Olson's old shack. Smoke curled from the stovepipe and glancing through the window he saw Jones busy at the stove. Stepping to the near-by rock-wall, he smiled as he noted that the flat stone that had served many other sojourners in the shack as a cache cover was fitted snugly into place over the hole. Laying the stone aside he peered into the aperture and his eyes widened as they encountered the numerous packets of paper money. Hastily removing them, he uttered an ejaculation of surprise. "Good God— here's that eighty thousan' Doc had in his cache—an' the thirty thousan' dredge company pay-roll—an' shore as hell—here's the Amalgamated's pay-roll along with 'em!" He shook his head slowly from side to side as he crowded the currency into his packsack. "The ways of these damn crooks is beyond my limited powers of comprehension," he muttered, as he replaced the stone as he had found it. "They doublecross one another without battin' an eye. Their duplicity is shore sad to contemplate." Stepping into his canoe he pushed on, landing a mile or so beyond to cache the packets of currency among the rocks, some distance back from the creek.

As he resumed his journey, he grinned. "I've got a hunch there's goin' to be repercussions of some kind shortly. If citizen Jones can show that he come by that hundred an' thirty-five thousan' honestly, he'll get every cent of it back. I'm no damn cache robber. But if he can't—if his title to it seems clouded or obscure, an' open to suspicion—he's goin' to get a lesson in rectitude that'll be good fer his soul. Besides which, I might be able to show some slight profit on the venture, myself."

An hour later he drew his canoe from the water at the landing, and entering the saloon, crossed to the bar where Cush was already setting out bottle and glasses.

"So you got back, eh? How's things down to Dawson?"

"Oh, about so-so. Downey's got another pay-roll robbery on his hands."

"An' I s'pose he'll be up here again huntin' the robber."

"Most likely. How's things on the crick? Has anything of note transpired during my absence?"

"If you mean has anything happened—there ain't. But somethin's apt to. I'm shore glad you got back."

"Yeah? What's on yer mind?"

"It's that there damn John Jones, he claims his name is, that moved into Olson's old shack. He ain't no one a man could trust. He don't never come up an' mix with the boys of a night. An' twict, now, One Armed John's ketched him sneakin' around in the bresh near One Eyed John's cabin. The first time whilst Doc was still out in the hills, One Arm seen him sneakin' away from there, an' he's pretty sure Jones had be'n in the cabin. It was long about noon when One Arm seen him, an' knowin' that there eighty-thousan' was cached there in the cabin I worried about it all day, figgerin' to slip over there when night come, an' see if it was still in Doc's cache.

"But 'long about suppertime Doc come back. He come over here that night—an' bein' as he didn't put up no squawk about bein' robbed, I guess Jones didn't locate his cache. Couple days later, One Arm seen Jones agin, layin' in the bresh watchin' the cabin. That was two, three days ago, an' I tipped Doc off that someone was prowlin' around his place, an' sence then he's stuck clost to the cabin—ain't even be'n over here of an evenin'. What I want to know, ain't it some kind of skullduggery if a man sneaks around through the bresh, like that?"

"Well, bresh-sneakin', per se, ain't hangable. The question of intent would be the decidin' factor. I'd say that in the absence of an overt act, or of tangible evidence of criminal intent—"

"Listen here!" Cush interrupted testily. "I don't want to hear no sermon. All I asks is, kin we hang that coot, er can't we? He don't spend a damn cent in here hisself. An' on top of that, he's keepin' a good customer away, besides."

Black John grinned. "Hell, Cush—if we start in an' hang everyone who don't patronize yer bar, here, we'd—"

ONE ARMED JOHN, his eyes staring wildly, burst into the room. "Hey—down to One Eye's shack! Doc's dead! He's murdered somethin' awful!"

Black John filled a glass Cush slid across the bar, and handed it to the man who brought up panting beside him. "Throw this into you an' get holt of yerself," he said. "Take yer time, now—an' tell us what you know."

The man gulped down the liquor. "It's Doc! He's deader'n hell!"

"Yeah—you told us that. S'pose you start at the beginnin'. How come you know he's dead?"

"I gits up this mornin' an' I ain't feelin' so good—like it's my guts er somethin' that's ailin me. An I figgers how mebbe Doc might fix me up, so I goes down to One Eye's shack an' knocks on the door. No one don't answer, an' I pounds some more, but it don't do no good. So I shoves the door open an' sticks my head in, an'—oh God, it's somethin' awful in there! Doc's layin' there dead on the floor, with his feet tied together, an' his arms tied tight to him, an' his shoes an' socks is off, an' his feet's be'n burnt, an' a rag's tied over his mouth! So I slams the door shet an' comes hellbent up here! It's that damn John Jones done it, all right. I ketched him sneakin' around there a couple of times. I'm shore glad yer back, John—'cause now, by God, we kin hang him!"

"The facts calls for an investigation," Black John said. "I'll go an' look things over. An' don't neither one of you say a damn word to anyone about what come off. If John Jones shows up, throw a gun on him, an' hold him here till I get back."

As he neared One Eyed John's cabin the sound of feet thudding the trail from down the creek reached his ears, and he stepped aside into the brush. A moment later, Jones dashed into sight, and as he reached the spot, Black John stepped directly in front of him, blocking the trail. "What's yer hurry?" he asked, as the man halted abruptly.

"Hurry! By God, I be'n robbed! That's what's my hurry!"

The big man eyed him coldly. "Yeah? Robbed of what?"

"Of what was in my cache—that's what!"

"That oughtn't to worry you much. Only a couple of weeks ago you told me you didn't have nothin' of any value—an' you couldn't have taken a hell of a lot out of that old claim of Olson's sence then."

"I lied when I said I didn't have nothin'! I didn't figger it was any of your business what I had. What the hell do you think I come up here fer—my health? I pulled off some damn big jobs, back there in the States—an' I fetched in the stuff with me—a hundred an' thirty-five grand in good cash money—that's what I had. An' now it's gone—every damn cent of it!"

"Tough luck!" Black John said. "Remember, I warned you about leavin' anything of value layin' around. I told you you'd better deposit it in Cush's safe."

"Yeah—an' you said there wasn't no crime allowed on the crick, too. Robbery's a crime, ain't it? What you goin' to do about it?"

"Do about it? Why, we're goin' to hang whoever is guilty— same as we always do."

"You got to ketch him first."

"Yeah, there's that angle, too. But that don't bother us much. If a man commits a crime on Halfaday, he always gets hung. Come on along with me. I've got a little chore to do, down here a piece. I figure you might be able to help me. Then I'll get to work on your case."

"What kind of a chore? Hell, we ort to go huntin' that robber 'fore he gits plumb away."

"He ain't likely to. Step on ahead. I'll foller." A short distance farther on Black John spoke again. "Turn off to the left. We're goin' over to that cabin, yonder."

The man halted abruptly and faced about. "What—what you goin' there fer?"

Black John noted that the man's face had gone white, and

that the words came haltingly from between tight lips.

"Oh, jest a little routine chore. Fact is, a man was murdered in there—sometime durin' the night, most likely. An' I want to sort of look around a little. Like I said, no one can commit a crime on Halfaday an' get away with it."

"Listen," the man said, wetting his dry lips with his tongue. "I—I don't want to go in there. I hate to look at dead men—gives me the creeps. I'll go up to the saloon an' wait around till you git through."

Black John shrugged. "Suit yerself. You've asked me to help you locate the man you claim robbed yer cache—an' I've asked you to help me out down here first. If you ain't willin' to help me, I won't go out of my way to help you—that's a cinch. An' without my help you ain't got a chance in the world of locatin' that cache robber. I ain't lost no hundred an' thirty-five thousan' dollars—but if I had, I'd shore as hell want all the help I could get to recover it."

For a long moment the man stood undecided, his hands slowly opening and closing. "All right, then," he blurted suddenly. "I'll go along with you. But, fer Pete's sake make it snappy. If the man's dead, like you claim, it hadn't ort to take no hell of a while to look around."

Opening the cabin door, Black John motioned the other to precede him. The man hesitated, drew slightly back, then with a visible effort, crossed the threshold and stepped aside to allow the big man to enter.

Hardened as he was to scenes of violence, Black John involuntarily shuddered at the sight that met his eyes. The doctor lay on his back on the floor, his legs and arms tightly bound with babiche line. A sleeve ripped from a shirt covered his mouth, and was knotted at the back of his head. On the floor was a pool of thick, sticky blood that had oozed from his bashed-in head. A bloody hand-ax lay close by where the murderer had tossed it. As One Armed John had said, the feet of the corpse were bare, the skin blackened and shriveled in spots. Close beside them a half burned candle protruded from the mouth of a bottle.

For long moments Black John stood there, his eyes taking in every detail of the macabre scene. Out of the tail of his eye, he noted that the other, his face paper-white, was staring down at the floor.

"Come over here an' take a look," the big man invited. "I've investigated quite a few murders, take it first an' last—but never as dirty a one as this."

"I—I can't look," the man gulped. "I—I'm sick to my stummick—an' I've got the shakes."

"You'll come over here an' get you an eyeful, like I said. You shore as hell ain't no help to me, standin' there shakin' yer buttons off. If I had as much as you have at stake, you bet I'd pitch in an' help."

"What—what you want me to do?" the other asked in a quavering voice.

"I want you to come over here where you can get a good look, an' remember jest what you see. Cush, he's the coroner. An' he'll want the testimony of two witnesses as to jest how things was when we got here."

THE MAN edged closer, his eyes staring glassily, his hands trembling violently. Black John's voice boomed in a rumbling monotone, seemingly speaking more to himself than to the other. "Pore Doc, he hadn't be'n amongst us very long. But the boys all liked him. He was a kindly soul—doctored 'em when they was ailin' an' never charged 'em a cent. It's shore sad that a man like him should came to an end like this. Tortured, that's what he was. Look at them feet—burnt to a blister where the damn fiend that done it held the candle agin 'em. An' look how that line cut into his arms there, where he strained agin it. Tortured to make him tell somethin' he know'd, most likely. An' then—mebbe he wouldn't tell, an' the murderer got mad an' bashed in his head with the hand-ax, there. But the chances is he did tell—an' then the damn cuss bashed in his head, anyhow. Whoever done this ain't very far from here, right now. An' when the boys hears about it—an' has a look at what come off here, there's one murderer that ain't even goin' to get the benefit of a miner's meetin'. There won't be no quick jerk on the end of a rope fer him. They'll take matters into their own hands an' it's a safe bet that the damn dirty cuss will be as long dyin' as Doc was—mebbe longer—an' prob'ly a damn sight more painful...."

"Shet up! Me, I'm gittin' outa here!"

"Not till you tell me what you done this for, you ain't," Black John said, in a hard, gritty voice, stepping between the trembling man and the door.

"I never done it!" the man cried, his voice rising to an hysterical falsetto. "It's a lie! I never seen this guy before!" His knees shook so violently that he suddenly collapsed onto the bench beside the table.

"That's lie number one. But it ain't gettin' you nowheres. You was seen on two different occasions, prowlin' around this shack, keepin' an eye on Doc."

"It's a damn lie! It must of be'n someone else."

"Where'd you get the hundred an' thirty-five thousan' you claim was stole out of yer cache!"

"I fetched it in with me—like I said—from jobs I pulled in the States."

"Shore you didn't get it out of the wall there, where Doc had it cached? You don't need to answer that one. I'll know in a minute, as soon as I look in the cache. You see, I happen to know that's the exact amount he had in there—eighty thousan' he fetched in with him, an' fifty-five thousan he gathered in sence."

The man's eyes flickered. "It's a damn—I mean—I—I lied. I never had no cache, with no one-thirty-five grand in it."

"Kind of a coincidence, ain't it—you namin' the exact amount Doc had in his cache? Do you still claim you never murdered Doc?"

"No, I never murdered him! I tell you I never seen him before!"

Black John picked up the hand-ax from the floor. He grasped it by the bit, and pointed grimly to the bloody handle. "Okay. I'll damn soon know whether yer lyin' or not. The finger prints on this handle stick out like a sore thumb."

"Finger prints!" the man cried, shrilly. "What do you know about finger prints?"

"I'll know all about these—an' yours, too, after I turn you over to the boys. As soon as I get out that powder Downey gave me, an' my camera—an' the ink pad, an' get your prints—the boys won't be very long makin' up their minds who murdered Doc."

The man leaned heavily against the table, his eyes staring straight ahead. "Don't—fer God's sake—don't let 'em torture me," he whined, in a low, mewling voice. "I done it. I killed him—but, he had it comin'. You claimed he was a kind man—but I know he was nothin' but a damn low-lived, dirty, double-crosser. He got jest what was comin' to him fer what he done to Jack Brower."

"Who's Jack Brower? An' what did Doc do to him?"

"He was a pal of mine, an' Doc murdered him! That's what he done—doublecrossed him an' then murdered him. That's where he got that eighty thousan' he fetched in with him."

"H-u-u-m. Go ahead an' spill it—an' it better be damn good to excuse a job like this."

"Jack Brower, he's in stir—see? Fer a job him an' couple other fellas pulled off in Windsor—they throwed the book at Jack. Give him life, an' ninety-nine years on top of it on a murder an' robbery rap. Well, this here damn cuss was the prison doctor. He know'd Jack refused to tell where he had eighty grand cached outside. After Jack had be'n in a few years, an' seen how there wasn't no chanct to crush out, this Doc, he puts a proposition up to him. He claimed he could spring Jack by givin' him some drug—like knock-out drops, that would make him look like he was dead—an' he'd sign the death certificate, an' Jack he could git some pal to claim his body. Then he'd fetch Jack to agin, an' they'd go fifty-fifty on the eighty grand.

"Jack he thinks it over an' figgers it's his only chanct, so he says okay. Then the Doc he tells Jack he's got to tell him where the cache is at before he springs him, figgerin' Jack might double-cross him when he got out. But Jack, he holds back on it, figgerin' the same way about Doc. Doc he keeps at him, p'intin' out that he might's well take a chanct, bein' as the eighty Gs wouldn't never do him no good, on account they got his sentence so high he can't never come up fer parole er pardon. Doc he swears he'll play square, an' finally Jack tells him where the stuff is cached, an' Doc goes an' gets it.

"Jack, he sends fer me, an' spills the whole scheme, makin' me promise to keep cases on Doc, an' knock him off if he tried to pull a fast one. An' seein' how there'd be eighty grand in it, I agrees. Well, Doc he don't dast to set back an' not do nothin', er Jack would sing about him coppin' off the dough—so one night, he slips Jack this here drug, an' Jack takes it—an' a couple of minutes later he's deader'n hell. Then Doc signs the death warrant, an' I claim the body, an' we git holt of an undertaker an' have it buried in a lot Doc bought fer it.

"I hit Doc fer a cut on the eighty Gs, figgerin' that when he shelled it out, I'd knock him off, an' cop it all—fer what he done to pore Jack. But the damn cuss give me the slip. I follered him to Seattle, an' clean on through to Whitehorse. There a guy tipped me off that he'd hit fer here. So I come on up here—an'—well—I guess you know the rest. What I mean, that damn skunk got jest what was comin' to him."

Black John nodded, thoughtfully. "On the whole, I'm inclined to agree with you. But on the other hand, your ethics is open to question, too. Like I said, the boys here on the crick feel kindly toward Doc, an' I couldn't answer fer their reactions on his murder, even with the mitigatin' circumstance you've mentioned. If you was to stay on the crick, the least you could expect would be a quick hangin'.

"In view of the facts you've stated, personally, I'd be inclined to sort of play one murder agin the other, an' slip you enough grub so you could cross the line, an' reach the Tanana. An' yet, on the other hand, if you don't stay here, how could you expect to locate that hundred an' thirty-five thousan' you stole out of Doc's cache?"

"To hell with that hundred an' thirty-five Gs! There's more where that come from—but I ain't only got one life!"

"That seems a sensible way to look at it," the big man admitted. "We'll slip around to my shack an' you can get goin'. The quicker the better—before the boys get holt of what come off here."

As the man was about to depart, Black John asked, "By the way—are you dead shore this Jack Brower was dead when you buried him?"

"Dead! Yer damn right he was dead! I know,'cause I helped the undertaker lift him into the coffin."

BLACK JOHN returned to One Eyed John's cabin, and gazed down at the corpse with puzzled eyes. "Downey claims the authorities dug up Brower's coffin an' found it empty. No one else would dig up a dead man. So Jones was either mistaken, or he was lyin', when he claimed Brower was dead. An' besides that, a dead man can't be runnin' around the country leavin' his finger prints on peach tins, an' booze bottles, an' crowbars. Therefore, he must be alive. Alive, an' playin' with Doc. He's hidin' out somewheres, an' when they pull off a job, Doc does the work, then Brower slips in an leaves his finger prints for the police to find. Then, if someone happens to get sight of Doc—like that guard did—an' identifies him, the police will turn him loose when they take his prints—jest like Downey did, there in the station.

"It's a damn slick racket, all right. But where the hell is Brower?" Stooping, he ran deftly through the dead man's pockets, in the hope of finding some memo, or notation that would reveal the accomplices whereabouts. In an inner shirt pocket he withdrew a small oiled silk bag. Opening it, he pulled out and unrolled an object so bizarre—so gruesome that he involuntarily drew back, dropping it to the floor. He stared down at it for a moment, then gingerly, he picked it up and examined it—*the skin of a human hand!*

Beautifully tanned, it was soft and pliable as silk, yet tough as good leather—a perfect glove that reached well beyond the wrist. Black John smiled grimly as his eyes focused on the small slit at the tip of the index finger. "So," he muttered, "that's the scar Downey couldn't account for. Doc was prob'ly in a hurry when he skinned out Brower's hand an' his knife slipped. An' that's why they didn't find notbin' but an empty coffin when they dug into Brower's grave." Slowly, carefully, he drew on the glove, flexing his fingers, turning his hand this way and that to admire the fit. "Downey's goin' to be mighty interested in this," he muttered. Then paused abruptly, as a slow grin twisted the lips behind the heavy black beard. "But come to think of it, why bother Downey with trifles?"

Carefully he removed the glove and returned it to its oiled silk wrapping. "With Doc's ontimely passin' them pay-roll murders will cease, an' it won't hurt Downey none to be keepin' his eye peeled for the man with the scarred finger. Besides," he added, as he pocketed the small packet, "a man can't never tell when some odd relic like this might come in handy."

Returning to the saloon he faced Cush across the bar. "Well," the somber-faced one asked, as he set out bottle and glasses, "what did you find out?"

"The facts are about as One Arm stated 'em. Accordin' to appearances Doc's demise is an ondisputable fact, an' was accomplished with sadistic ferosity by—"

"If that means he's dead, One Arm told us that a'ready. What I mean—how about his cache?"

"Empty as a bar maid's promise!"

"Well, it was that damn John Jones done it, all right! An' now we kin call a miner's meetin' an' hang him. But first off, we'd better hit down to Olson's shack an' grab him before he gits clean off'n the crick with that there money Doc had!"

"There's no doubt in my mind that Jones is the culprit, an' that he richly deserves a good thorough-goin' hangin'. But I have my doubts as to his ability to leave the crick with Doc's wealth. You see, Cush, on my way down to Dawson, I stopped to chat with him for a few minutes, an' told him if he had anything of value he'd better deposit it here in the safe. He assured me that he had nothin' that anyone would bother to steal. So on my way back this mornin' I took occasion to examine his cache, jest by way of verifyin' his statement. I found a certain discrepancy in his statement, in that the cache contained certain funds—packages of bills that had a strangely familiar appearance. It struck me that they greatly resembled the packets that I had previously seen in Doc's cache—so I removed them, and recached them, pendin' an investigation as to their rightful ownership."

Cush eyed the big man across the bar. "Yeah? Well, this investigation about rightful ownership has went about as fer as it needs to. Doc's dead—an' Jones will be as soon as the boys gits their hands on him. That leaves you an' me. I seen that pack of Doc's as quick as you did, that time he first come here. You told me yerself they was eighty thousan' in it, that time you looked in his cache. This here's a fifty-fifty proposition. So, when you fetch them bills in from where you cached 'em, I want my forty thousan'—an' not a damn cent less."

Black John grinned into the somber eyes. "Why shore, Cush— fifty-fifty's okay with me. You don't think I'd doublecross you, do you? I'll fetch your forty thousan' in this evenin'."

BLACK JOHN ADVISES

OLD CUSH, PROPRIETOR of Cushing's Fort, the log trading post and saloon that catered to the wants of the little community of outlawed men that had sprung up on Halfaday Creek, close against the Alaska-Yukon border, shoved his square, steel-rimmed spectacles from nose to forehead, folded a limp three-months-old newspaper, laid it carefully away on the back bar, and set out a bottle and two glasses as Black John Smith entered and crossed to the bar.

"I was readin' a piece in the paper about over in Paris where a hell of a lot of folks lives down in the sewers. Now what I claim—who in hell would want to live in a sewer?"

"Well," observed Black John, deliberately pouring his drink, and watching the little beads rise and rim his glass, "right off-hand, Cush, I can't think of no good reason why anyone would pick a sewer as a place of residence. But I s'pose it's all accordin' to how they was raised. In the first place, you got to remember they're Frenchmen."

"Oh," said Cush, as he poured his own drink. "But even at that, John, why would they like to live in a sewer?"

"Ever been to Paris?"

"No."

"If you had," replied Black John loftily, "it wouldn't be so hard fer you to onderstand their preference."

"But it must be dark as hell, an' wet, an' stink down there."

"Oh, shore," Black John agreed, "all them things would have

to be taken into consideration. But there's folks, Cush, that would gladly overlook them small inconveniences let the sake of bein' fashionable."

"Fashionable! Cripes sake, John, you don't mean it's fashionable if anyone was to live in a sewer!"

"Well, it wouldn't be in New York, er even mebbe in Chicago—but over in Paris it's different. In spite of what you might think, Cush, them Frenchmen is great readers, an' they read about how it's fashionable in places like London an' New York, an' other civilized towns, fer to live in the suburbs. Now Paris is onfortunate in that it ain't got no suburbs to live in, so them that's bound to be fashionable in spite of tall moves into the sewers."

"But Cripes—a sewer ain't no suburb!"

Black John regarded the other with eyes full of pity. "If yer education had been broadened to include Latin, Cush, you wouldn't keep fallin' into them errors. In Latin the word 'sub' means under, an' the word 'urb' means city. Now, whatever other defecks them Frenchmen has, they shore know their Latin—an' livin' in them sewers proves it. Education's a great thing, Cush—onct you've got it."

"Huh," grunted Cush, "eggication is bad enough, when it makes folks use big words instead of little ones, but on top of that, if it makes 'em want to live in a sewer, I'm damn glad I ain't got none of it." He swallowed his liquor, refilled his glass, and made an entry in his day book. "This last one is on you," he said. "Here comes someone. At that, though," he admitted, "it's handy to have some eggucated fella around to kind of explain things."

It was spring on Halfaday. Along the creek the young leaves of the willows and birches and aspens showed vivid green against the sombre background of spruce. The creek, running bank-full, burbled merrily after its long winter silence, and the feel of the mild air was good as it wafted through the open doorway in which a stranger now stood hesitant. For a moment the two men at the bar regarded the newcomer in silence. He was a well set up six-footer, whose blue eyes were taking in the details of the room.

"Why—he's nothin' but a kid!" exclaimed Black John. "Come on in, youngster, an' belly up to the bar. The house is buyin' a drink."

The lad crossed the floor as Old Cush slid an empty glass toward him.

"Thanks just the same," he said, accompanying the words with an engaging smile, "but I don't drink."

"Sech habit, prob'ly won't hurt you none, if persisted in,"

grinned Black John. "Me an' Cush seems never to have acquired it, so you'll pardon us if we fill up."

"Why sure, go ahead. It's just that I never learned to like it—been too busy playing football and baseball, I guess. What place is this?"

"Cushing's Fort, on Halfaday Crick, Yukon Territory," replied Black John. "Yonder's Old Cush hisself, an' my name's Smith—Black John, fer purposes of identification."

"I'm Bob Farnum. I was working my way to the Klondike with Jack Dalton. There were four of us, packing in over the Dalton trail with horses. We've had to keep crossing and re-

crossing since we hit the
White River. Can't cross
except early in the
morning when the
river's low because of the
cold nights, and yester-
day morning, I got lost
hunting one of the
horses, and when I got
back to the river, the
others had crossed and
gone on. I followed
down on this side till I
came to the mouth of
this crick, and found a
trail leading up it, so I
followed it."

"You come up the crick a-foot?"

"Yes. Pretty tough going in some places, with the soggy snow, and bayous to wade."

"I'll say it was. Where's yer pack?"

"I haven't got any pack. The outfit went on down with the horses."

Old Cush set his glass on the bar and regarded the young man intently. "When have you et?" he asked abruptly.

"I haven't eaten since night before last," smiled the boy. "You see, in the morning we ford the horses across first and eat af-terward, so we'll be sure the river won't rise before we make the crossing. By the time I got back to the river, it was too high to cross, so I followed down this side. But I never caught up with the outfit."

"Set down in one of them chairs," ordered Cush, "an' git them wet clothes off'n you. The klooch'll warm up some grub an' fetch it in d'reckly, an' I'll dig you out some dry stuff in the tradin' room."

The lad hesitated. "I'll just wring these things out and put 'em back on," he said. "The fact is, I'm broke. What little money I had is in my duffel bag and that's gone on with the outfit. If you'll stake me to a good meal, though, I'll sure appreciate it. I'm hungry as a wolf."

"You'll wring 'em out an' hang 'em on a chair," retorted Cush, "an' there ain't no question of pay about it. A man wet to his neck, an' no grub in his belly is liable to ketch the pneumony, er the rheumatiz, er somethin'. Git to work now, an' do like I say."

"It's a wonder Jack wouldn't of waited till you got back, instead of pullin' out on you," said Black John. "Did you find the horse you was huntin'?"

"No, I lost his trail among the rocks of a slope where the snow had melted off. But you can't blame Dalton for going on. The fact is, we were short of grub. Two horses that had grub packs on 'em got drowned upriver. We lost the packs, and we were all on short rations. We had agreed that it was every man for himself in case we got separated. There could be no waiting. Dalton's pretty hard-boiled. The Indians, the Chilkats and the Sticks, sure are afraid of him."

"Yeah," Black John agreed, "Jack's a good man on the trail. He'll get through if anyone kin. An' I s'pose he thinks everyone else is jest like him. The way he handles them Siwashes, though— some day one of 'em's goin' to git him. What do you aim to do now—foller on down after Dalton?"

"Well, I don't know just what to do," replied the lad as he proceeded to remove his wet clothing. "Back home the papers were all full of this Klondike gold rush, and the fortunes that are being cleaned up, so I decided to get in on it But Dalton has been telling me that there are thousands of people pouring into the country over the Chilcoot and the White Pass, and that not one out of a hundred of them will get his ante back. He says the Klondike diggings are over-crowded already. He believes that a man would stand a better chance out on one of the cricks along the White River."

Black John nodded. "Them Dawson diggin's is shore crowded," he admitted. "An' there ain't no reason why the White River country wouldn't be as good, if not better than anywheres else. 'Gold's where you find it', the old sayin' is. Step over behind the stove. Here comes the klooch with the grub. Cush'll be in d'reckly with some dry clothin'."

The youngster, holding his wet shirt before him, slipped behind the huge stove, as a young Indian woman entered and deposited a huge plate of stewed moose meat, a pot of tea, a bowl of gravy, and a heaping plate of bread on a card table and departed. Cush came in from the trading room, his arms laden with clothing topped with a coarse towel.

"Rub hell out of yerself now, an' climb into them duds, then tear into that platter of grub—an' don't be afraid of it, there's plenty more where that come from. Cripes, a big husky kid like you that ain't et sence you have, an' mushin' the way you've been, had ort to be able to swaller a moose, hoofs, horns, an' all!"

HALF AN hour later the boy mopped up the last of the gravy with the last piece of bread on the plate, and shook his head protestingly, as Old Cush roared for the woman to bring more grub.

"No more, please," he grinned. "Honestly—I couldn't swallow another mouthful. I never tasted anything so good in my life, but there's a limit. I sure want to thank you. This is the first time I've felt really comfortable for more than a week. We've been going on pretty short rations."

"You can fergit about the thankin'," replied Cush, "an' yer welcome to stay here as long as you like."

"Is there gold on this creek? Could I stake a claim somewhere around here?"

"Yeah," Black John replied, "there's gold on Halfaday, an' there's gold on most of the feeders. Most any claim you'd stake would pay wages. Lots pays better 'n wages. An' there's been a few real strikes made. A man could do a lot worse than stake a claim on Halfaday. But—"

"I'll bet he could," interrupted the youth, smiling frankly. "I like you men, and I believe I'll stake a claim here. I'll probably be an awful nuisance at first, asking questions and all. I don't know a thing in the world about mining, except what Jack Dalton told me on the trail. But I can learn. The trouble is, I haven't got any outfit. What little I had has gone on down the river with Jack Dalton." He appealed directly to Cush. "I already owe you for a big meal, and the clothes I've got on," he said. "If you'd trust me for enough supplies to get started, I'll pay you as soon—"

"You don't owe me fer a damn thing," interrupted Cush, mopping at an imaginary spot on the bar, "an' what's more yer credick's good here fer anything you want."

"That's right," seconded Black John, "an' you can hole up with me till you git located. This here gold diggin' ain't no compli-cated business to learn—mostly it's harder on the muscles than what it is on the intelleck—an' I could see when you was stripped a while ago that yer well muscled."

The lad chuckled. "But as for intellect, you aren't so sure, eh?"

White teeth gleamed behind the black beard as Black John's smile widened. "Not yet," he admitted, "but the matter is rela-tively onimportant. Cush, there, has got along fairly well with one which it would be outrageous hyperbole to refer to it as infinitesimal."

Old Cush slanted the youth an apologetic glance. "Don't mind him," he said. "As long as the big words holds out, John'll keep on talkin'—whether he says anything, er not."

"All of which reminds me," laughed the big man, "that it's a fine day, an' if you'll fetch them wet clothes along, we'll step over to my cabin an' hang 'em on a limb where the sun'll hit 'em. An' then, if you ain't too tired, we'll slip up the crick a ways an' look over a few locations."

With the wet clothing wrung out and hung up to dry, the two entered the cabin where Black John indicated a neatly made bunk across the room from his own.

"That's yourn," he said, "fer as long as you want it."

The lad seated himself on the edge of the bunk as Black John settled into a chair and filled his pipe. "You men have been fine to me," he said. "Sometime I hope I'll be able to—to show you that I appreciate it."

"Don't let that bother you none, son," replied the big man, punching at his pipe stem with a wire that he took from a nail. "So you come to the big country after gold, eh? Well, you might's well learn right on the start—you ain't goin' to have no snap. I've seen some of them newspapers from down in the States, an' from what they print, it looks like we was all shovellin' gold out of the grass roots, up here. We ain't—by a damn sight. The gold that's got is got by damn hard work."

The other nodded. "I'm not looking for a snap," he replied. "I'm not afraid of hard work. I got a taste of what a man's up against, coming in. I can take it. The fact is, I've got to make a strike."

"Some girl, I s'pose," commented Black John. "Some girl that wouldn't think of marryin' a pore man, but is perfectly willin' to let him hit out into this damn country to freeze, an' drown, an' starve so she kin have a million er so to blow in when he gits back with it—if ever. If he don't git back, there's plenty of other men, that's mebbe got their million made."

The youngster grinned. "Nope. No girl. Never had much time for girls. Too busy with football and baseball. I've got to get an education before I take any girl seriously. I'm planning to study medicine. But I want at least three years in the university before I go to medical college. A man needs that for a foundation. I've had one of those years. Everything was going along fine. Then my dad lost his position through no fault of his own, and had to take a job that pays him less than half of his former salary. So as far as I'm concerned, college is out—unless I can finance myself. With the newspapers full of this gold country news, I decided that the quickest way for me to get the money, was to come up here and dig it out of the ground. I'm only nineteen. If I can make a strike within the next year, or two, I can go back and get my education. See?"

Black John nodded. "Yeah. I see. But s'pose you don't strike nothin' that pays better'n wages? Er even if you was to do better, an' hit a location that done only fairly well. It would take you several years to git enough together—mebbe ten years er so. Then it would be too late."

"It's the chance I've got to take. There was no job I could get back home that would pay any better than wages."

"That's so," admitted Black John. "Anyways, up here you've got a chanct to hit it out big. But layin' all that aside. Now, take me. I don't mind sayin' that I've struck it lucky—here an' there. I've got more dust an' cash than I've got any present use fer. I like yer looks an' the way you talk. I'm willin' to take a gamble on you. Why not set there an' figger out about how much you'll be needin' to finance them six more years of college you was tellin' about, an' I'll advance you the money. You kin pay it back, a little to a time, when you git yer medical practice established. I won't miss the money—an' it'll save you a lot of time."

THE LAD shook his head. "No," he said, emphatically. "I can't do it. Don't think I don't appreciate your offer. It's fine—one of the finest things I have ever known a man to do—me a perfect stranger, and all. How do you know that I'm not a grafter of some kind—an out and out crook, maybe?"

Black John grinned. "I told you I was willin' to take a gamble." he said. "Fact is, son, I've had more er less experience with crooks, of one kind an' another—an' somehow, you don't come up to specifications. A man can't tell how he gits to know a crook when he sees one. It ain't the eyes, like I've heard some folks claim. Hell, I've know'd folks with shifty eyes that was square as a die, an' I've know'd others that could stare a hole through a stone wall—that I wouldn't trust 'em on the other side of. An' it ain't the way they talk, neither. I know men that blisters the paint off'n a bar every time they open their mouth that I'd trust with my last cent. An' I know others that their talk is so damn pious that the hour of prayer in a girl's school would sound like rank blasphemy beside of it, that I wouldn't trust with a plugged nickel."

The other smiled. "The fact is, I'm not a crook. If I took your money I'd pay it back, if it took me all my life to do it. But, I need a lot more money than just enough to pay for my education. My dad is the finest old boy that ever lived, and he's in trouble. We always had plenty to live nicely on, and he never begrudged me or my sister anything within reason. What was his, was ours. Now—he's not living so nicely. My sister is working to help eke out the family resources, and my mother is worrying her heart out. She's just as fine as Dad is—and she tries not to let him know she worries. But well, it's up to me to pull 'em out of the hole—see? This gold rush looked my best bet—and I took it. I'll make good, too. You'll see. I don't need a million. Fifty thousand will set Dad up in business, and educate me too."

Black John nodded slowly. "Yeah," he said. "I see. An' damned if I don't believe you will make good."

II

BLACK JOHN LED the way up the creek, pausing now and then at some claim to chat with the owner, introduce young Farnum, and explain to him the manipulation of windlass, sluice, riffles, and pans. Presently he entered a narrow crevice in the rough rock wall, by means of which a tiny creek flowed into Halfaday. This crack, varying in width from four feet to as many yards, zigzagged between living rock walls which towered perpendicularly to the narrow strip of blue sky high above the tiny creek bed. Five hundred feet farther on the walls drew suddenly apart to form a narrow valley, some hundred yards in width, whose floor lay level for a mile or more, then slanted sharply into the high hills.

Black John pointed to a small, one roomed cabin that stood near the center of the valley, close beside the bank of the little creek. "That's Buck Hammond's old cabin," he said. "Fella name of Veely lived in it fer a while after Buck pulled out. If I was you, I'd stake on this here feeder. Buck, he took out about a hundred thousan' in a year's time. Could of took out a lot more, but he married Old Man Price's daughter down to Dawson, an' the old man wanted Buck should manage some properties he had on Bonanza. Took him into pardnership, an' I guess Buck's worth a couple of million, by now. This Veely, too—he could of done all right fer hisself, but we hung him."

"Hung him!"

"Yeah, he killed a fella in a row over a stud game, an' a miners' meetin' voted a hangin' onto him. You can move yer stuff into the cabin an' stake you out a claim. You won't be needin' no windlass er sluice fer a while till you git down into the gravel, an' when you do you kin move 'em over off'n Veely's old claim. This here crick looks like the best bet on Halfaday. Mostly the newcomers passes it up not noticin' that crack in the rock, er else not explorin' it if they do. She's spotted, though, like most of the other cricks. Most any claim you'd stake will pay wages er better, an' if you hit it lucky you'd can prob'ly clean up a hundred thousan' er so in a few years' time."

Examination showed the cabin could be made habitable with a little cleaning up, and the addition of more dirt on the roof. The youngster was enthusiastic. "I don't know how to thank you and Cush for what you're doing for me," he said. "I'm just beginning to realize what a man would be up against in this country if he didn't find friends. Why, it would be almost hopeless!"

"Well, most chechakos is long on hope," observed Black John. "It's about the only recommendation most of 'em's got. At that, though, they git about what's comin' to 'em, in the long run."

"Are you sure you weren't saving this little valley for yourself? I don't want to impose on you men. I'd rather take my chances out there on the main crick than do that."

"You ain't imposin' on no one," replied Black John. "Like I told you, I've struck it sort of lucky in several different ventures, an' I don't aim to do no hell of a lot of bone work this summer. It don't seem to agree with my kidneys, er mebbe it's my liver, er spleen, er gall bladder, er some sech part. I find I can keep toll'ble well if I jest sort of favor myself, an' I don't aim to jeopardize my health with no hard work. Come on, we'll pick out a location, an' I'll show you about stakin', an' then we'll be gittin' back."

"Don't we have to record a claim, or something, after you've got it staked?"

"Oh, shore. I'll help you with that, too. You can record it with Cush, an' then, when someone goes on down to Dawson, he'll record a whole batch of 'em to onct."

WITH HIS claim duly staked and recorded, young Farnum spent the next two or three days packing supplies to his cabin. Two weeks later he showed up at the fort and proudly laid a limp gold sack on the bar. "I wish you'd weigh that up," he said. "I'd like to know how I'm doing."

Cush weighed the dust and returned it to the sack. "Fifteen ounces an' a quarter," he said. "That's a little better'n wages to start off with, which ain't doin' bad, fer a chechako."

"Take it, and credit my account. There's a few more things I need."

"There ain't no hurry about yer account," Cush replied. "You can jest let it ride, if you want to."

"But I don't want to. What's the use of my carrying that dust around when it belongs to you? Take it, and I'll pay the rest the next time I come. And don't forget to charge me with that big meal and those clothes I got the first day I landed here."

"OK.," said Cush, emptying the dust into the till and making an entry in his book. "But that meal of vittles, an' them clothes is on the house. I don't aim to trade on a man's miseries."

Black John entered and joined the youngster at the bar, as Cush set out the bottle and glasses. "Too bad Cush don't handle none of 'em belly washes like ginger ale er pop," he grinned. "It must be lonesome as hell if a man don't drink. But at that," he added quickly, "a young fella's a damn sight better off without it."

"Don't mind me," laughed the lad. "Go ahead."

"How you doin'?" asked Black John, downing his liquor.

"I've taken out fifteen ounces and a quarter," Farnum answered. "Cush just weighed it."

"Well, that ain't so bad fer the top gravel," observed Black John. "Jest keep on goin', an' when you git down a ways, if she don't start to git better, sink a new shaft."

In the long days of early June, daylight is almost continuous on Halfaday. Men began to drift in, and young Farnum stayed on into the evening, listening to the talk, and enjoying his first contact with human beings for nearly two long weeks.

Several men became increasingly loud and boisterous as their liquor took hold, one in particular who answered to the name of Stonewall Sheridan, pounded the bar with his fist, and loudly ordered a round of drinks. Men ranged themselves at the bar as Cush set out bottles and glasses. Sheridan filled his glass, and as he was about to raise it, his eyes fell upon young Farnum, who had dropped into a chair beside one of the tables, and was idly riffling a deck of cards.

"Hey, you—there!" called Sheridan. "Didn't you hear me order the drinks?"

The youngster met the man's glance with a smile. "Go right ahead," he said. "Don't mind me. I don't care for anything, thank you."

"You don't care fer anythin'! Meanin', you won't drink with me, eh?"

"I'd drink with you, if I wanted a drink," replied the lad, still smiling. "It's just that I don't drink liquor."

"Mamma's boy, eh? You don't drink licker! Well, by God, you might think you don't, but you do—when I'm buyin' a round! Git up on yer hind legs an' belly up here!"

The smile faded from the youngster's lips, and his face flushed slightly. But he made no move to rise from his chair. His lips parted, but he seemed at a loss to reply.

Picking up his glass, Sheridan stepped toward him. "Take it where you set, then!" he roared. "By God, when I buy you'll drink, if I've got to pour it down you!"

Old Cush's eye noted the exact position of a heavy six-gun that lay ready to hand beneath the bar, as Black John Smith suddenly confronted Sheridan in mid-floor. The blue-gray eyes glittered coldly as they met the angry eyes of the other. "Jest what was you aimin' to do?" he asked in a low, level voice.

"I'm goin' to pour this licker down that young cub's throat! I'll learn him not to drink with me! This ort to be good—" he added with a loud laugh, "the first drunk he's ever been on! We'll fill him clean up to the neck."

"You—an' who else?" The men who knew Black John noted the deadly evenness of his voice.

"Well, hell—we'll all be in on the fun."

"Yeah? Well, I don't like to spoil no man's fun—but I'm warnin' you not to lay a finger on that kid. When he told you he didn't drink, he meant it."

The other's lips twisted into a snarl. "Who says so?" he demanded.

"I do. I'm steppin' back to the bar now. You can heed the warnin' er not—jest as you like. But if you don't heed it, you're goin' to let yerself in fer a mess of the damndest, most boisterous fun that you've run acrost in a hell of a while. The boys'll ondoubtless enjoy it more'n what you will, 'cause the joke, Sheridan, will be on you."

Deliberately, Black John turned his back on the other and resumed his place at the end of the bar. Tense silence reigned for a moment, as Sheridan stood in the middle of the floor, his rage-narrowed eyes shifting from the flushed face of the youngster in the chair to the row of stony faced men at the bar. Reading nothing of sympathy in their eyes, he turned abruptly and resumed his place beside the others.

"If this is a Sunday School," he growled, "we'd ought to be singin' a hymn."

"Suit yerself," retorted Black John. "They sing 'em at funerals, too."

The drink was downed, someone else bought a round, and once more the loud talk was resumed, Sheridan's the loudest of all. With each succeeding drink he became louder and more boastful. It was as though he sought by bluster to efface the fact that he had not forced Black John's hand.

"Yessir," he bragged loudly, "when it comes right down to pullin' off a job, I've got all you cheapskates backed clean off the boards! Why hell, take that Clean All soap factory pay-roll job I pulled in Chi. Seventy thousan' in cold cash. I slipped down to New Orleans an' blow'd every damn cent of it in three months! Then over in Baltimore, I took a branch bank fer forty-six thousan', an' hopped clean acrost to Frisco an' took the Express Company fer thirty thousan' more, after stoppin' off in Brooklyn an' gatherin' seventeen thousan' off'n a brewery. I've got eighty-five thousan' in Cush's safe right now. How many of you gravel hounds can match it? Them was high class jobs, I'm tellin' you. Here I understand a man kin git famous for snatchin' as little as forty thousan' off'n some soldiers."

Men glanced toward Black John, whose boast it was that he had once held up a major and three soldiers over in Alaska and relieved them of a forty thousand dollar pay-roll. But the big man had either missed the slur, or chose to ignore it. He stood at the end of the bar in casual conversation with Cush, while out of the tail of his eye, he was regarding young Farnum, upon whose face the flush of embarrassment had given place to an unwonted pallor. He remained seated at the table, but his fingers had ceased to toy with the cards. His fists were clenched, his lips pressed into a thin straight line, and his blue eyes, narrowed to slits, were fixed upon the loud-mouthed braggart at the bar. Presently the youngster rose abruptly, crossed the floor hurriedly, and disappeared through the doorway.

A few moments later Black John, too, sauntered from the room and took up a position at a corner of the building. "Now what the hell?" he muttered to himself. "If he's gone on up to his claim, that's O.K., but if I ever seen cold, killin' rage in a man's eyes, it was in his. An' that ain't so good in a kid—they ain't got no judgment. Funny thing—seemed like this rage sort of hung fire; he didn't git like that till after Sheridan had quit botherin' him. He might be comin' back, an' no tellin' what the fool kid would do."

And the kid was coming back, as hurried footfalls from the direction of Black John's own cabin soon proclaimed. As the lad rounded the corner of the building, Black John suddenly confronted him.

"What's yer hurry, son?" he asked as his glance strayed from the frowning brow above the narrowed eyes to the black six-gun tightly clutched in the youngster's right hand. He recognized the gun as one that had reposed on the shelf beside the clock in his own cabin—the gun with which Snook, alias Cleveland, the poisoner, had shot himself.

"I—I'll kill him!" exclaimed the youth in a nervous, half-hysterical voice. "Or he'll kill me. He's got a pistol. I saw it bulging at the front of his shirt. I'll—"

"Yeah," smiled Black John soothingly. "I seen that, too, son—when I bluffed him back to the bar. I thought he might pull it on me, in which case it would of been jest too damn bad fer him. Cush would have stopped his clock before he'd got his gun out of his shirt—an' we don't want no shootin's on Halfa day. Better jest give me the gun, son. He ain't a-goin' to bother you no more."

"Bother me! Good gosh, it wasn't that! He's the man that is responsible for all our trouble; it was that seventy thousand dollar soap factory robbery that cost my dad his position. He ruined my dad, and caused my sister to go to work as a clerk, and my mother to worry her heart out, and—"

"Yeah—an' so what?"

"And he stands up there and brags about it! I—I'll—"

"Let's jest step on over to the cabin an' talk it over first," said the big man quietly, and reached out his hand.

WITHOUT A word the lad turned over the gun and followed Black John up the trail to the cabin.

"Now," said Black John, "how come yer dad lost his job on account of this here robbery, er burglary, or whatever it was?"

"He was general manager of the Clean All factory, and after the robbery the directors let him out because they said he hadn't taken proper precautions for the protection of the big pay-roll. It wasn't true. He had taken exactly the same precautions that had been taken for years. They had always been considered adequate—then, when it happened, Dad was the goat."

"Yeah, that's often the way things turns out. I s'pose them directors figgered that in order to make a showin' to the stock-holders they had to put the blame on someone. Trouble is with them corporations, they ain't got no tollerance. But it looks, son, like you was gunnin' fer the wrong man. If yer plumb blood-thirsty that-a-way, you'd ort to go an' shoot up that board of directors. This here Sheridan, whatever his faults may be—an' to hear him talk, he's prob'ly got plenty—can't be blamed di-reckly fer yer dad's losin' his job. That there was a side issue that he couldn't of foreseen. There he was, mindin' his own business—"

"Minding his own business!" exclaimed the other, his eyes widening in surprise. "Why, he was committing a robbery!"

"Yeah," agreed the big man in a matter of fact tone. "That was his business, an' he was mindin' it. The adverse effect on yer dad prob'ly never occurred to him."

"But," queried the youth, regarding Black John with a puzzled frown, "how does he dare to come right out and boast of all these crimes?"

"Well, he hadn't ort to be blamed too hard fer that. Lots of folks, especially when they git a little drunk, er drunker, has got a bragful nature."

"But how does he dare to do it? Aren't there any police in this country?"

"Oh, shore—there's police, all right. But they're pretty busy down along the big river, what with all the chechakos that's pourin' in on 'em. They don't bother Halfaday much. They know damn well that me an' Cush will keep the crick moral."

"Moral!"

"Yeah. You see, son, layin' as we do right up agin the line, makes it handy fer the boys to sort of dodge back an' forth, as circumstances seems to indicate. Quite a lot of the boys along the crick is outlawed, fer one reason er another, their characters, like this one of Sheridan's, havin' been smirched by some performance er other. So they come to Halfaday. What any man done before he come here ain't none of our business, but what he does after he gits here is every man's business. That's why we don't stand fer no crime on the crick, it would fetch in the police, an' shootin' it out with a man is a crime, accordin' to our code. That is, if it's carried out deliberately—like you was goin' to shoot it out with Sheridan. You would have been tried by a miners' meetin', an' prob'ly hung. Which wouldn't of helped yer dad none, nor yer sister, an' would of added a heap of worries to them yer ma has already got."

THE YOUNGSTER nodded thoughtfully. "You're dead right," he admitted. "I was a fool. I certainly am indebted to you for more than I can ever repay. I don't know—I never wanted to kill anybody before—but hearing him bragging about the thing that ruined my dad—ruined all of us—my blood seemed to boil— I—I went kind of nutty, I guess."

"Ruin," observed Black John, "ain't never complete, until such time as there can't nothin' be done to avert it. An' comittin' a felonious shootin' on Halfaday is one of the world's worst ways to avert ruin. What you want to do, son, is to take the bull by the horns an' milk him dry."

"How—what do you mean?"

"Well, accordin' to his own tally, an' I happen to know that it's a fact—even if he did state it—he's got eighty-five thousan' dollars in Cush's safe. Good liquid money, too—me an' Cush kind of run it over. It looks like if you had that eighty-five thousan' it would finance yer education, an' leave plenty over to set yer dad up in some good business, don't it?"

"Why—certainly! But I haven't got it. And I'm not going to steal it—even if he did."

"Shore you ain't. In the first place you couldn't, if you wanted to. An' besides, it would be reprehensible an' onethical to a surprisin' degree. An' on top of all that, larceny in any form, or an attempt at larceny, is also hangable on Halfaday. But if you was to sell him yer claim fer the eighty-five thousan', it would be all open an' aboveboard, wouldn't it?"

"Is the claim worth that?"

Black John regarded the younger man thoughtfully. "What difference does that make?" he asked.

"Well, it's like this. I told you I wouldn't steal his money—and I won't. If I were to sell him a claim that I didn't believe was worth anything like the price I asked for it, it would be just as much stealing as though I held him up at the point of a gun. I believe that a man has got to stay square. That's what I like about you—you're so doggone square and open and aboveboard in everything you do. And you certainly saved me from making a fool of myself." He paused, and then asked abruptly, "What makes you think he'd buy my claim?"

"Well, a little salt might help him make up his mind."

"Salt?"

"Yeah, kind of sprinkle a little dust in the gravel to make a good showin'."

"Not me."

Black John laughed, "Shore you wouldn't, son. I was jest soundin' you out. It would be extremely onethical. I'd hate to see you do it—an' that ain't no lie. It's refreshin' to meet up with a youngster like you. You was raised right. I was raised right, too—but it was quite a while ago, an' some of the raisin', mebbe, has had a chanct to wear off. Take it, though, with a claim like yourn, you won't be needin' to salt it none. It's more'n likely to be good. That's why I located you on it. I liked you from the start. Two claims on that feeder has turned out good. Buck Hammond took out a hundred thousan', an' could have took out more if Old Man Price hadn't needed him. An' Veely could have done likewise if we hadn't had to hang him. It ain't at all outside of the probabilities that you kin take out somewheres between one an' two hundred thousan' in the next few years. Buyin' any claim is a gamble, but it's a reasonable one. If a man buys claim at a figger based on what the claim is doin' at the time he buys it, it's a fair bargain, ain't it?"

"Sure it is—if the claim hasn't been salted."

"Saltin' is out—as fer as you're concerned. Listen, now, an' I'll put you wise, to somethin' about that crick. Let's see, how fer down are you—how deep is yer shaft?"

"I'm down about seven feet. When I go back I'm going to tear down Hammond's old windlass and erect it above the shaft. It's got to where I can't throw the stuff out any more, without getting half of it down my neck."

"Seven foot, eh? Well—one more foot, an' yer goin' to know whether yer claim's a real strike, like Hammond's an' Veely's, er jest a wages proposition. All them claims on that feeder pays wages, er a little better, down to about eight foot."

"That's what mine's been doing."

"Well, most of 'em jest keeps on the same way clean down

to bed rock. But like I told you, that feeder's spotted. There's pockets of damn good stuff. If you begin gittin' into better stuff at seven an' a half er eight foot, you'll know to a certainty, you've struck it lucky. It ain't never failed yet on that feeder. If you begin throwin' out richer stuff in the next day or so, you kin figger yer proposition's goin' to clean up anywheres between one an' two hundred thousan', in the next few years.

"Now," continued Black John, prodding at his pipe stem with a wire, "you could do one of two things. You could stick here an' work the claim fer several years; er you could sell out to someone at a reasonable figger—say eighty-five to a hundred thousan'. The buyer would be takin' a gamble, of course—there ain't nothin' certain but death. But the chances is all in his favor that the investment would be sound. You would save several years' time in the matter of yer education. Yer dad could save that time in startin' up in business again. Yer sister could quit workin'. An' yer ma could quit worryin', an' three, four years of worry shore raises hell with a woman. Looks to me, son, like a good quick sale at, say, around eighty-five thousan' would be right down your alley."

"Sure it would!" exclaimed the youngster, his eyes shining. "Gosh, I can hardly wait to get back to the claim! Maybe I won't start in tomorrow and make the dirt fly! Day after tomorrow, I mean—it will take me all day tomorrow to rig that windlass. The best part of it is, I wouldn't feel under any obligation to restore that seventy thousand to the factory. He said he blew all that money in New Orleans. Of course, the rest of his money was stolen, too—but—"

Black John laughed. "Don't be a damn fool, kid. Did you ever stop to figger that if you was to trace back the pedigree of most all the money you ever handle you'd prob'ly find that it had be'n stole, at sometime er other? I have, an' most of it wouldn't have to be traced back so damn fer, neither. But it don't seem to irk my conscience none, at that."

A SHORT time later Black John stood in the doorway of his cabin and watched the youngster hasten eagerly up the creek in the direction of his claim. The bearded lips parted in a smile. "Good kid," he muttered. "It would be too damn bad fer a kid like him to linger too long on Halfaday." Then he sauntered over to the saloon, to find the customers gone, and old Cush preparing to close for the night.

"Where you been?" asked Cush, as he set out the bottle and a couple of glasses. "When I seen that you'd took notice of that there bulge in Sheridan's shirt, I figgered you'd slipped over to the cabin to heel yerself."

"No, there ain't nothin' in mixin' it up with a wind-bag like him. An' besides, I'm sort of savin' him fer a special purpose."

"Special purpose?" queried Cush. "What kind of a special purpose would a damn cuss like him be good fer?"

"Well, he's got eighty-five thousan' in the safe. I figger mebbe he might want to invest it."

"Invest it in what?" asked Cush, a gleam of interest showing in his somber eyes.

"In the kid's claim, fer instance."

"You mean his claim up Buck Hammond's crick? Hell, that claim ain't never goin' to pay out much better'n wages."

"It could pay out even less than that an' it wouldn't grieve me none," grinned Black John, swallowing his liquor, and refilling his glass. "That is, in case Sheridan was to buy it."

"But why would Sheridan fall fer a deal like that? Cripes, John, that kid couldn't put over nothin' like that on him!"

"Mebbe not. But I've got a kind of a hunch that within the next few days, Sheridan's goin' to fall all over himself tryin' to buy that claim. He'll prob'ly git the idee, somehow, that it's worth more'n what it really is. An' that reminds me, Cush, that if I was to make you any propositions at sech times as this here Sheridan would be apt to overhear 'em, you fall in with 'em—see? No matter how unpromisin' they sound, you agree to 'em. An' by the way, jest hand me a sack of dust out of the safe an' charge it up agin me."

"What in hell you goin' to do with a sack of dust this time of night?" asked Cush as he pushed the sack across the bar.

"Use it fer bread," replied Black John.

"Bread! You drunk, er crazy, er somethin'?"

Black John grinned. "Ain't you come to the place in the Good Book yet where it says to cast yer bread upon the waters an' you'll find it agin?"

"Seems like I rec'lect some sech sayin', but it didn't mention nothin' about dust. If you heave that poke in the water, the only way you'll ever git it agin is to dive fer it."

"Yer too literal minded, Cush," laughed the big man, as he pocketed the little sack and headed for the door.

"I might be literary minded—but I ain't no damn fool," retorted Cush as he followed the other to the door, and watched the huge figure merge into the semi-darkness of the upcreek trail.

III

IN THE EARLY evening of the second day following, young Farnum reappeared at the fort, his eyes fairly aglow with excitement. Finding Cush and Black John in the saloon, the youngster tossed a small sack on the bar. It was not nearly so limp as the one Cush had previously weighed.

"Weigh it up, Cush," he cried, "and take out the balance of what I owe you!" He turned to Black John. "By Gosh, I believe I've made a real strike! It's working out just exactly the way you predicted it would if the claim was going to be a good one—just like you said both those other rich claims worked out—the gravel began suddenly to get richer between seven and eight feet. I worked like the devil yesterday rigging that windlass, and this morning I started early and I hadn't got down six inches till the stuff began to get richer. I could even see the gold as I shoveled it into my bucket—catch little glints of yellow nearly every shovelful. I worked long and hard today panning the buckets as I took them out. I never threw a bucketful onto the dump. I certainly am tired tonight, but I couldn't help coming down to tell you the good news—and to find out how much I'd taken out."

"It's jest crowdin' of thirty-four ounces," Cush announced as he returned most of the dust to the sack, and made an entry in his book. "An' yer all squared up, an' got dust in yer poke, to boot."

Black John reached out and grasped the youngster's hand. "I'm shore glad she turned out that-a-way, son," he said. "If she repeats agin tomorrow, yer all set. A good quick sale now, an' you won't need to interrupt that there education of yourn. An' won't them folks—yer dad, an' yer ma, an' yer sister—be proud of you! They kin all quit worryin' then."

"You bet! I'll be glad to sell out. I thought about it a long time, last night in my bunk. If I can get a good price I'd be foolish to stay here and work the claim. I'd be losing a lot of valuable time."

"Shore you would," agreed the big man heartily, "an' there's yer folks to think about, too. But hold out fer yer price. Don't take a damn cent less'n, say, eighty-five thousan'. That'll be plenty fer you—an' the purchaser could be lookin' forward to a damn good profit, besides."

"I'll hold out," replied the lad. "I'd be a fool not to take your advice, after all you've done for me. You know all about this country—and—and you're so darn square! I certainly was lucky to fall into the hands of an honest man. Why, you could have kept still about that claim, and when I struck that better gravel, you could have persuaded me to sell out to you for just a few thousand. Or you could have asked a partnership in the claim for helping me locate it, and I'd have been glad to agree. Even now I feel that you ought to—"

"No, no!" Black John interrupted. "I don't want no part of it. Like I told you, I've had a few lucky ventures of my own. Like you said I kind of know the ropes, up here. Don't worry none about me, son. I'll git along fine. An' now you better slip on back an' git you some sleep. Hit her another hard lick tomorrow, an' me an' Cush would kind of appreciate it if you come down an' tell us how you come out—if you ain't too tired. We've kind of took a likin' to you, an' we'll be interested to know. Come on down early, like now—before the boys comes driftin' in. It ain't necessary the news should git spread all over the crick, er you might have a stampede in on top of you."

"Sure, I'll come down," replied the lad. "It's little enough I can do for you men. I'd come if it were twice as far. Gosh—I—I'll never forget what you have done for me! It means a lot to meet men like you. Sometime a fellow might be tempted to—to do something underhanded or shady—and he'd think of you fellows—and what you'd do under the circumstances—and he'd be ashamed to—"

"Yeah," interrupted Black John hurriedly, "that's right, son. We're glad you feel that-a-way. But you better trot along now, an' ketch you some sleep. You'll have a hard day, tomorrow."

OLD CUSH was seized with a sudden fit of coughing, and Black John glared at him across the bar.

"Must of breathed in a bug," Cush explained, recovering, and reached to the back bar for the bottle and glasses. "This un's on the house."

"I'll be going now," said the lad. "See you tomorrow. And oh yes—there's one thing I forgot. I don't suppose it amounts to anything—but the other day, just before I came down here, I distinctly remember of pulling my ladder up out of my shaft and laying it on my dump. But the next morning it was in the shaft. Someone had been down in there."

"H-u-m," uttered Black John, combing at his beard with his fingers. "That's kind of odd, ain't it? But I wouldn't worry none about it if I was you. What happened, someone prob'ly come along when you wasn't there an' slipped out a sample pan, to find out how you was doin'."

The youngster laughed. "It's a good thing it was before I got down into that good gravel," he said. "They probably don't think I've got much of a claim."

"Shore they don't," agreed Black John. "Serves 'em right fer their underhandedness. So long. An' by the way, don't let Sheridan know you're anxious to sell out. Make him come to you."

Old Cush filled his glass, and eyed the big man across the bar. "Ain't yer ears kind of burnin', John?" he asked. "Cripes—I damn near choked to death—him thinkin' about what you'd do if something crooked come up! If he know'd what you'd do, an' done it, he'd be damn lucky to keep out of jail. An' you was careless as hell about that ladder."

"What the hell you talkin' about?" grinned the big man. "Shut up—here comes One Armed John. I want to have a little talk with him."

When One Armed John had filled the glass Cush slid toward him, Black John opened the conversation.

"How's fishin'?" he asked.

"It ain't so bad. I ketched a good mess, today—sold 'em to Pot Gutted John."

"How's Sheridan doin' down on his claim?"

"All right, I guess. He don't do no hell of a lot of work. Mostly he jest sets around."

"Ever stop in an' talk to him?"

"Oh, sometimes, when I'm down that way. I don't like him much. He's always braggin' about what he done. Hell, you'd think, hearin' him brag, there couldn't no one rob no one unlest it was him."

"The statement seems ambiguous, but we'll let it pass," grinned Black John.

"Shore, he's the damn biggest talker I ever heard. He don't

like it much on Halfaday. Claims there ain't nothin' doin' here. He claims he don't have to work no more. He's got enough so's he can set back an' take it easy, if he could find some good proposition to invest his money in. He kind of fingers to go down to Dawson an' look around fer an investment. I was talkin' to him this mornin'. He says he'd ruther stick around on Halfaday, on account of the police might be lookin' fer him, but there ain't no investments here."

"Well," Black John replied, "it's a fact that investments ain't exactly what you might call rife on Halfaday. But there's one I kin think of that might interest Sheridan. The kid has struck it lucky, an' he might be willin' to sell out."

"You mean the kid that's staked up on Hammond's feeder?"

"Yeah, he's the one."

"He's a damn good kid. I wouldn't like to see him git skun by a damn cuss like Sheridan."

"Me an' Cush wouldn't, neither," said Black John. "Fact is, we was sort of figgerin' on mebbe buyin' the kid out ourself. But if Sheridan is huntin' an investment, we wouldn't neither one of us stand in his way."

"Besides," persisted One Armed John, "I don't believe there's another damn claim on that feeder that would go much better'n wages. Hammond an' Veely got the only good ones there was. Hell, that whole crick's been prospected from one end to the other."

"That," replied Black John, fixing the other with a meaning look, "is my opinion exactly—an' that's the main reason why I wouldn't stand in the way of Sheridan's investin' in one of 'em."

A slow grin widened One Armed John's lips as the idea percolated into his none too active brain. "You mean he might buy out the kid's claim?"

"He might, if he could be made to think it would be a good investment. The kid took out fifteen ounces the first two weeks he worked it, an' then today he took out thirty-four ounces, an'

I look fer him to repeat tomorrow. He'll be in here at six o'clock tomorrow evenin' with his clean-up fer the day. He's pannin' it as fast as he takes it out."

"You mean," exclaimed One Armed John, "that he salted it? But hell—he couldn't of! In the first place he didn't have no dust to salt it with, an' if he had, a green chechako like him wouldn't have sense enough to salt a claim."

"Them's the exact sentiments I want you to put acrost to Sheridan. It hadn't ort to be hard to do. He knows the kid was broke when he come, an' he knows jest how green he is. It takes dust an' savvy to salt a proposition, an' the kid ain't got neither one. Therefore, if he's takin' out around thirty ounces a day, an' better, he's got somethin' that's worth mebbe a million. But he's so damn green he don't know how much it's worth. He might be induced to sell fer right around a hundred thousan', if he could git spot cash. What I want you should do is to slip down the crick kind of casual, tomorrow mornin', an' confidentially slip the word to Sheridan. Tell him jest what I told you about what the kid's takin' out, tell him his claim is actin' jest like Hammond's an' Veely's done on the same feeder—an' you might estimate that them two took out somewheres around a half a million apiece. It would be a lib'ral estimate, but Sheridan is a lib'ral talker hisself. An' you might slip him the tip that Cush an' me is all het up about buyin' the kid's claim. Tell him that the kid will be here at six in the evenin', an' if he's took out anywhere around thirty ounces, we're goin' to raise a hundred er a hundred an' fifty thousan' to buy him out. Do you git the idee?"

"Shore, I git it. I'll stop in there in the mornin'. It'll work out all right, 'cause I promised to fetch him a mess of fish if I ketched any. But even yet, I don't savvy how the kid could of salted his claim."

"The ways of Providence is sometimes devious in the extreme," replied Black John, "an' it ain't always given to mortals to fathom 'em."

"Oh," agreed One Armed John, regarding the speaker with vast respect, "in that case, mebbe he could of."

When the one armed one had departed, Old Cush, who had been busy with an account book, returned the book to the back bar.

"I know, now, what you meant the other night about throwin' bread in the water an' gittin' it back, like the Good Book says— but what I can't figger, if there's any water in the kid's shaft how in hell is he gittin' that dust back?"

"Literal acceptation is the tenet only of the theological fundamentalist," replied the big man.

"Oh—works like a pump, eh?"

"Yeah—sort of hot air pump," grinned Black John. "But, shut up—here comes some of the boys."

"All right, John, but about that poke of dust—it weighed up seventy-six ounces, an' I charged half of it up agin me. If yer aimin' to give that kid a start, I want to be in on it. He's a good kid—square as hell."

IV

THE NEXT EVENING when young Farnum arrived at the fort, Black John and Cush stood talking at the bar, and he noted that the man, Sheridan, was seated at a table, apparently absorbed in the contents of an old newspaper.

Cush weighed the sack of dust the youngster tossed onto the bar, and returned it. "Thirty-seven an' a half ounces," he announced.

"Getting better as it goes down," said the lad happily. "I'm certainly glad I made a strike."

"Shore," agreed Black John. "You must be pretty tired, though, workin' like you've been the last few days. If I was you I'd hit back fer the claim an' git you some sleep."

"Just what I'm goin' to do," smiled the lad. "I just came down, as I promised, to let you know how I was doing."

"We're obliged," said Black John. "It was mighty interestin'. So long."

The moment the lad passed through the door, Black John leaned forward and spoke to Cush in an undertone, one which, however, he was certain would carry to the table where Sheridan was still engrossed in his newspaper, apparently oblivious to anything that went on about him.

"That young punk has struck a shore winner," he announced, with suppressed excitement. "His claim is doin' jest what Buck Hammond's an' Veely's done—didn't show much till the eight-foot line, then all to onct showed big. We've got to git that claim, Cush! It would be a crime to pass it up. I'm tellin' you it'll go half a million!"

"W-e-e-l-l," drawled Cush, taking his cue, "mebbe not quite half a million, John."

"The hell it won't! That's what them other two done."

"Yeah, but every claim mightn't go quite that big. It's bound to go way up there, though. Why in hell couldn't one of us of struck it?"

"Our luck wasn't runnin', an' his was—that's all. We shore staked claims enough on that feeder all around Hammond's when he made his strike, an' none of 'em went much better'n wages. An' the same when Veely struck it. That feeder's spotted—either a claim's rich as hell, or it won't go no better'n wages. I tell you we've got to git holt of it!"

"Yeah, we shore have," agreed Cush. "What would he let it go for, I wonder?"

"I offered him fifty thousan' fer it yesterday, an' he turned me down," replied Black John. "But I'm bettin' he'd grab a hundred thousan'. I'd even be willin' to go a hundred an' fifty, if we had to. Cripes, Cush, if Red John, er Pot Gutted John finds out he's made a strike, they'd pool up an' buy it in a minute—they've got the dust to do it, an' they know all about them other claims.

We've got to work fast. Tell you what we'll do. We'll wait till tomorrow evenin' when he comes down to show us what he's took out, like he promised—an' then we'll git him over to my cabin an' make the deal. We'll have the hundred thousan' in cash an' dust—an' I'll bet he'll grab it. If we have to, though, we'll go a hundred an' fifty, like I said. What do you say?"

"Well—that's a sight of money, John. But of course at them figgers, we couldn't lose. I'll go you."

"O.K.," said the big man, with an air of relief. "Don't say a damn word to no one about it. I'd shore as hell hate to have anyone beat us out on this deal."

"I won't say nothin'," agreed Cush. "P-s-s-t—here comes some of the boys."

Several men from up and down the creek drifted in, and Sheridan joined them the bar. Drinks were had, and as usual, when he was drinking, Sheridan became loquacious.

"Tellin' you about me," he said, "I don't like it none too good in a place like this, where there ain't nothin' to do but work. A strong back an' a weak mind, that's what this here gold minin' takes. A man can work like hell, an' he don't git nowheres. Take me, I belong somewheres where a man with money an' brains can set back an' let both of 'em go to work fer him. Take it down around Dawson, now—I'll bet that, with all the propositions that's goin' on down there, a man could find some damn good investments."

"Yeah, I s'pose he could," agreed Long Nosed John. "But then agin, the police might pick him up, too. That is, if he was wanted somewheres."

"That's true—an' that's where the brains would come in," replied Sheridan. "It don't look to me like a man would have to be so damn foxy to keep clear of a lot of hick cops. Hell, I've pulled my stuff right under the noses of the best police in the world! When a guy out-guesses them city dicks, he's goin' some. I only got picked up onct, an' I beat that rap easy. It cost me plenty, but I never done no stretch. Hell—with brains an' money, a guy kin pull anything, an' believe me, I've got 'em both. I've got what it takes!"

"You go shootin' off yer head around Dawson like you do up here, an' yer goin' to need everything you've got to keep clear," opined Red John with a grin.

"That's where the brains comes in," retorted Sheridan. "Knowin' when to talk, an' when not to. I kin keep still as a clam, when I have to. Guess I'll be pullin' out right now. Belly up, boys, an' I'll set 'em up. An' then I'll be on my way." Crossing to the table, where he had been sitting, he retrieved an empty packsack from the floor and swung it to the bar. And then he continued, addressing the proprietor, "Cush, you can count me out my eighty-five thousan', an' I'll be on my way. I'll stop at my camp an' git the rest of my stuff. Tonight I've got an itchin' foot. If I change my mind, later, I'll be back."

With the money in his packsack, the man strode to the door. "So long," he called. "No hard feelin's. I like you boys all right, an' if there was any way to set my brains an' money to work on Halfaday, I'd stay right with you, but there ain't."

"Someone ought to knock the damn wind-bag off before he gits to the river," opined a man. "It wouldn't be sech a bad haul, at that."

Black John frowned. "Anyone tryin' it, would shore be out of luck," he observed. "We ain't had a hangin' in quite a while."

V

NEXT MORNING AS Black John and Cush were pouring their first drink, young Farnum burst excitedly into the saloon, a packsack on his back.

"I've got it!" he cried. "Sheridan came up to my cabin last night and bought me out! Eighty-five thousand, in cold cash! Gee—it's more money than I ever hoped to see!"

"Come acrost with all he had, eh?" asked Black John.

"He didn't want to, but he finally did. He started in at sixty thousand, and I held out for a hundred. Gradually he got up to seventy-five, but I told him I wouldn't take a cent less than the hundred thousand. At last he offered me eighty-five, and I took it, just as you advised me to—and here I am with the money right in this sack. Now I can hit for home, and everything will be fine again. Gosh—I'll bet I'm the happiest boy in the world!"

"That's great!" agreed Black John. "An' yer in luck agin, too. My canoe's all packed fer a trip to Dawson. I found I had to go down there on some matters, an' I was jest about to start. You kin go on down with me, an' when we git to the big river, we'll hail the first upriver steamboat we come to, an' put you aboard. Cripes—you'll be gittin' home with a damn good stake, almost before yer folks had the chanct to miss you."

"I don't know how I can ever thank you and Cush," said the youngster. "You're two of the finest men I've ever known."

"You don't need to thank us," replied Black John. "We didn't do nothin' that ought to be mentioned. You struck it lucky, an' that's all there is to it. Come on—fetch yer sack along. We'll be goin'."

Ten days later, Black John stepped into the saloon, and Old Cush set out the bottle and glasses.

"Git him on a boat?" he asked, as the big man poured his drink.

"Shore did. The *Sarah* come along an' I put him aboard her. The kid struck it lucky agin. Camillo Bill was aboard, goin' outside fer a visit, an' I told him how much the kid was packin' out with him, an' he promised to look out fer him, an' see that he turned that cash into a bank draft at Seattle. Seen anythin' of Sheridan? I been kind of wonderin' if his money an' brains had got to work fer him yet?"

"Oh, shore—he come b'ilin' in here couple hours after you an' the kid left an' started in h'istin' one drink right after another. He collected some of the boys, an' he got 'em all drunk whilst he bragged an' blow'd about how he'd put one over on me an' you. I didn't say nothin' much, jest looked kind of sorriful, like a man would that had got beat out of his half of a half a million. He looked right sorry when I told him you had went down to Dawson with the kid. He wanted to strut an' brag in front of you, too. Well, he stayed drunk fer three, four days, then he hit out fer his claim, an' I ain't saw him sence. He'll prob'ly be showin' up before long, though."

And Sheridan did show up, that very afternoon. He stepped into the bar-room, and at sight of Black John swaggered up to the bar, and ordered a round of drinks.

"I s'pose Cush has broke the news to you?" he taunted.

"News?" queried Black John.

"Why sure—about me beatin' you two out, buyin' the kid's claim!"

The big man stared at the other with puckered brow. "Why yes—it seems to me that Cush did say somethin' about you buyin' some claim er other, now that you mention it. How does it suit you?"

The other's expression changed suddenly, and he ordered another drink. It was as though a sudden chill had struck to his very innards, and he strove to conquer it.

"It's all right to make out like you don't give a damn," he grinned. "You've got a damn good poker face. But you've got to admit I beat you. Fact is though, spite of me havin' that good proposition, I don't like it here on Halfaday. I'd rather be where there's more folks—women, an' all that. I don't want to be no hog. I give eighty-five thousan' fer that claim, I'm willin' to double my money on it."

"I wouldn't wonder," said Black John.

"What do you say—you an' Cush give me a hundred an' seventy thousan', an' take the claim."

"I ain't lookin' fer no investments, myself," replied Black John. "I don't know how Cush feels."

"I got all I can 'tend to here," said Cush.

"I'll make it a hundred an' fifty thousan', fer a good quick sale."

"That ought to show a good profit on the deal, if you could find a customer," admitted Black John.

"What will you give?" asked Sheridan.

"Who, me?" Black John countered. "Why I wouldn't give a damn fer that whole feeder. I don't believe there's a claim on it that would pay any better'n wages."

The man's face went livid, as he stared into the gray-blue eyes above the black beard.

"How about Buck Hammond an' Veely?" he demanded in a voice that shook.

"Who?"

"Buck Hammond, an' Veely—the two that took out half a million apiece on that feeder!"

Black John's lips parted in a grin. "What you doin', tryin' to kid me? Er mebbe it's somethin' you et. Hold on—it might be that you've stole the manuscript of our drayma."

"Drayma! What the hell do you mean—drayma?" cried the man, his voice faltering now so that he found difficulty in controlling it. "I heard you an' Cush talkin' about Hammond's an' Veely's claims right here in this room—that day I set there pretendin' to read a newspaper. An' you said them claims had paid half a million apiece."

"Eavesdroppin', eh?" replied Black John. "Eavesdroppin' is underhanded as hell, Sheridan. It had ought to come under skullduggery. But if that's the time you mean—all you done was to overhear me an' Cush practicin' our lines in a little drayma we're workin' up fer the Fourth of July. It's a nice little drayma, Sheridan—you'd enjoy it. *Brains an' Money* the name of it is, er *I've Got What It Takes.* Better stick around an' take it in, Sheridan. The tickets is eighty-five thousan' apiece—an' yourn's all paid fer."

BLACK JOHN FINDS
A MISSING HEIR

CORPORAL DOWNEY LOOKED up as Black John Smith stepped through the doorway of his office at detachment head-quarters in Dawson. "Hello, John!" he greeted. "How's things on Halfaday Crick?"

"We ain't got no kick comin'. Most of the boys cleaned up pretty good this spring. I brought down thirty-two hundred ounces to bank here. Cush's safe was gittin' a bit crowded. How's things along the river?"

"Sort of quiet, right now," Downey replied. "Except for routine work we seem to be gettin' a breathin' spell."

The big man dropped into a chair and filled his pipe. "I fig-gered crime mast be at a low ebb," he grinned. "We ain't had even so much as a tort feasor show up on Halfaday in quite a while. Kind of looks like the moral tone of the Yukon has took a turn fer the better."

"I guess," laughed Downey, "that the fact that everyone's busy with the clean-up has got more to do with it than the moral tone of the Yukon. The first steamboat from upriver docked this mornin' an' dumped a fresh batch of chechakos onto us. I expect when they get to stirrin' around we'll find plenty to do. There's bound to be crooks of one kind or another amongst 'em."

"Yeah, them damn chechakos always seems to pan out a few crooks to the boatload."

Both glanced up as a tall man with sharp angular features

paused in the doorway. Unbuttoning his overcoat he drew a pair of gold rimmed eyeglasses attached to a black ribbon from his waistcoat pocket and adjusted them on his nose. From an inner pocket of his coat he produced a wallet and carefully selecting a card advanced to the desk and tendered it to Downey.

"I wish to consult with the officer in charge," he said.

Downey glanced at the card and raised his eyes. "I'm in command of the detachment," he said. "Downey's the name. What can I do for you, Mr. Binford? You're a lawyer, I see."

"Yes, working in conjunction with the firm of Hoag, Hoag, McBirney, Throgmorton, and Hoag, barristers of London, England."

"Sounds like callin' hogs, don't it?" grinned Black John, his glance taking in the details of the man's garb.

Binford glared at him. "The firm stands at the very top of the legal profession in London," he said, stiffly, and turned again to Downey. "More than a year ago they delegated to me the task of locating an heir of the late Lady Ainslee-Higginbothom, one Percival Lansdowne Montague Sprague."

"Them English shore as hell goes in fer names, don't they?" interrupted the irrepressible Black John.

Ignoring him, the man continued. "Briefly, the facts are these: some eight years ago this Percival, the younger son of Sir Joshua Sprague, Lord Montbarton and Herps, left London under a cloud. He was at the time twenty-four years of age. Some five years later circumstances developed which cleared his name, and his aunt, Lady Ainslee-Higginbothom, by way of making partial amends for the injustice done him, revised her will leaving him a considerable sum of money. A year and a half ago she died, and it has developed upon her barristers, the Messrs. Hoag, Hoag, McBirney, Throgmorton, and Hoag, to find young Sprague and turn this money over to him. There is reason to believe he fled to Canada, but my search throughout the Provinces has been unavailing. Realizing that a great number of people have been attracted to the Yukon by the lure of gold, I

came here in the hope of finding him among these thousands. It is to this end I am appealing to the police."

Corporal Downey nodded. "Glad to help you anyway we can, Mr. Binford. It's like huntin' for a needle in a haystack, though. We've got several hundred missin' persons on the list now. I'll put his name with the rest."

"But!" exclaimed the man, "have you no record of his entry into the Yukon? I was informed in Ottawa that the police keep a record of all persons entering here."

Downey smiled. "Oh, sure, we keep a record, all right. I'll look him up. If he came in under his own name we'll prob'ly have him listed. But if he skipped out of London under a cloud he prob'ly hasn't used his own name since." Stepping into another room Downey consulted the records and returned. "No one by the name of Sprague is listed," he said. "If you've got his description it might help some."

"Of course I realize he is probably living under an assumed

name. I have memorized his description. In fact it has been uppermost in my mind for more than a year. Wherever I mingle with people I search their faces, hoping against hope that I may some day encounter his among them. Although I have, of course, never met him, I feel sure I should recognize him on sight. He stands five feet, ten inches in height. He weighs, or did weigh at the time of his disappearance, about twelve stone. We may assume that in the eight years that have elapsed he may have added to that weight. His hair is red, his eyes blue, and his aquiline nose had once been broken. Despite the best efforts of skilled surgeons the injury is still noticeable in a slight depression on the bridge."

Downey jotted down the description. "All right," he said. "Give me his name again an' we'll keep an eye out for him. Where are you stoppin', in case we'd want to get in touch with you?"

"At the Northern Hotel. I shall remain in the hotel very little, though, as I intend to pursue my search in such places as men are wont to foregather. I shall be greatly obliged for whatever assistance you may be able to lend me."

"That's all right," the officer assured him. "We'll do what we can. It's all in the day's work. I'll let you know if we run onto anything."

THE MAN departed and a few minutes later as Black John rose to go his glance rested for a moment on the card that lay on the desk. "It looks like even a lawyer would have more sense than to come huntin' someone in the Yukon dressed in store clothes with a long overcoat floppin' around his legs. An' them shoes! Did you notice them shoes, Downey? Looked like they was made of hen skin, an' they was fastened on with buttons—like a woman's! He'd be plumb bushed if he'd lose his button hook to hell an' gone up some crick."

"Yeah, but a lawyer ain't no smarter'n any other chechako when it comes to gittin' around in a new country. I guess he won't be goin' out on many cricks, though. That red on his nose with the little blue veins showin' through it ain't sunburn. That nose cost him somethin'. He'll do most of his man huntin' in Dawson."

"Well, so long, Downey. Jest dropped in to say hello. I'll be gittin' along down to the Tivoli an' see if I kin scare up a game of stud. Come on up to Halfaday an' see us sometime when you git tired of winnowin' out these Yukon goats from the sheep."

Stepping into the Tivoli and finding no sourdoughs there, Black John sauntered to the bar where the lawyer, Binford, had just refilled his glass from a bottle of whiskey that stood before him. Calling for a drink the big man regarded the other with a smile. "Drink up, Binford, an' have one on me," he invited.

Adjusting his eyeglasses the man favored the speaker with a stony stare. "Aren't you the—er, person who was in the police station a few minutes ago?" he asked in a chilly tone.

"Yeah, I'm the character. You've got a good eye fer faces, Bin. You ought to find yer man. Smith's the name—Black John, to be more explicit. I couldn't help overhearin' the spiel you was givin' Downey, an' it occurred to me that mebbe I might be of some assistance to, you in locatin' this Percy what's-his-name."

"Percival Lansdowne Montague Sprague," corrected the lawyer. "But really Mr.—er—Smith, I have, as you know, already enlisted the aid of the authorities."

"Yeah, that's right. But you ain't be'n here long enough to find out that there's a hell of a lot of country hereabouts—an' damn few authorities. There's lots of cricks in the Yukon with men on 'em that the police never seen. I move about more er less, an' I thought it might be possible that I could stumble onto yer man. That is, of course, if there was enough in it to make the effort worth while."

"You say you believe it probable that you can locate—"

"I said 'possible', not 'probable'," interrupted Black John. "As a lawyer you'll ondoubtless appreciate the difference. You will, note, too, that I referred to the matter of emolument."

"Ah, yes—to be sure—to be sure!"

"Yeah—I'd want to be reasonably sure of gittin' it."

The man downed his liquor at a swallow. "Did I also hear you invite me to join you in a drink?"

"You did," grinned the big man, shoving the bottle toward the other, who promptly refilled his glass.

"In the matter of remuneration I may say that my own fee is entirely contingent upon my success in producing Percival Lansdowne Montague Sprague. Since engaging my services, upon recommendation of a certain member of parliament for whom I had won several lawsuits, the Messrs. Hoag, Hoag, McGirney, Throgmorton, and Hoag have, from time to time advanced certain moneys to cover necessary expenses incident to my search. But they have remained adamant against any suggestion of the payment of even a portion of the fee until I have accomplished the desired result. It is unjust—damnably unjust. But as the fee will be considerable in the event of success, I felt justified in undertaking the commission even to the neglect of my regular practice. The amounts they have advanced have been barely sufficient to cover my own expenses, and will in no wise allow my advancing any expense money to another. In fact I was obliged to draw upon my own funds to finance this trip to the Yukon. I shall of course be reimbursed, but the London barristers seem very niggardly in the matter of expense funds, demanding itemized accounts of moneys expended—so that I am at times sorely at a loss to remember how these funds had been disbursed."

"Had to kind of pad her up, here an' there, eh?" grinned Black John. "Well, that's fair enough. An' you don't need to worry about advancin' me any expense money. I ain't exactly broke. What I was referrin' to in particular was the honorarium in case of success. How much would there be in it fer me if I locate yer man?"

Binford swallowed his liquor and refilled his glass. "Well," he hazarded, "what would you say to—to a thousand pounds?"

Black John laughed. "There ain't much a man could say to a little jag of chicken feed like that."

"What?"

"Meanin' that the sum is in no wise allurin'. I guess you an' me can't deal, Bin. But don't let it worry you none. There's no hard feelin's. You made an offer. I turned it down—an' there ain't no more to be said. The fella I've got in mind mightn't be the one you want, anyhow. So jest fergit it."

"Do you mean that you have someone actually in mind? That you know where Sprague is?"

"W-e-e-l-l, I wouldn't go so fer as to state it as a positive fact."

THE MAN gulped his liquor and hastily refilled his glass. "Listen," he said. "Time is a matter of vital importance in this search." He paused abruptly as the bartender approached, moved the bottle and glasses aside and swabbed up a few drops of spilled liquor. As he moved on Binford lowered his voice. "Can't we take our drinks to one of the tables where we will have some semblance of privacy?"

"Shore thing," agreed Black John, picking up bottle and glasses, and leading the way to a table in a far corner of the room. "There won't no one disturb us here. What's on yer mind?"

"As I said, time is a vital factor," began the lawyer, as they seated themselves with the bottle and glasses between them. "By the terms of Lady Ainslee-Higginbothom's will her nephew must be found within two years of her death. And of those two years, only five months now remain. If he has not been produced within the specified time the entire legacy of sixty thousand pounds is to be divided into two equal funds, one to be used in establishing a foundation for research into the diseases of cats, in London, and the other to found a hospital and retreat for homeless mongooses, in Rangoon, India. It seems that Lady Ainslee-Higginbothom spent many years in India as wife of some Government official."

"Sixty thousan' pounds," mused Black John. "That's right around three hundred thousan' in real money. The sum is worth contemplatin'. An' how much are you to receive fer findin' this heir?"

"Five thousand pounds."

"An' if I found him an' delivered him to you I was to git one thousan'—an' you'd keep the other four."

"Well, you must remember that I have worked on this case for a year and a half."

"Yeah? Well, Bin—you keep right on workin' on it fer the next five months, an' see what it gits you."

The man drank and refilled his glass. "How would two thousand strike you?" he asked, at length.

"Not very forcible. It looks to me like a fifty-fifty proposition."

"Very well," Binford agreed. "If you can produce Percival Lansdowne Montague Sprague within the specified time I will agree to split my fee with you—each of us to receive twenty-five hundred pounds."

"That's more like it, Bin. It's a deal. But I want it set down in black on white. There's a lawyer a couple of doors up the street. We'll git him to draw up the agreement."

"I'm a lawyer," reminded the man. "I can draw up—"

"But I ain't," interrupted Black John. "An' jest between you an' me, Bin, I don't trust 'em very fer—as a breed."

Binford flushed and frowned. "How about this lawyer up the street? Is he supposed to be particularly honorable or honest?"

"Hell, no! None of 'em is! But I'm the one that's hirin' him, an' whatever crookedness he's got will be on my side. All I want's an even break."

BLACK JOHN paid for the drinks and the two left the saloon to return an hour later, each with his copy of the agreement. "What did this here Sprague skip out fer?" asked Black John, as they resumed their seats at the table.

"It was the result of a midnight brawl at the door of some tavern, or pub, in London, the name and address of which I have in my notes. It seems that he and his elder brother, since deceased, and another young blood whose name escapes me for the moment, engaged in fisticuffs with one Archibald St. Claire Ellington, Bart., and that during the course of the affray, Ellington was felled by a blow from a fist and killed. All were more or less drunk at the time—the younger Sprague drunker than the others. The body was found a few minutes later by a party which was leaving the tavern, and Ellington, being a person of some consequence, the newspapers kicked up a great to-do about it the following morning. And of course the police got busy at once.

"It seems that the elder brother, who, by the way, succeeded to the title upon the death of his father two years later, per-suaded the younger that it was he who had felled Ellington, and that his only chance to avoid conviction for manslaughter was to leave England before the police solved the crime, which they were almost certain to do. He gave Percival two thousand pounds and managed to slip him aboard a tramp ship success-fully disguised. Scotland Yard solved the case to its own satis-faction, fixing the crime upon the younger Sprague, who of course could not be found.

"Two years after succeeding to the title of Lord Montbarton and Herps, the elder brother died after having dissipated the family fortune in riotous living, and shortly thereafter, the other young blood who had witnessed the manslaughter died also.

"It seems, however, that there had been a third witness to the brawl, the driver of a hansom cab, often employed by the Spragues in their carousals. Upon his deathbed, a year after the demise of the elder brother, this cabby called for the authorities and dictated a statement which he swore to and signed, to the effect that he had witnessed the killing of Ellington, and that it was the elder brother, and not the younger that had struck the fatal blow. He explained how, with the aid of the other two, the elder Sprague contrived to fix the blame upon his brother—for which aid he paid handsomely until the day of his death.

"Immediately upon ascertaining these facts Lady Ainslee-Higginbothom advertised far and wide for young Sprague's return. Obtaining no results, she caused a clause to be inserted in her will, bequeathing to him the sum of sixty thousand pounds in the event of his being found within two years after her demise. She died nineteen months ago.

"There you have the matter in a nutshell. I have all the facts together with many others in my portfolio. And now, may I ask where Sprague is living at the present moment?"

"He's on a crick a couple of hundred miles from here. I'll hit out fer there in the mornin'. Ought to be back with him in three weeks."

"Are you quite sure he's our man?"

Black John grinned and winked knowingly. "That ain't the name he's goin' under, at present. An' I can't say fer shore he's actually Sprague. But from the description you give Downey he ought to be a good workin' model. It might be he'll turn out better'n the original."

"Why—what do you mean?" Binford asked, eying the other with a puckered brow.

"W-e-e-l-l, the thought occurred to me that if we was to produce the rightful heir, this Percival Lansdowne Montague Sprague, in person—all we git out of it is a lousy twenty-five hundred pounds apiece. But if we could dig up a good phony—one that would pass muster—we might kind of work along with him, an' split the legacy three ways."

The lawyer stared at the big man astounded. "You mean," he gasped, "we could produce someone other than Sprague, who would impersonate him and claim the legacy?"

"That was the thought I was playin' around with. Whether it would work er not depends on how much dope you've got on Sprague—how much you know about him. There's goin' to be a hell of a lot of questions asked that's got to be answered to the satisfaction of them London barristers before they'll fork over the dough—but with all them important deaths to our credit, it looks like we might put it acrost."

"You mean we could divide the whole legacy between the three of us."

"I wouldn't see the sense in draggin' in no outsiders."

"That would give us twenty thousand pounds apiece," muttered the lawyer thoughtfully. "Why—we might do even better than that! If this person could be induced to accept, say ten thousand for his share, you and I could split fifty thousand between us."

"Yer grasp of the situation does credit to yer legal trainin'," grinned Black John. "It sort of shows me up as a tyro."

"It might be done," breathed the other. "I have voluminous information concerning Sprague. It was forwarded to me by the London barristers so that by adroit questioning I could expose any impostor. If this person you have in mind will pass physically for Sprague, and if he possesses ordinary intelligence, I believe I will be able to instruct him so that he may be able to convince the Messrs. Hoag, Hoag, McBirney, Throgmorton, and Hoag that he is in fact the man they seek. It is reasonable to suppose that no member of the firm is acquainted with him personally, as they were merely his aunt's barristers. The fact that his near relatives are dead, and that he has been absent from London for a long time are strong points in our favor."

"Yeah, that's the way it looks to me. This party might not be no mental giant, but if I git him back here in three weeks he'll have time to memorize all the dope you've got. My first thought was to dye my hair an' whiskers red an' play the part myself, but—"

"Oh, that would never do! You are at least three inches too tall. You must weigh all of fifteen stone. And your nose is not aquiline, nor has it apparently ever been broken."

"Yeah, I run them drawbacks over in my mind. Of course, I could diet off a few stone, an 'git someone to bust my nose fer me so it would hump up kind of aquiline. But I shore as hell couldn't shrink my height none."

"Then, too, your—er—manner of speech is—er—perhaps not exactly suited to the part."

"Yeah, prob'ly a bit rough an' ready fer a lordlet. But you've got to remember, Bin, this Sprague has be'n missin' fer eight years. His speech has had time to kind of bog down on him."

That night Black John played stud with the sourdoughs, and early the following morning he took leave of Binford promising to return within three weeks with his man.

"And—er—it has occurred to me," said the lawyer, "that possibly if this man were properly approached he might even be induced to accept, say, five thousand pounds for his share."

"He might, at that," grinned Black John. "When it comes to figgerin', Bin, you've got me beat a mile."

II

OLD CUSH, PROPRIETOR of Cushing's Fort, the combined trading post and saloon that ministered to the wants of the little community of outlawed men that had sprung up on Halfaday Creek, close against the Yukon-Alaska border, looked up from the month-old newspaper he was reading as Black John stepped through the doorway of the saloon.

"What—back a'ready!" he exclaimed, as he hastened to set out bottle and glasses. "Cripes, I wasn't lookin' fer you fer a week yet! What ails you that you didn't pull off no drunk in Dawson?"

"I'm not a drinkin' man," grinned Black John, "an' besides I run onto a little deal by which I hope to turn an honest penny. Where's Red John?"

"Down to his claim, I s'pose. What's he got to do with it?"

"I have decided," the big man announced, "to make him a lord."

"A lord? You mean like that lordship that come to Halfaday that time—with the trick specs that I thought was broke 'cause they didn't have but one glass in 'em?"

"Exactly."

"Humph," grunted Cush, in disgust, "Red John would make a hell of a lord! An' how could you make one out of him, anyhow?"

"You'd be surprised," grinned Black John. "It's a long story an' will have to await a more propitious time. So long, Cush, an' if you don't see neither one of us fer quite a while, don't worry."

A shadow darkened the doorway and Red John himself stepped into the room.

"Speak of the devil, an' up he pops," Black John chuckled. "Step up. I'm buyin' one." As the other ranged himself beside him the big man stepped close and examined his nose, running an exploratory forefinger along its ridge. "Yup—aquiline's the word—be'n broke, too."

"What the hell's ailin' you? Shore it's be'n broke. It was years ago—a bloke hit me."

"An' yer hair's ondoubtedly red," continued Black John, ignoring the explanation. "An' you stand about five foot ten. An' you'll go about twelve stone. You'll fit the part to a T."

"Listen," scowled Cush, "if this is some kind of a drayma yer figgerin' out—you can't pull none in here. The last time you done it I damn near got shot!"

"The first act," replied Black John, "will be staged in Dawson." He turned to Red John. "How would you like to make a play fer sixty thousan' pounds sterlin'?"

"What kind of a play? An' what's my nose an' hair an' weight an' height got to do with it? An' is it legal? I like it here on Halfaday, an' wouldn't want to git mixed up with the police."

"It's so damn legal that we've got a Montreal lawyer on our side," Black John replied.

Red John grinned. "But, cripes, John—every crook that gits caught has got a lawyer on his side!"

"Mere hirelings! This lawyer is no hireling. He's a colleague—a collaborator."

"Oh—sort of accomplice, er accessory before the fact, eh?"

Black John frowned. "Yer choice of terms is ill advised, savorin' somehow of crime. The enterprise of which I speak might possibly be considered by the prudish to overstep the bounds of strict integrity. But in the broader view it's middlin' honest.

"The plan is simple. A party in England died leavin' sixty thousan' pounds to another party who had be'n missin' fer several years. By the terms of this will, the party must be located within two years of the death of the testator, whose English barristers have be'n tryin' to find him. To this end they engaged the services of one Binford, a lawyer of Montreal, who is to receive five thousan' pounds in case he digs up this heir.

"The fact that nineteen months of the stipulated two years has already passed, has made brother Binford kind of anxious to close the deal an' collect his dough. Durin' a casual conversation with him I gathered that this missin' heir's physical specifications coincides with yours to an alarmin' degree. So the thought occurred to me that it ondoubtless lies within our power to extricate these barristers from their preplexin' predicament an' at the same time, turn the venture to some slight profit to ourselves. The idea bein' that you impersonate this missin' heir.

"When I broached the plan to Binford he grabbed it, hook line an' sinker, assurin' me that if your physical characteristics was okay, he could easily coach you up on what facts you'd need to know, providin' you was possessed of ordinary intelligence. An' I don't mind statin' that them physical characteristics ain't got me worried a damn bit."

"What do you mean?" scowled Red John, "that I'm too dumb to remember what this lawyer tells me?"

"W-e-e-1-1, when a man embarks on a venture he's got to sort of take all contingencies into consideration. A chain, as the sayin' goes, ain't no stronger than its weakest dink."

"Listen!" exclaimed Red John, bristling. "If that's all that's botherin' you—fergit it! Where's this lawyer? I'll damn soon show you I kin learn a part—an' play it, too! What you figger, I s'pose, is to collect this money an' split it three ways."

"Exactly."

"All right—who'm I s'posed to be? Where did I come from? An' when? An' why? An' how?"

"Binford will give you all the facts," Black John replied. "If I should try to explain it I might confuse you, as my own knowledge of the details is sketchy, at best. Throw a light pack together an' we'll hit out fer Dawson. I may add, though, that the matter of remuneration might be gone into a little further. The amount involved is sixty thousan' pounds, which fer your enlightenment I'll state is right clost to three hundred thousan' dollars in real money. It was Binford's idea to pay you five er ten thousan' pounds fer your part in collectin' this dough, leavin' the remainder to be divided equally between him an' me. But upon thinkin' the matter over, the arrangement hardly seems equitable. When it is you who are to play the leadin' role why should we, who are mere pawns in the game, grab off the lion's share of the profits? It somehow bears all the earmarks of an onderhanded transaction. It even savors of bad ethics. An' as a matter of principle I'd ruther the bulk of this fund remained safely on Halfaday.

"So I suggest that you hold out fer at least fifty-five thousan' pounds—which sum, of course, me an' you splits fifty-fifty. That leaves Binford five thousan' fer his trouble which, takin' the man's character into consideration, seems to me a liberal—even a generous fee. Damned if I'll stand fer seein' any of our local boys gypped by no Montreal lawyer!"

"Let's git goin'," replied Red John. "I'll be ready when you reach my claim in the canoe."

III

INQUIRY AT THE hotel disclosed the fact that Binford was on Bonanza looking over some mining properties with a view of making an investment with the proceeds of a legacy he was expecting within a very short time. The clerk said that Binford had left word for Black John to meet him either at the hotel or the Tivoli within a day or so.

As it was early in the day the two men from Halfaday repaired to the Tivoli, where they passed the time at the bar to such good purpose that by suppertime both were pretty well oiled.

Red John paused suddenly and stared owlishly across the rim of his lifted glass into Black John's eyes. "John," he announced solemnly, "I can't go on with this."

"What!"

"No, sir—I can't do it. My conscience is prickin' me. It ain't right. It's agin all them precepts of rectitude I learnt at my nurse's knees—"

"You git yer mind off 'n nurses' knees till after this here deal is out of the way!" exclaimed Black John.

"No. I mean it, John. Honest, I do. Listen—if we don't git that sixty thousan' quid someone else would—some that's rightfully entitled to it—an' mebbe needs it. If it was someone that already had plenty, I'd say go ahead—but s'pose it's some old folks, er a widow woman, er even some little children we'd be bilkin'. I can't do it, John. I can't go on with it. It jest ain't in me to snatch the bread from the mouths of widows an' orphans— much as I'd like to."

Black John nodded solemnly. "Yer attitude is a worthy one, John, an' it shows yer honest to the core. I wouldn't stand fer hornswogglin' no sech parties as you've mentioned out of their money, no more than you would—an' you know it! Hell, John— ain't I right now protectin' you from bein' gypped out of yer just an' lawful legacy by that damn Binford who, by means of questionable methods, is tryin' to hog the major portion of it fer himself? As a matter of fact, the only ones who lose in thish—this transhaction is a bunch of cats an' mongeese."

"What?"

"Yes sir," replied Black John, the effect of the Tivoli's potent liquor showing in his thickening speech, "yessir, thash—that's a fack. The rizzzidgary—wait a minute." He paused and staring fixedly into the bar mirror, pronounced very deliberately, "The r-e-s-i-d-u-a-r-y l-e-g-a-t-e-e-s in this case are a hospital fer sick cats in London, an' a home fer indigent rangoons in Mongeese, India."

"Haw, haw, haw!" roared Red John. "Yer drunker'n hell, John! The mongoose is an animal, an' Rangoon is a city!"

"Be that as it may," replied Black John with dignity, "that's what I'm tellin' you."

"An' besides, the plural of mongoose is mongooses—not mongeese."

"I'll concede the p'int—about rangoon bein' the plural fer India. But the plural of mongoon is certainly rangeese."

"Cripes," laughed Red John, "I'll bet you the drinks you don't know what a mongoose is!"

"I'll take you," replied the big man, with a superior air. "A mongoon is a goose—I mean a mongoose is a goon that eats rats an' snakes. The name bein' derived by affixin' the prefix 'mono', meaning 'one', to the word 'goose', meanin' 'goose', an' indicatin' thereby that it's the sole an' only geese that is carniverous. I'll have a little more of the same—an' you kin pay fer it."

"Like hell I will! A mongoose ain't a goose, at all. It's—"

"Cut out that 'ain't'!" interrupted Black John with a disapproving frown. "Don't fergit that, startin' today, yer a lord, er an earl, er duke, er somethin'—an' believe me, them lads talks their part!"

"Okay," grinned Red John. "Until this worthy enterprise has been consummated I shall confine my loculation within the accepted bounds. I shall eschew the vernacular, choosing only such words as my memory tells me will conform to the best usage, don't cher know. And—now, my good man, allow me to disabuse your mind of a rawther absurd misapprehension. The mongoose is not a bird, at all."

STARK SURPRISE at the unexpected flow of words caused Black John, in his more or less befuddled condition, to blink foolishly into the other's face. "Who the hell said it was?" he argued, striving mightily to collect his scattered wits.

"You just stated that it was a goose—"

"So's a tailor's goose—but it ain't a bird."

"The mongoose," continued the other, "is a ferret-like animal—a native of India, where it is highly esteemed because of its ability to kill rats and snakes. I happen to be more or less familiar with the little beggars, as an aged aunt of mine, Lady Ainslee-Higginbothom, brought a number of them to England when she returned from a long residence in India where her husband was something or other in the Government. She was very much attached to them, primarily, I presume, because of her antipathy to rats and snakes. Fine old girl—Aunt Hig. Devilish uppish, and all that—but a good old heart in her! I was a bit wild in those days, I fawncy—but she always took my part—a grand old girl!"

Black John, perfectly sober now, was staring in open-mouthed astonishment. "Who—who did you say? What was this aunt's name?"

"Lady Ainslee-Higginbothom, of Bywater, Kent. She was an Ainslee, of Ainslee Downs, Surrey."

"An' your name?" asked the big man, eagerly. "Who the hell are you?"

The other grinned. "Red John Smith—to you—of Halfaday Crick, Y.T."

"An' before that it wasn't, by chance, Percival Lansdowne Montague Sprague, second son of Sir Jushua Sprague, Lord

Montbarton and Herps?"

It was Red John's turn to stare in astonishment. "What the hell is this?" he rasped angrily. "A trap?"

"Yeah," grinned Black John, "a trap all set an' baited—to ketch a crooked lawyer in. Listen, Percy—keep yer shirt on—you ain't wanted no more fer that manslaughter in front of that tavern in London eight years ago. They know, now, it was yer brother done it—he knocked Archibald St. Claire Ellington so cold with his fist that he stayed cold. Then him an' the cabby an' the other guy that was along framed you, bein' as you was too drunk to remember what come off. They bruised up yer knuckles so you'd believe it was you hit him, an' when the papers kicked up a stink yer brother slipped you a couple of thousan' pounds an' hustled you aboard a ship. Scotland Yard run the thing down, an' what with the lies them other three told, an' the fact that you was known to be a scrapper when drunk, they pinned the job on you. But yer brother's dead now—an' so is the other guy. The cabby's dead, too—but before he kicked out he spilt his guts, he squawked the whole story in a signed deathbed statement. Yer brother had been payin' him to keep his mouth shet.

"But the cabby was like you—he had a conscience. Only he never found it out till he come to die. You're settin' pretty, Percy—you an' me. We'll show that damn crooked lawyer where to head in at! Kin you beat that fer onderhanded deviltry—him tryin' to ring in some phony heir to beat you out of yer rightful inheritance? It shore beats hell what some folks will stoop to!" Pausing abruptly, he glanced toward the door. "Shut up!" he exclaimed, in an undertone. "Here comes Binford now!" Motioning to a man who had just entered the saloon, he called loudly. "Come on over here, Bin! I'm buyin' one! I want you to meet my friend, Percival Lansdowne Montague Sprague. He's the party I was tellin' you about." As the two shook hands he glanced at Red John. "This is Mr. Binford, the lawyer I mentioned."

"Ah, yes, Mr. Sprague," Binford repeated, with a sly wink, as his keen eyes appraised the other from top to toe. I believe you'll do—'pon my word, I do!"

"I shall try," smiled Red John.

"To be sure—to be sure! And I have no doubt very successfully, too. But let us go at once to my room at the hotel. There is much to be done, my good man—with the barber, and the tailor, and the haberdasher. There is also much for you to learn. I trust you have a retentive memory."

"Fairly retentive, I believe," replied the other, as the three left the saloon.

"Ah, a well-modulated voice—and a fair command of English, I see. That is fine! In fact it could not be better. I anticipate no difficulty whatsoever. With the memoranda I have it should be easy for you to answer all questions to the satisfaction of my London colleagues, the Messrs. Hoag, Hoag, McBirney, Throgmorton, and Hoag."

"So old Hoag has taken the boys into—"

Black John silenced Sprague with a vicious dig in the ribs with his elbow, and the remark passed unnoticed by the lawyer, who went on to explain:

"As the amount involved is a rather large one, I think it very likely that one of these barristers will come to Montreal for a personal interview with you. Of course they will doubtless endeavor to persuade you to journey to London. But you must absolutely refuse to do that. To be sure—under no circumstances must you go to London! There would be many unforeseen pitfalls into which they might lead you—acquaintances of other days—relatives—places with which you are supposed to be familiar—a hundred and one dangers which we could not possibly foresee."

"I shall not go to London," said the other with determination.

"Very good. We have little to fear even from a personal interview on this side of the water. I have all information necessary for a successful coup. In the first place, your name is—"

"Percival Lansdowne Montague Sprague," interrupted the other, and for several minutes he proceeded to recite the names of numerous relatives and acquaintances, and of places. He mentioned certain dates, and mentioned the given names of the various members of the firm of London barristers who were representing his aunt's estate. He detailed the events leading up to the incident before the tavern, the address of which he mentioned. He even called the cabby by name, saying he was one they frequently employed.

BINFORD HALTED in his tracks and glared at Black John. "What is the meaning of this?" he demanded. "Who is this man? How could he possibly know these things? I certainly did not mention them to you! You could not possibly have gained access to my papers—of that I am certain. Why—he has mentioned facts that I myself did not know!"

Black John grinned. "Why the hell wouldn't he know 'em? He was there, wasn't he? He's Percival Lansdowne Montague Sprague, in person, ain't he? Who would know—if he didn't?"

"Do you mean," gasped the lawyer, that this man is actually Percival Lansdowne Montague Sprague?"

"Well," asked Black John in well feigned surprise, "who the hell did you think he was?"

The lawyer blew up. "You—you crook! You doublecrosser! You have produced the rightful heir—who can lay claim to the entire legacy—when our agreement was that—"

"Listen—you!" thundered Black John, glaring at the man. "You told me who you was huntin', an' I found him! What do you mean—agreement? You told Corporal Downey right in the police office who you was lookin' fer—an' I heard you! Deny that, if you kin! We'll leave it to Downey!"

"But—why—you—you damnable scamp! Our agreement called for your producing an impostor—one who should impersonate the real heir! We were to pay him five or ten thousand pounds and divide the balance between us!"

Reaching into his pocket, Black John drew forth his copy of the agreement drawn by the Dawson lawyer and shook it in the irate man's face. "Here's our agreement!" he roared. "We'll show it to Corporal Downey—an' see if he kin find where it says anything about any phony heir!"

"But—the verbal agreement we made subsequent to that!"

Black John shook his head in resignation and turned to Sprague. "Kin you beat that, Percy?" he asked with a wink. "Ain't it hell the abysmal depths of evil into which an onprincipled lawyer will plunge? Why—the very fact that I have produced the rightful heir is a good an' sufficient answer to his vile calumny! Let us depart from here an' leave this—this swine to wallow in his own filth! We will have nothing further to do with this person. He has proven himself to be beneath even the utmost contempt of honest men. We will proceed at once to the police detachment and request Corporal Downey to get in touch with them London barristers—that mess of McBirneys an' Throgmortons, an' the mouthful of Hoags. We will ignore this lawyer. An' by the way, I must file this copy of my agreement with him where it will be brought to the attention of the London barristers. For should they honor Binford's spurious claim to havin' be'n instrumental in locatin' you, I'm entitled, by the terms of this agreement, to receive one half of any amount due him. An' I'd ruther it would come direct from all them Hoags an' company than take a chanct on collectin' it from Binford, who has proven himself thoroughly onprincipled an' ontrustworthy."

THE LAW VISITS
HALFADAY CREEK

IT WAS HOT for June, and Ma Bergson, ample-bodied pro-
prietress of the Little Gem Restaurant, wiped beads of sweat
from her brow with a corner of her apron. With the spring
clean-up behind them, men were drifting in from the creeks in
anticipation of the week-long jamboree that would appropri-
ately celebrate the two national holidays—Dominion Day and
the Fourth of July.

Relict of Ole Bergson, a Swede prospector who had been
buried in a landslide at Forty Mile, Ma had moved upriver with
the stampede and opened the Little Gem with capital gladly
advanced by the sourdoughs. These sourdoughs had long since
been repaid—and roundly and affectionately cursed for fools
when they had refused to accept profit on their investment. For,
when occasion demanded, Ma Bergson's words could be as
blistering as her kitchen stove.

The saloons and gambling houses of Dawson were doing a
rushing business. Night and day, Ma Bergson moved with heavy
efficiency back and forth through the swinging door that
separated the blistering hot kitchen from the dining room with
its long lunch-counter, and its double row of little tables, one
eye on her profits, the other on the welfare of her customers.

The Bessemer Kid stepped through the doorway and seated
himself on a revolving stool at the counter behind which Ma
Bergson stood, her back against the long sideboard laden with
its display of pies, cakes, and doughnuts reposing beneath the

glass
domes
that pro-
tected them from
the swarming flies.

Shifting a toothpick to
the opposite corner of her mouth,
Ma eyed the Bessemer Kid: "Jest like
all the rest of 'em. Can't wait till Dominion
Day comes. Got to come in, three, four days
ahead, an' git tanked up so when it does git here you won't know
if it's Dominion Day or Chris'mas. If men could cash in on the
sense they ain't got, Dawson would be the richest camp in the
world. You better fill up with good grub while yer in shape to.
Couple days from now, after that red-eye gits to workin' on you,
you won't have the stomach to hold grub, nor the dust to pay
fer it."

The Bessemer Kid grinned broadly. "Not this time, Ma.
Honest, I ain't goin' to take a drink—er, mebbe jest two er three.
I be'n workin' all winter fer Jimmy the Rough, an' since Chris'mas
I ain't blow'd a cent—honest I ain't."

"Jimmy was in fer grub a month ago, an' he tells me you made
him a good hand."

"Jimmy's a good guy to work for."

"All the sourdoughs is. They know the game. It's the chechakos that's the man-killers."

Fumbling in his pockets, the Kid tossed three little moosehide sacks onto the counter. "Weigh 'em up, Ma. We finished
the clean-up yesterday, an' Jimmy paid me off."

The woman weighed the dust, and after a laborious mathematical calculation, glanced up. "A hundred an' seventy-six ounces, Kid. It figgers twenty-eight hundred an' sixteen dollars. Enough fer a grubstake—if the Klondike Palace, an' the Tivoli, an' the rest of 'em don't git it all."

"They ain't goin' to git none of it—mebbe jest an ounce or two. You keep it fer me, Ma. Will you? Jest give me a couple of ounces."

Ma Bergson's thick fingers patted at her tightly drawn yellowed gray hair as she eyed the youth. "You mean you want to bank this dust with me?"

"Sure I do."

"Till when?"

"Why—till—till I want it."

"Stick 'em back in yer pocket," ordered the woman, shoving the sacks toward him across the counter. "Till you want it!" she repeated contemptuously. "That'll be 'long about midnight. You'll come rollin' in here, lit up like a steamboat, an' beller fer yer dust. Take it to the Tivoli. Curly'll bank it fer you. Er take it to the Klondike Palace. Cuter Malone'll bank it—an' you never will see it again."

"No, Ma, I mean it. I want to save that dust. Like you say, it's a grubstake. Bank it for me. Come on. Jest weigh me out a couple of ounces, an' you keep the rest. Don't give me none of it, even if I want it, till after the Fourth."

THE WOMAN regarded him intently. "You mean that?" she asked, her thick lips hardening about the toothpick. He nodded several times.

"Sure, I mean it."

"All right, sonny," she replied, picking up a sack and shaking some dust onto the scale. "I'm givin' you ten ounces. Two ain't enough. But, mind you, them ten ounces has got to last you clean through the jamboree. I'm holdin' a hundred an' sixty-six ounces fer you—twenty-six hundred and fifty-six dollars. An' what I mean, I'm holdin' it! After the Fourth you kin come here an' git it. But you've got to be stone-cold sober when you come, an' don't you fergit it! You kin barge in here an' holler yourself hoarse, an' demand it, an' threaten me fer it, an' git down on yer knees an' pray fer it—but not an ounce do you git. What you will git is a good thick cup bounced off'n yer head, an' you'll land out there in Front Street on the seat of yer pants. When I do a thing, I do it, an' I don't fool! An', what's more you don't git no receipt, neither."

"No receipt?"

"Not the scratch of a pencil fer you. Any time my word ain't as good as my writin' I'll go jump in the river. Yer dust'll be here when you need it. An', what I mean, there won't be no mortgage agin' it—no chippies, nor bartenders, nor tin horn gams comin' to me with I.O.U.'s agin' it, like if you'd git soused an' show 'em a receipt where I'm holdin' a hundred an' sixty-six ounces fer you. No sir, if you go tryin' to borry agin' this dust, yer goin' to find out how Ma Bergson kin lie like a gentleman. If anyone comes around askin' me have you got some dust banked here, I'll tell 'em you ain't got an ounce an' never did have. Put that in yer pipe an' smoke it! An' you better make that ten ounces do you. You can't even eat here, on the hundred an' sixty-six!"

The Bessemer Kid grinned. "I guess you could git plenty tough with a guy, at that, Ma. Anyways I ain't worryin' none about my dust. Give me some coffee an' sinkers. An'," he added, glancing about the room, "where's Millie at?"

Ma Bergson opened the till, lifted out a heavy revolver, placed the three little sacks in the back of the drawer, returned the revolver to its place, and closed the drawer. "Millie ain't here no more," she replied, without meeting his glance. "Nope. She quit. Biscuit shootin' got too tame fer a girl like Millie. Hours was too long an' not enough bright lights in it. Goin' to learn a dance act, an' put on a show. Yup. Song an' dance act with Louie Beckwith. He talked her into it. Told her—"

The Bessemer Kid's face went white. "Louie Beckwith! You mean Louie the Decker? That tin horn gambler that hangs around Cuter Malone's? They say he sells dope to the girls!"

"Yeah," agreed the woman, in a hard, dry voice, "an' the gamblin' an' dope peddlin' ain't the half of it." She paused, rested her thick hands on the edge of the counter, and regarded the Bessemer Kid through eyes that stared coldly between little rolls of fat. "What did you want of Millie?" she asked.

"Why I—it seemed like she was kind of different from the rest—prettier—an' that's why I be'n savin' my dust. I figgered, mebbe, if I got enough fer a grubstake, I could make a strike, an' then, mebbe we—mebbe I could coax her into gittin' hitched."

"Millie's a hard worker. She'd make a good woman fer a man, if she'd git that dancin' out of her head."

The Bessemer Kid's glance strayed to the open door past which check-shirted men were moving, calling rough greetings, as they made the rounds of the saloons. "Yeah," he assented, in a dull, detached voice. After a moment of silence he turned lack-luster eyes toward the woman. "Give me my dust, Ma," he said. "I changed my mind about bankin' it."

The woman shrugged her thick shoulders and pulled the drawer half open, exposing the heavy revolver. "All right, Kid," she replied, with no attempt to disguise the sneer in her voice. "I guess Millie might's well go where she's headed as to hook up with a quitter."

"Quitter!" exclaimed the Kid, flushing to his hair roots. "What do you mean, quitter?"

"It was only about an hour ago that Millie walked out on me," said Ma Bergson, with seeming irrelevance. "She thought she was goin' to meet up with Louie the Decker to practice a song an' dance act. The little fool! She fell fer what he told her about him bein' a dance artist lookin' fer a pardner to team up with. An' how they could clean up big money with their show. I told her she was a fool, but she wouldn't listen. She likes dancin', an' thought I was tryin' to hold her 'cause I needed her help, what with everyone in from the cricks, an' all. I'm goin' to need the help, all right." She paused, and again the thick shoulders shrugged, heavily. "But what of it? In a week, or a month, there'll be a new face on the line, that's all."

The Kid stared wide-eyed into the woman's face. "You say she was here till today? That she quit only—"

"I said an hour ago," snapped Ma Bergson. "She went to the Klondike Palace. She thought it was to practice a song an' dance act. It'll take a sight longer'n an hour to learn her the difference. What was it you ordered, Kid? Oh, yeah—sinkers an' coffee." Turning, she raised a glass dome from the sideboard and slipped three doughnuts onto a plate which she placed before the Kid. She moved heavily toward the kitchen, leaving the drawer half open. When she returned a moment later, bearing a thick cup of steaming coffee, her customer was gone. Glancing toward the half-open drawer, her thick lips tightened more firmly upon the toothpick as her eyes rested on the little moosehide sacks beyond where the gun had been. "He had his choice," she muttered, grimly. "The gun, or the dust. Good luck to him." She returned the three doughnuts to their place beneath the glass dome, and slowly sipped the cup of black coffee.

II

IT WAS MID-AFTERNOON when the Bessemer Kid stepped through the doorway of the Klondike Palace and strolled unobtrusively to the bar. Through a broad, arched doorway he could see the dance-hall where, to the monotonous jangle of the tinny piano, several couples were waltzing indifferently. Across the room, a croupier dozed behind his idle wheel, and a man dealt faro against three cheap players.

A girl in a low cut gown and short skirts that disclosed a long run in her cheap silk stocking, strolled over from the piano and regarded the Kid languidly from between lids heavy with mascara. "How about a dance, baby? The music's swell."

"It's too hot," growled the Kid, and ungraciously turning his back on her, ordered a drink. The girl made a snoot at him and strolled back to loll against the piano.

As the Bessemer Kid poured his drink, his glance rested on Cuter Malone, the beefy proprietor, who stood with his back against the huge iron safe toward the open end of the bar, a big yellow diamond flashing in the cravat that showed above his fancy vest, and the inevitable black cigar cocked at an angle between his thick lips. With an air of bored magnificence he was watching the play at the faro layout across the room.

Ma Bergson had said that Millie had gone to the Klondike Palace. But nobody was practicing a song and dance act. Nobody was doing much of anything. It was a dull hour of a hot day.

The big revolver beneath the Bessemer Kid's shirt pressed uncomfortably against his belly. He glanced down to see if it made a noticeable bulge. Louie the Decker was nowhere in sight. He was wondering where to turn next, when a low buzzing sound attracted his attention. The sound came from the rear, and he saw Cuter Malone turn and lift a tray from the back bar. A bartender eyed the gross figure questioningly, and Cuter shook his head.

"I'll handle this one," he said, in a low voice, as he placed a wine bottle and two glasses upon the tray. The bartender turned away, and out of the tail of his eye, the Kid saw Cuter glance swiftly about the room, remove a small phial from the pocket of his vest, pour a few colorless drops into one of the glasses, and return the phial to his pocket. Then, he picked up the tray and lumbered through the opening at the end of the bar.

The Bessemer Kid became instantly alert. Here was something wrong, plenty wrong! He downed his drink, and moved unnoticed toward the rear, ostensibly toward a door far back, above which appeared the legend: *Gents' walk*. At the break of the long bar a wooden half-partition ran at a right angle, partially cutting off a section of the huge room which was devoted to poker and stud. There were no players at the green covered tables, and as the Kid stepped around behind the partition, he saw that Cuter had paused before a narrow door. Holding the tray in one hand, he was fitting a key into the lock with the other.

Drawing the six-gun from beneath his shirt, the Kid cocked it and moved swiftly and silently along the partition until he stood directly behind the thick-bodied proprietor. The lock clicked, and the door swung inward. Cuter stepped through and, turning to close the door with his foot, found the muzzle of a forty-five six-gun boring into his short ribs. His eyes bulged, and a peculiar throaty gurgle rumbled between his lips as he sought to back away from the prodding gun.

Glancing beyond him, the Bessemer Kid saw the figure of a girl bent forward upon the table, her face buried in her arms. Her shoulders heaved in great gasping sobs as she shrank from the gaze of the pasty-faced man who sat across the table regarding her with a sardonic grin. Neither had noticed the Kid, screened as he was by Malone's gross body.

The proprietor filled his lungs to bellow for help as his eyes encountered the narrowed eyes of the Kid.

"Go ahead, yell, Cuter," the young man urged, in a hard, low voice. "Yer flunkies'll come an' they'll git me. But not before two or three of these soft-lead slugs will plow through yer belly. An' not before the balance of 'em make a sieve out of that white-faced rat behind you."

THE BREATH wheezed from Malone's lungs in an audible sigh as the Kid kicked the door to and heard the lock click behind him. "Thick walls, an' a thick door, Cuter. You'll have to yell loud, now. I've heard of this room. Sound proof, they say. An' they say there's be'n men murdered in here, an' them in the barroom never heard the shots."

With unsteady hands Malone set the tray on the table and sank into a chair—sank back away from the prodding gun. At the first sound of the Kid's voice the girl had raised her head, and as it ceased, she leaped wildly to her feet:

"Oh—get me out of here! Take me away from here! Please, Kid—hurry!"

Stealthily the left hand of Louie the Decker reached for the little wall button behind him. A shot roared and with a thin scream of pain, the man grasped his left wrist and stared in horror at the shattered hand from which blood jetted in tiny spurts, spraying the table top.

The Kid's gaze met the terror-wide eyes of Cuter Malone who cringed in his chair also staring at the thin red spurts. "I don't know," he said, speaking rapidly, "if he touched that buzzer or not. Or if they could hear that shot. But if anyone comes to the door you tell 'em everything's okay in here—an' make it sound right. Make it sound right, Cuter! It'll take 'em quite a while to bust down that door, long enough fer me to fill that thick belly of yours full of slugs."

At a slight rattling of the latch Cuter rose heavily to his feet, removed a plug set into the thick wall close beside the door, and placed his lips to the aperture: "We're all jake in here," he said in a husky whisper. "Never mind the buzzer. We changed our mind."

Replacing the plug, he sank back into his chair and watched Louie the Decker futilely try to staunch the spurting blood with a handkerchief. The girl cowered against the wall, paper white, eyes staring, clenched fists drawn tightly against her breasts, breathing rapidly between parted lips.

With his back to the door, the Bessemer Kid glanced toward her. "All right, Millie," he said. "Tell me."

The girls eyes flashed from Louie the Decker to the thick figure beyond the blood-spattered table. "I—I can't!" she faltered. "I can't tell you. He said I would—it was horrible!" She buried her face in her hands.

The Kid's glance shifted to Malone: "Have a drink, Cuter," he invited. "You look like you need one."

The man moistened his lips, but made no move to comply.

The Kid's eyes narrowed: "I said 'Have a drink,'" he repeated, and the man reached for the bottle and picked up a glass. "The other glass," came the hard voice of the Kid. "The one with the drops in it."

Malone's eyes flickered, and the hand that held the glass trembled. "It's knockout drops," he croaked, thickly. "My heart's bad. It might kill me."

"It's easier to die that way than with a slug in yer belly," reminded the Kid, advancing the muzzle of the gun. "I'm givin' you yer choice. In about ten seconds I'll start shootin'."

"Give me some drops," pleaded Louie the Decker, as he watched Malone reach for the other glass, fill it, and drain it at a swift gulp. "My hand's hurtin' fierce!"

"No drops fer you," rasped the Kid. "You're goin' the hard way. I'm sorry it ain't hurtin' twice as bad."

"The girl lied!" shrilled the man. "It was a song an' dance act we was goin' to rehearse! I was only kiddin' her a little!"

The Kid smiled thinly. "Yeah? Where does knock-out drops come in—in a song an' dance act?"

"I don't know about no drops! If there was drops, they was

Cuter's doin's. I don't know nothin' about it!"

"You lie!" growled Malone, his voice sounding unnaturally thick, as he glared with dull eyes at the other. With an effort, he met the Kid's gaze. "You guessed it," he snarled. "We was goin' to break her in fer the line."

There was a swift movement and a nickel-plated gun flashed above the edge of the table. The Kid's gun roared again, and Louie the Decker lurched sidewise, slipped slowly from his chair, and lay very still upon the floor, the nickel-plated gun clutched in his hand.

The Bessemer Kid turned to Malone. "If anyone heard that shot an' comes to the door, you tell 'em like you done before," he ordered.

"No one heard the shot," mumbled Cuter. "The other time it was the buzzer. He touched it before you shot."

"Have another drink," commanded the Kid. "Drops an' all. The drops are in yer vest pocket in case you've fergot."

"It might kill me, what with my heart, an' all," protested Malone.

The Kid shrugged. "It's all the same to me, if you die. I'm givin' you a break. These slugs is bound to kill you. But it'll suit me jest as well if you take a good long sleep. I'm gettin' out of here—gittin' her out, too—an' I ain't takin' no chances. You'll either be dead or asleep before I open that door an' I don't give a damn which. You goin' to take the drink? Or do I start shootin'?"

Malone hesitated, then as his glance strayed to the grotesquely crumpled body upon the floor, he reached for the phial and shook a few drops into the glass, filled it with wine, and swallowed the potion. The drug took rapid effect. His body sagged deeper into the chair, his head rolled uneasily and came to rest with the chin on his chest. When the man's breathing became regular and heavy, the Bessemer Kid tapped in the wall plug with the butt of his gun so tightly that it could not be withdrawn by hand, and secured Malone's keys. A moment later, he locked the door from the outside, slipped the keys into his pocket, and piloted the girl swiftly out the back door, unnoticed by anyone beyond the partition.

FROM HER position behind the counter, Ma Bergson glanced past the Kid into the tear-reddened eyes of the girl, as the two stepped into the restaurant. "Git yer song an' dance learnt?" she asked. "When does the show start? I want to git me a ticket."

"Don't rub it in, Ma," Millie pleaded. "You were right. I was a fool."

"What you goin' to do, now?"

"Go back to work—if you'll take me, I've got more sense than I had."

"Where's Louie the Decker?"

"He won't bother her no more," answered the Kid. "I shot him. He's dead."

Ma Bergson nodded, slowly. "I mistrusted somethin' like that might happen, when I seen my gun was gone. How about Cuter Malone?"

The Bessemer Kid shrugged. "He might be dead, too. He was asleep when we left him, on a chair in his little back room. He drunk some knock-out drops that he fixed up fer Louie to slip Millie. I made him drink 'em himself, a double dose of 'em. He seen me kill Louie there in the room, an' he know'd I'd shoot. So, when I give him his choice, he took the drops. But he claimed they might kill him, on account of his heart. I locked him in the back room. Louie's layin' there, too. There won't no one dare to bother 'em fer a long time."

Ma Bergson sniffed: "If his heart's all them drops would work on, Cuter Malone's safe enough. He ain't got no more heart than a rock. But, when he wakes up, he's goin' to be seein' red. You kids can't stay in Dawson. Cuter's got rats workin' fer him that'll do jest like he tells 'em to—an' believe me, he'll tell 'em plenty!"

"I ain't afraid of him," retorted the Bessemer Kid. "He can't run me out of camp."

Ma Bergson shrugged her thick shoulders: "Suit yerself. There's no fool like a dead fool. They'll find you with a knife in yer back, some mornin', or a bullet. At that, you'd git a better break than Millie."

"I'll go to the police. I'll tell Corporal Downey what come off."

"If you go to the police, it'll be that dumb Constable Brink you'll be tellin', not Downey. He's off on patrol. But even if he was here, he couldn't do nothin'. Cuter would have plenty of witnesses that he wasn't even in that room. Use yer head, Kid. There's a lot of bull-headed dead men. An' once Cuter's mob git you out of the way, think what might happen to Millie."

"Where can we go?" cried the girl, desperation showing in her eyes.

"I'd say Halfaday Crick is yer best bet."

"But," objected the Kid, "I thought they was all outlaws, up there!"

Ma Bergson smiled, bleakly. "Well, what do you call yerself? If you ain't an outlaw, now, yer goin' to be one, when Cuter Malone wakes up an' finds you've skipped out where his rats can't find you. He'll run to the police with a squawk you could hear a mile an' he'll tell his own story. There's gold on Halfaday, Kid. An' you've got a grubstake. Take an old fool's advice, an' go there."

The Kid's face lighted with sudden interest. "Sure I've got a grubstake! But I—we ain't—" he stumbled to an embarrassed halt, and flushed deeply as he glanced at the girl. "I was goin' to—to tell you about it, Millie. I figgered if I made a strike you might, mebbe, marry me. I was huntin' you when Ma told me where you was at. So I went an' got you."

The desperation had gone out of her eyes now. She looked at him for a long moment, smiling a little. "Yes," she said at last. "I'd have married you at Christmas, if you'd asked me one more time. I was just, kind of—of putting you off, Kid. Then, when you went back to the crick, I thought you were mad. I thought that if I could get in a show you'd come and see me dance—and maybe you'd ask me again."

"Well, then that's settled," interrupted the practical Ma Bergson. "Them drops ain't goin' to keep Cuter Malone sleepin' ferever. You two has got to git married before you hit out. The arch deacon was in here fer dinner an' he told me he was headin' fer Moosehide to see how the Siwashes is gittin' along. He's down there now. You two hit the trail fer Moosehide. It's only four mile. I'll throw an outfit together, an' slip down with it in a canoe. I'm gittin' heavy. Them rock trails is hard on my feet, any more, if I'm carryin' a pack. The boys in the A.C. Store'll pack the stuff to the river fer me. The arch deacon'll marry you an', come dark, you kin hit upriver in the canoe. Here, give me back my gun—'fore you git outlawed some more. There'll be a rifle in yer outfit. An' I'll fetch along the balance of yer dust. Git goin', now. Halfaday Crick's upriver, up the Yukon, an' then on up the White. But, when you pull out of Moosehide, keep on goin' downriver in the canoe till dark, then swing acrost, an' head back upstream. That'll throw them reptiles of Malone's off yer trail. I'll manage to pass the word, somehow, that you hit out fer Circle, er Birch Crick, on the American side. That'll keep 'em busy till snow flies, if they aim to follow you."

"But," protested the Kid, "that's a lot of trouble fer you to go to, Ma. Can't you send someone else down to Moosehide with the stuff? You'd have to walk back, an' s'pose the canoe'd tip over with you, or somethin'?"

"Listen!" exclaimed Ma Bergson. "Who's runnin' this? I'll have you to know that I was runnin' these rivers in a canoe when they was pinnin' 'em on you three cornered! An' as fer walkin' back—a four-mile walk'll do me good. I'm gittin' too fat in this restaurant. Besides, chances is, the arch deacon wouldn't marry you without I told him to, not havin' no license, nor nothin'. He's know'd me fer years. Married me to Tom Foster, first, an' then to Bergson. Cripes! He's stunk up my cabin with his Siwash meetin's on more'n one crick! It's time he done me a good turn. He'll marry you, all right, when I tell him it's a 'mergency."

"But, them outlaws? How about takin' Millie amongst 'em?" asked the kid.

"Huh," snorted Ma Bergson, "a woman's a sight safer on Halfaday than she is in Dawson! Them boys up there might be outlaws, but they ain't skunks! You tell Black John Smith, an' Old Cush I sent you, an' tell 'em why."

That night, as the canoe bearing the Bessemer Kid and his bride of a few hours was forging slowly upstream, Cuter Malone, amply supported by witnesses, was unfolding to Constable Brink the tale of a murder over a card game in his little back room. And John Doe, alias the Bessemer Kid went down on the book as the murderer of Louis Beckwith, alias Louis the Decker.

III

IT WAS WELL into the twilight of a long summer day, some two weeks after the big celebration in Dawson, that Corporal Downey, of the Northwest Mounted Police, drew his canoe from the water and ascended the steep trail to Cushing's Fort, the combined trading post and saloon that served the little band of outlawed men that had collected on Halfaday Creek, close against the Yukon-Alaska border.

Still a young man, Corporal Downey was the terror of evil doers, and the friend of the square-shooting sourdoughs. He was also a friend of Black John Smith, a huge man whose boast it was that he had upon a certain occasion, and at the point of a gun, relieved a major and three common soldiers of a forty-thousand dollar payroll, near Fort Gibbon, Alaska—an incident that the big man professed to regard more in the nature of a sporting event than a crime. As no mention of the occurrence had ever come from the American authorities, Black John's skirts were clean in the Yukon. Despite his oft repeated statement that "on Halfaday we don't neither help, nor hinder the police", there had been times a-plenty when Black John had been of invaluable assistance to the young officer.

Stepping into the room, Downey was greeted heartily by the big man, who stood at the bar shaking dice for the drinks with Old Cush, the proprietor. "Hello, Corp'ral! Step right up! Yer jest in time. Cush is goin' to buy one. What's on yer mind? Some activity in the ranks of the sinful?"

"No, jest a routine patrol. We've got a couple of robberies on the book, an' one murder."

Black John brightened.

"A murder, eh? A good one?"

Corporal Downey grinned. "If any murder can be called good, this one can. One of Cuter Malone's mob got knocked off—a damn tin horn gambler they called Louie the Decker. We've suspected him of dope-peddlin' an' plenty more, but we've never been able to get anything on him to go to trial with."

"Ain't found out who done it, eh?"

"We know who done it. Cuter give Brink the low-down."

"Huh," snorted Cush, "it would be low down, all right, if Cuter Malone had a finger in it. Who was this here party?"

"Young punk they call the Bessemer Kid. Accordin' to Cuter, an' about a dozen witnesses, this Kid run up against Louie the Decker in a two-handed card game, in Cuter's back room. When the Kid begun to lose steady, he claimed Louie was second dealin' on him, an' pulled a gun from under his shirt, an' let him have it. Brink's be'n workin' on the case, but he ain't had much luck. This Bessemer Kid has disappeared."

"What does Brink want of him?" queried Black John. "To give him a medal, er somethin'?"

Corporal Downey, his face serious, shook his head. "A murder's a murder, no matter who the victim is. We all know the North is well rid of Louie the Decker. But that ain't sayin' that anyone had a right to shoot him down in cold blood because he suspected him of cheatin' at cards. We'd have picked Louie up, sometime, an' put him away, accordin' to law."

Black John nodded: "Yer right, in the main, Downey. A murder's a murder, no matter who the victim is. But every killin' ain't a murder."

"This one was," Downey replied, "accordin' to all Brink's evidence."

"Ain't you worked on it, yerself?"

"No. It's Brink's case. I'm lettin' him handle it. He wrote it on the book. I'm givin' him the chance to write it off. Of course, if I should run onto the Bessemer Kid, I'd take him in."

A swift glance passed between Black John and Old Cush—a glance that was not lost on Corporal Downey.

"Well," ventured Cush, breaking the momentary silence, "mebbe you would; an' then agin, mebbe you wouldn't."

"What do you mean?" asked Downey, his eyes narrowing slightly. "I've brought in tougher birds than that punk."

"Oh, shore," agreed Black John, "if this here Bessemer Kid was tough, we'd know you'd fetch him in. Did you talk to Jimmy the Rough an' Ma Bergson?"

"Jimmy the Rough, an' Ma Bergson! What have they got to do with it?"

"Well, this Bessemer Kid, he worked fer Jimmy. An' Ma Bergson, she could tell you a story of that killin' that wouldn't match up very good with Cuter's. An' she'd show you the gun Louie the Decker was shot with. She keeps it in her till, down to the Little Gem, in case someone would try to pull a stickup on her."

Corporal Downey regarded the big man thoughtfully. "If I didn't have the evidence of my eyes to the contrary, I'd say you hadn't got over yer Dominion Day drunk, yet. Ma Bergson—the finest old girl in the Yukon—with the gun in her possession that killed Louie the Decker! It don't make sense. Whose gun is it? An' who does she claim shot him?"

"It's hers. An' she claims, jest like Cuter, that it was the Bessemer Kid done it. She knows it was him."

"Has she told Brink?"

Black John grinned. "She knows Brink, same as we all do. An' she knows there ain't a damn thing between his two ears but solid bone. She wouldn't tell Brink nothin'. She'd tell you, though, if you was to ask her. An' Jimmy the Rough would tell you what kind of a hombre this Bessemer Kid is. Men gets to know one another pretty good by the time they've wintered together in a one-room shack, an' worked side by side fer half a year."

CORPORAL DOWNEY glanced from the face of the speaker to the somber face of Old Cush. He knew these sourdoughs— knew that they were doing a good, and a difficult job in keeping Halfaday free of crime. He had confidence in their judgment, and in their ability to size up situations and men. And he had confidence in the judgment and the honesty of Ma Bergson, and Jimmy the Rough, who also were sourdoughs. "Do you know about this murder?" he asked.

Old Cush answered: "We know all about the killin'. We don't know nothin' about no murder. Ma Bergson told John about it when he was down to Dawson fer Dominion Day. An' he talked to Jimmy the Rough."

Downey drummed for a moment on the bar with his fingers. "What's Ma's version of it?" he asked.

Black John's glance met the shrewd eyes of the young officer squarely. "Mebbe you'd better git that straight from Ma Bergson, herself, like I done. In the meantime, if I was you, I'd sort of talk things over with the Bessemer Kid, an' the girl. They kin tell you an earful."

"The Bessemer Kid! An' the girl?" exclaimed Downey, his eyes narrowing, slightly. "Is there a girl mixed up in it? Cuter didn't mention any girl to Brink."

"He wouldn't—the dirty low-lived skunk. They mentioned cards, instead."

"An' the Bessemer Kid is here, on Halfaday? An' this girl is with him?"

"Yup. They're here," Black John replied. "Got a couple of claims staked on a feeder, about four mile up the crick. Livin' in Whiskey Bill's old shack. Ma Bergson sent 'em up here. When I was down to Dawson she told me all about it—asked me to sort of keep an eye on 'em. The girl, she's pretty as a picture on a calendar. Her name's Millie Avery, on her recordin' papers, an' his is John Avery. They call him the Bessemer Kid, on account he used to live in Bessemer, Alabamy."

"Is she his sister?"

"Hell, no! His wife! An' there ain't no quibblin' about that part of it, neither. You know Ma Bergson. She kin blister the paint off 'n a bar, once she sets her tongue to it, she's that out-spoken when the circumstances demands it, but she wouldn't never of started them young folks off into the hills together onlest they was married, you kin bet on that. She herded 'em down to Moosehide, after the shootin', an' made the arch deacon hitch 'em up proper. They couldn't wait fer no license. But the arch deacon has know'd Ma fer a dozen years, er more. He knows she's a square shooter. So when she tells him to stretch a p'int—he stretched."

Corporal Downey grinned, broadly. "This case is becomin' complicated," he opined. "It looks to me like Ma Bergson an' the arch deacon has got themselves involved as accessories after the fact."

Black John chuckled: "Go tell that to Ma, an' listen to what she tells you back. Yer ears won't only burn, Downey, they'll sizzle, an' curl up, an' drop off, like bacon off 'n a stick."

Downey returned the grin. "Guess I'll go on up to their claims in the mornin' an' hear what they've got to say."

"BACK, EH?" greeted Old Cush, as the officer stepped into the saloon the following evening. "I don't see you fetchin' no culprit along."

Corporal Downey shook his head. "No," he said, "from what I've be'n able to gather, everyone can stay right where they are, as far as I'm concerned. I'll check up with Ma Bergson when I get back to Dawson, jest to make sure. I believe, though, I've got the facts about as they happened. I can generally tell when folks is lyin'."

"You ain't even fetchin' him down to stand trial, then?" asked Black John.

"No. What would be the use? If he was acquitted, Malone's mob would get a line on where he is, an' they might manage to knock him off. Or worse yet, take out their revenge on the girl. Or they might possibly be able to convince a jury that Louie the Decker really was killed over a card game. You can't never tell about a jury—'specially when it's apt to be made up of chechakos, an' there's a mob like Cuter's hangin' around to in-timidate 'em."

"Jest leavin' the case open, eh?" asked Black John. "How's he booked—by his right name, John Avery?"

"No, as John Doe, alias the Bessemer Kid. They didn't know his right name in Dawson. It's Brink's case. He wrote it on, let him write it off. We don't like open cases on the book, but if I'd have taken Cuter's report, instead of Brink, I wouldn't have entered no murder till I'd done some investigatin'. I'll tell the inspector about it, private, next time I see him, an' if he insists on havin' the case brought to trial an' wrote off, I'll come up after the Bessemer Kid, myself. I believe, though, the inspector'll look at it like I do."

"Yeah," agreed Cush, "an' it's the way any of you Mounted Police that really belongs in the North would look at it. Brink, he's a han'some fella. He'd look right nice on a horse."

"That's right," agreed Black John. "Back in the provinces, somewheres, he'd ort to do well on a horse." He paused for a moment, and added: "That is, providin' they could find him a horse that could think."

Corporal Downey's patrol report made no mention of the

Bessemer Kid, and some two weeks after his return to Dawson, Constable Brink submitted a proposed patrol for himself that would take him up Sixtymile, up Florence Creek, across a divide to Vancouver Creek, down Vancouver to the White, and back by way of the Yukon. Corporal Downey scanned the route, and approved the patrol, as neither Florence nor Vancouver creeks had ever been visited by the police.

His eyes were sharp.

"It's a good patrol," he said, as he handed the sketched route back to Brink, "but it ain't such an easy one, for a man that don't know the country. If you'd get up there, an' should happen to foller up the wrong crick, or cross the wrong divide, there's no tellin' where you'd fetch up—if anywheres. Think you can make it without gettin' lost?"

Constable Brink flushed at the implication of incompetence. "Of course I can make it! I've got a map. It don't take much brains to follow a map or carry a canoe over a divide."

"That's right," Downey admitted, with a grin. "Brains is more useful in not follerin' the map—or rather, in knowin' when not to foller it. The maps of the back country is made up mostly from hearsay an' guess work. The ones that makes 'em scatters cricks, an' divides, an' mountains, an' lakes where they think they ort to be, which ain't always where they are. Another thing—all cricks, an' all divides look alike on paper. But there's cricks that's too rough, or too shallow fer a canoe, an' there's divides that no livin' man could get a canoe over when he come to 'em."

"You always seem to get through, somehow."

"Yeah, I git through. But sometimes I sure know I've be'n somewheres. Go ahead. Make the patrol. You've asked for it."

IV

UPON AN EVENING a month later, a weary and bedraggled Constable Brink was paddling down a creek when a glimmer of light through the thick foliage of the bordering willows caused him to urge his canoe forward at redoubled speed. Sweeping around a bend, he beached the craft at a landing, ascended a short, steep slope, and regarded the low log building with scowling disapproval. His map showed no trading post on Vancouver Creek. Yet this was undoubtedly a trading post. "If this ain't Vancouver Crick, where the hell am I?" he muttered, savagely.

Advancing to the doorway, he paused and glanced into the lighted room where a huge, bearded man stood facing a somber-faced one across a bar. Constable Brink had never been on Halfaday Creek, but he had seen both Black John Smith and Old Cush in Dawson on numerous occasions, and he stifled a curse at the realization that this must be Cushing's Fort, and the creek he had blundered onto was Halfaday, and not Vancouver. For some moments he stood, unseen by the two at the bar, toying with the idea of slipping back to his canoe and continuing down the creek. He could report that he had reached the White River by way of Vancouver, and thus avoid revealing the humiliating fact that he had been lost for ten days, and had inadvertently doubled on Corporal Downey's patrol.

In the saloon the big man was speaking: "He'll be dead by mornin' unless we kin git his temperature down. No man kin live through a night with the fever he's got."

"Oh, I don't know," the other replied. "I give him a big dose of quinine. He'll prob'ly pull through."

"Quinine! You might as well fed him so much chalk!"

"Is that so! My doctor book claims quinine'll cure chills an' fever, so that's what I give him."

"Chills an' fever! You an' yer damn doctor book! That man ain't got chills an' fever, no more'n I have! It's pneumonia he's got. An' ondoubtless double pneumonia!"

"I don't care if he's got double pneumony, or even triple," argued the man behind the bar. "He claimed he had a bad chill, an' now he's got a bad fever! An' if that ain't chills an' fever, what is? Quinine'll fix him up fine, sure, onless he up an' dies on us."

"That's jest what he'll do if we can't git his temperature down," retorted the big man. "It's a hundred an' six."

"That's nothin'," scoffed the other. "He kin go twict that before he b'iles!"

"Of all the damn fools!" exclaimed the bearded one, in disgust. "Anyhow, I'm goin' to git somethin' to eat, an' then I'm goin' back there. I kin give him cold water sponges, an' Millie kin keep wet blankets on him, an' we kin take turns settin' up with him. At that, I don't believe he's got a Chinaman's chanct."

Constable Brink stepped abruptly into the room and advanced to the bar. "I heard you mention the name Millie," he said. "Millie who?"

Both men turned to face him, and Black John grinned broadly as he eyed the torn and disheveled uniform. "Well, if it ain't Constable Brink, or what's left of him! You shore look like you've be'n somewheres, an' didn't hardly git back. What you doin' on Halfaday?"

"I thought this was Vancouver Crick, till I came around the bend an' saw this light. Then I knew it wasn't."

"Cripes, Vancouver Crick's way west of here. What would you be doin' on Vancouver Crick? There ain't nothin' there."

"I'm on patrol," Brink explained, "an' Halfaday is the last place I wanted to show up at. Downey was through here not so long ago, an' he'll rag the devil out of me for doublin' on his patrol."

Black John grinned. "Yeah, I expect he will. But, it's his own fault, at that. He's in command at Dawson. He'd ort to keep you rookies that ain't dry behind the ears fer camp duty, an' send someone on patrol that knows the country."

Constable Brink flushed to the hair roots. "How's a man ever goin' to learn the country if he don't git out of camp? I asked fer the patrol."

"Well," observed Black John dryly, "you got it. Of course, if a man asks fer trouble an' gits it, he ain't got no kick."

"**YOU HAVEN'T** answered my question," Brink said. "Who is this Millie I heard you mention?"

"She's a girl that lives up the crick," replied Cush. "Why?"

"Well, there was a murder in Dawson, an' I've be'n workin' on it. Fella they call the Bessemer Kid murdered Louie the Decker in an argument over a card game in Cuter Malone's back room. The Bessemer Kid skipped out, an' the same day one of Ma Bergson's hash-slingers disappeared, too."

"An' you figger they pulled out together, eh?" queried Black John. "What does Ma Bergson think?"

"She don't know nothin' about it. I grilled her three, four times, an' she don't know a thing."

"Ma's kind of dumb," said Cush. "What does Downey think about it?"

Brink frowned. "He was off on patrol when it happened. He got back Dominion Day, an' right after the Fourth, he started on another patrol—the one that took him up here. So he don't know much about it. He prob'ly thinks I ort to have got the Bessemer Kid, though. That's the main reason I asked fer this patrol, to give him a chanct to work on it."

"This Louie the Decker," observed Black John. "I know'd him, by sight. An', believe me, he wasn't no ornament to any camp. I'd say it's a good thing fer the country that this Bessemer Kid knocked him off. It's too bad he didn't finish the job, an' clean out the rest of the Klondike Palace gang—Cuter along with 'em."

"If a man's got a bad reputation, it's no excuse fer someone murderin' him."

"So you figger it was a murder, eh?"

"I know it was," retorted Brink. "Malone, himself, gave me the facts, an' supported 'em with a dozen witnesses. It was an unprovoked murder, if there ever was one. An' I'll git the Bessemer Kid, if it takes me ten years!"

"Do you know these folks when you see 'em?" the big man

asked abruptly. "The Bessemer Kid, an' this Millie?"

"I know Millie. She used to wait on me sometimes in the restaurant. I never seen the Bessemer Kid."

Black John nodded, thoughtfully. "Well, you'll be seein' him, tomorrow," he said.

Old Cush scowled ferociously at the speaker. "What do you mean?" he snapped. "You gone crazy?"

The big man shook his head. "Nope. I ain't crazy. Nor, neither I don't mean nothin' but jest what I said. This here party is an officer of the law. We know the Bessemer Kid is here on the crick. An' we ain't doin' right to keep on hidin' him. We shet up whilst Downey was here, an' he went away without knowin' the Bessemer Kid was within a thousan' mile of Halfaday. I ain't never felt right about it sence. But this here policeman, he's smarter'n what Downey is. He smelt a nigger in the woodpile as soon as heard the name of Millie spoke. He's right about her skippin' out with the Kid."

He paused, and the frown on Cush's face resolved into a look of perplexed anticipation, as he realized that the speaker was talking with a purpose in mind. Nevertheless, he doubted the wisdom of passing Constable Brink any information concerning the Bessemer Kid, even though he held a vast respect for Black John's shrewdness. Gazing directly into the eyes of Constable Brink, the big man continued: "They're livin' together in a shack about four mile up the crick. Like I told you, you kin see him tomorrow. But, I'm doubtin' if you'll ever arrest him. The fact is, he's so sick that, if he ain't dead by mornin' he will be by tomorrow night."

Brink's eyes widened with excitement. "The Bessemer Kid right here on Halfaday!" he exclaimed. "An' Downey let him slip through his fingers!"

"That's right," admitted Black John, a note of contrition in his voice. "Mebbe we'd ort to of tipped Downey off, but we didn't. I hope he won't think hard of us."

"Don't matter what Downey thinks!" cried Brink. "The main thing is that he had the chance to pick the Kid up, an' muffed it. But he won't slip through my fingers! I guess Downey'll know who's a policeman, now! He's slippin'. Wait till the inspector hears how I picked him up right under Downey's nose, you might say! This case'll show him up, all right!"

"Pore Downey," said Cush, a note of compassion in his voice. "He'll shore take it hard—gittin' beat out by a rookie."

Black John had difficulty in suppressing a grin, as Brink replied, sententiously, but with a gleam of triumph in his eye: "Yeah, he'll take it hard, all right. But he's got to learn that the best man's bound to win in the long run. Why can't I go up to the Bessemer Kid's tonight?"

Black John shook his head. "Nope. It wouldn't do no good an' it would upset Millie terrible. She's up there alone with him—an' him dyin'. I'm goin' to hustle back there as soon as I've et. Cush, he'll fetch you on up the first thing in the mornin'. I'll give you my word the man'll be there. He couldn't be nowheres else. He's burnin' up with fever."

Old Cush nodded agreement. "Yeah, he's runnin' a fever, all right. Better wait till mornin' an' give the quinine a chance to work on him. Chances is, he'll be better by then, if John don't choke him to death with that thermometer."

"Fair enough," agreed Brink. "Let's eat. If the Bessemer Kid's as sick as what you claim, I guess he'll be there in the mornin'."

EARLY THE following morning, Constable Brink, accompanied by Old Cush, headed up the creek. An hour and a half later, they approached a shack before the door of which Black John sat whittling at a chip.

"How is he?" Brink asked.

The big man shrugged. "Jest about breathin' his last. Millie's in there with him. We couldn't do nothin' about that fever. We sponged him with cold water, and kept wet blankets on him all night, but it didn't seem to do no good. His breath is comin' in short jabs like—an' so feeble you can't hardly hear it. You kin go on in if you want to."

Brink stepped into the room. In the darkened interior he made out the figure of a woman who sat sobbing softly by the side of the bunk. Upon it lay a young man whose fever-tortured body was covered with a wet blanket. His chest labored pitifully to pump air into his gasping lungs.

Minutes passed as the officer stood silently watching the dying man, whose chest efforts became gradually feebler until they ceased entirely. Beside the bunk, the young woman sobbed audibly, and leaning over, stared for a moment into the lifeless face. She raised her eyes to Brink.

"He's gone," she said, simply, and drawing the blanket over the man's face, turned from the bunk.

Approaching it, Brink raised the corner of the blanket and stared down at the still features. He nodded, and turned away. "He's dead, all right," he concurred, and as he stepped past the sobbing woman, he noted that she drew way from him. "You don't need to fear me, Millie," he said, in a tone meant to be reassuring. "It wasn't you murdered Louie the Decker. It was him. He's dead, now, an' the case of the Bessemer Kid is closed. It was me that wrote it on the book an' it's me that's writin' it off. I kep' on the case till I ran my man down. It ain't my fault he died, jest as I caught up with him. I'm hittin' back to Dawson, now, to report to Corporal Downey that I located my man, right where he overlooked him. You kin go back with me, if you like. There ain't nothin' on you, back there."

Without meeting his eyes, the girl shook her head. "No," she replied, between dry sobs, "I—I'll stay here. These men have been kind to me, and I wouldn't want to go back there now."

SOME SIX weeks later, Corporal Downey accosted Black John in the Tivoli Saloon, in Dawson. "I was sure sorry to hear about the Bessemer Kid's death," he said. "You know, I kind of liked him, an' the girl too. When I got back I had a talk with Ma

Bergson, an' what she said checked exactly with what them two young folks told me, up there on Halfaday. I don't blame him fer knockin' Louie the Decker off. Under the circumstances, he couldn't have done nothin' else. Like I told you, though, what with all the witnesses Cuter could muster, a jury might have convicted him."

"The case is closed, now, ain't it?"

"Oh, sure, the case is closed. Brink, he closed it, an' he don't never give anyone a chance to think he didn't. You ort to hear him brag about it. An' he never forgets to mention that he located his man on Halfaday right after I'd be'n through there an' missed him. How's the girl doin'? Brink says she stayed up there."

"Yeah," grinned Black John, "she stayed. She's doin' fine. The Bessemer Kid, too. They both sent their best regards to you. They've got their shack up, an' they're doin' right well with the claims. Told me to tell you to be shore an' stop in the next time yer on the crick."

Corporal Downey was staring in open-mouthed astonishment. "What the devil do you mean, the Bessemer Kid doin' fine? He's dead, ain't he?"

"Not so you could notice, he ain't. You see, Downey there must of be'n some slight misunderstandin' somewheres, the time Brink was up there. This fella that was sick—the one that died of pneumonia, or whatever he had—it turned out that he wasn't the Bessemer Kid, at all. He was a young fella that had the claim next to theirs, an' when he got sick Millie helped take care of him. Me an' Cush done what we could, too, an' when Brink come into Cush's, that evenin', an' heard me mention Millie's name, an' how I was goin' back an' help her nurse the sick man, he spotted her for the girl that had skipped out with the Bessemer Kid.

"I seen, in a minute, how Brink would go bustin' up there to investigate, an' how he couldn't help but blunder onto the Kid, him right on the next claim, or mebbe even right there helpin'

Millie with the sick man. So I done some fast thinkin' an' when I found out Brink didn't know the Kid by sight, I told him right out, that the Kid was on the crick. Cush near throw'd a fit, till he seen I had somethin' up my sleeve—then he shet up.

"Well, somehow, mebbe from somethin' I said, Brink he got the idea that this sick man was the Bessemer Kid. So I went back to the shack, that night, to doctor him, an' Cush fetched Brink up there the next mornin'. They got there jest before this fella died.

"I'd had a kind of a talk with Millie, durin' the night, sort of explained the setup to her. Smart girl, that Millie. Anyways, we figured it wasn't none of our business if Brink thought the Bessemer Kid was dead. Nor neither it wasn't fer us to go contrary to what a policeman writes down in his report. So we buried this fella, that day, in the graveyard, an' we put up a slab fer him with the name *Bessemer Kid* burnt into it, good an' plain, bein' as that's who Brink claimed he was. You'd ort to come up an' see it, sometime. It's a dandy!"

"I will," promised Corporal Downey, with a broad grin. "An' when it comes to fast thinkin', my hat's off to you, John. What you goin' to have? I'm buyin'."

"It didn't irk my brain none to outguess Brink. He's a damn fool. But," he added, as he filled his glass from the bottle the bartender set before them, "he got his case wrote off the book, at that."

DEAD MAN'S NUGGET

CORPORAL DOWNEY LOOKED up from his desk with a grin of welcome as Black John Smith stepped into his little office at detachment headquarters in Dawson. "Hello, John! What you doin' down here?"

The big man settled himself into a chair, selected two cigars from his pocket, rolled one across the desk toward Downey, and lighted the other. "Oh, I come down with One Armed John. He can't handle a canoe on a long trip, so I come along with him. He's be'n complainin' fer a week about havin' pains an' aches in his belly, so I told him he better go to the hospital an' let 'em find out what's ailin' him. We got in late yesterday afternoon an' after stoppin' at the Tivoli fer a couple of drinks, he went over to the hospital an' I set in a stud game with Bettles, an' Moosehide, an' some of the boys."

"When you goin' back?"

"Damn if I know. If they've got to operate on One Arm I'll stick around an' see how it comes out, an' mebbe take him back up to Halfaday with me. But if it's jest a case of the doctor prescribin' some medicine fer him, we could ketch the *Sarah* in a couple of hours an' have 'em put us off at the mouth of the White. That would save quite a bit of upriver paddlin'. How you gettin' along? Are the sinful keepin' you busy?"

"Yeah, plenty busy. There's nothin' very important, right now. A prospector got murdered up the Klondike a while back. We know who done it—but we can't prove nothin' on 'em."

Black John grinned. "That's the trouble with the law. You know who done it—but they git off scot free because you can't prove it. On Halfaday, if we know who done a hangable act, by God, we go ahead an' hang 'em."

"Yeah—but that ain't accordin' to law."

"It's accordin' to common sense, though. Anyways it serves the practical an' laudatory purpose of puttin' the malefactor where he can't repeat his peccadillo agin some other innocent party. Who killed who—an' why?"

"Couple of fellas named Neff an' Walters killed a man named Green on the next claim to theirs. We know there was bad blood between 'em. Green's claim was pretty good—an' the one Neff an' Walters worked in pardnership wasn't payin' wages. They wanted to buy Green out, but he wouldn't sell. So they slipped over to his shack one night, an' brained him with a club. They prob'ly robbed him, too. We found what looked like an empty cache near Green's shack—but we couldn't get a damn bit of evidence. Green had no enemies except them two. An' no stranger had be'n seen on the upper Klondike. It's jest one of them cases where you know damn well who done it—but you can't prove it. I took a chance an' arrested 'em, hopin' to bluff a confession out of 'em. But they jest laughed at us—an' told us to prove it. We couldn't. So there wasn't nothin' to do but turn 'em loose."

"H-u-m—tough babies, eh? Would the amount they was s'posed to have got off'n Green be important—er merely negligible?"

"We don't know how much it was. Prob'ly not much. Green had be'n bankin' around two hundred ounces a month, here in Dawson, and it was about time fer him to fetch in another deposit when he was knocked off. Neff an' Walters would be the only ones to know about this, except the bank."

"Huh—a piddlin' amount to knock a man off fer. This here Neff an' Walters seems to be parties of no character."

DOWNEY FROWNED. "Dangerous men," he said. "You better keep yer eyes on 'em if they show up on Halfaday. They didn't go back up the Klondike when we turned 'em loose a few days ago. They hung around the Klondike Palace fer a couple of days an' then disappeared."

Black John nodded. "Yeah, they don't seem like nobody a man would pick out fer neighbors. What do they look like? In case they'd show up at Cush's an' fergit what their real names was?"

"Neff, he's the tough one of the two—stands about five foot eight. He's heavy-set. Got a scar on his right cheek, an' a mean look in his eye. Walters, he's tall an' thin an' nervous. His left eye twitches when he talks, an' he sort of keeps glancin' at Neff like he was afraid of him. I figgered he'd squeal when we ques-

tioned 'em separate, an' I could see that Neff was afraid he would, too. But he didn't."

"Well, I'll be trottin' along," Black John said. "If One Arm's in shape to travel I don't want to miss the boat. If he ain't, I'll be seein' you agin. So long."

Stopping in at the Tivoli for a drink on his way to the hospital the big man was surprised to see One Armed John standing at the bar. The one-armed one greeted him.

"Hello, John! Where you be'n? I be'n huntin' all over hell fer you!"

"I've be'n over chawin' the fat with Downey. How about you? Did the doctors up to the hospital decide to disembowel you, er what?"

"How do you mean—disembowel? They looked me over, an' I got some medicine, an' that's all there was to it. The *Sarah's* pullin' out in about an hour. We got time fer a few drinks, an' then what's the matter with ketchin' her? It'll save a hell of a lot of paddlin'. An' besides, I'm tired livin' in a damn city!"

II

LATE THAT EVENING the *Sarah* nosed into the bank just below the mouth of the White River and put the two, together with their canoe and their duffel, ashore. Half an hour later, as Black John was forking a juicy beefsteak in the frying pan, One Armed John fumbled in his packsack, produced a bottle of ample size, drew the cork, and took a drink, puckering up his face in disgust as he returned the cork to the bottle.

"What the hell's that yer drinkin'?" asked the big man, eyeing the bottle.

"That's my medicine," the other replied. "It shore tastes like hell—but they claim it'll cure what ails me."

"Who claims it will?" demanded Black John.

"Why—the bartender down to the Eldorado."

"The bartender at the Eldorado!" roared the big man, in disgust. "Damn you! I've got a notion to kick your pants clean into the middle of the river—an' you in 'em. Here I fetch you all the way down from Halfaday to see a doctor, an' instead of goin' to the hospital, you go to the Eldorado an' consult a barkeep. Let's see that bottle!"

When the one-armed one handed it over Black John held it close to the firelight and read the label: Dr. Cooley's Kidney and Liver Cure. Good for all diseases of the Kidneys, Liver, Gall Bladder, and Prostate Gland. Will dissolve stones in the Kidneys or Bladder. Will POSITIVELY CURE Stomach Ulcers, Stoppage of the Bowels, and all ailments of the Great or Small Intestines. Dose, for adults: One tablespoonful before meals. Two may be taken in extreme cases. Children and infants in proportion.

"Good medicine, ain't it?" asked One Armed John, as the other handed the bottle back. "By God, a medicine's got to be good if it'll cure all them things! I feel better a'ready—an' this is only the second dost I've took. Besides, it cost two dollars a bottle—an' that shows it ain't no cheap medicine, like pain killer. I fetched a dozen bottles along, an' when I git 'em all took I'd ort to be in damn good shape, hadn't I, John?"

The big man nodded. "Yeah. Anyone that could live through a dozen bottles of that stuff would have to be in damn good shape. Come on—let's eat."

The meal was finished in silence and as the two filled their pipes Black John said, "So you never went to the hospital at all, eh? You went to a bartender, instead?"

"Oh, hell no, John! I went to the horspital, all right. Stayed all night—but they never done me no good there. Jest between you an' me, John—a horspital is a hell of a place to go. It's like this—after we had them couple of drinks in the Tivoli, I started fer the horspital. I stopped in to the Antlers an' had a couple of more. An' I had a couple at Cuter Malone's. An' then I stopped in to the Eldorado, an' damn if there wasn't a fella tendin' bar there that use' to tend bar down to Forty Mile! So we had some more drinks, an' when I told him where I was headin', he says how I better keep away from there. 'I'm warnin' you,' he says. 'All them horspital doctors wants is a chanct to cut folks open. You allus hear 'em talkin' about doctors practicin'—well, that's what they do—practice cuttin' folks up. Damn if I'd let 'em practice on me,' he says. 'Cripes,' he says, 'if it ain't nothin but yer guts that's botherin' you, I know a medicine that'll cure you in less'n a week!'

"I tells him I guess I better go on up to the horspital, 'cause that's where you claimed I better go. So I does. I'd had quite a few drinks by that time, but I makes it, all right—after gittin' into the cannery, first, by mistake.

"There was a lady in the office, settin' back of a desk, an' she asks me what I wants, an' I tells her I want to git cured. She says 'what's the matter with you?' An' I says, 'How the hell do I know? That's what I come here fer—to find out.' She says, 'Yer drunk, ain't you?' An' I says, 'Shore I be—an' if you'd drank what I have you'd be a damn sight drunker'n me.' But, on top of that, I says, 'My guts is ailin' me, an' I want to see a doctor.'

"She says how I better come back in the mornin', but I tells her if I wait till mornin' I'll be a damn sight drunker'n what I be now. 'So trot out yer doctor,' I says. She says have I got any money; er am I a charity patient? 'Yer damn whoopin' I got money!' I says, an' I thumps my poke down on the desk in front of her so hard she jumps. When I picks the poke up agin she says do I want a room? An' I says, 'What the hell do you think I want— a stall?' She says she thought mebbe I wanted a ward. 'Not by a damn sight!' I says. 'I was a ward, myself, onct, to a Methodist preacher, till I skipped out on him—an' what the hell would I want with a ward on Halfaday?'

"So she makes out a kind of a ticket an' shoves it acrost the desk an' says I should sign it. An', by God, I was that drunk I come near signin' my right name to it! A man's got to watch hisself around them horspitals—they're tricky as hell.

"So she taps on a little bell she's got settin' there on the desk an' a young lady comes in all rigged out in a white dress an' a white cap on her head. The other lady tells her to take Mr. Smith—that's me—to Number Thirteen. 'Not by a damn sight!' I says. 'It's bad enough to come to a horspital,' I says, 'without drawin' no Number Thirteen, to boot! So they both laughs, an' she says, 'All right, Number 'Leven, then.'

"So I follers this other lady down a kind of a hall, like, an' she opens a door, an' I goes into a room which it's got a narrow iron bunk in it, an' a little iron stand beside it, an' a chair, an' a kind of a cupboard—all painted white. This young lady, she waits by the door. 'Is there anythin' you want?' she says. 'What have you got?' I says. She says, 'What?' An' I says 'If you ain't got nothin' but straight whiskey you don't need to bother, 'cause I fetched a quart along.' So then she goes away, an' I shets the door, an' pulls off my boots, an' has me a good stiff snort, an' sets the bottle on this little iron stand where it's handy, an' climbs into the bunk.

"**I MUSTA** be'n middlin' sleepy, 'cause the next thing I knowd it was daylight, an' my head was achin' me a little, an' I had a hell of a taste in my mouth. So I retch over an' got my bottle an' takes a good long pull at it. When I seen it was goin' to stick I begun to feel better, an' then the door opens an' a damn good lookin' young woman, all rigged out in a white dress like the other one, comes in an' gives me a look. 'Git yer clothes off!' she says. 'Not by a damn sight, young woman!' I says. 'How do I know where yer husban's at? An' besides, there ain't no lock on that door. You git to hell outa here! That's how I lost my arm,' I says, 'an' damn if I'm goin' to lose the other one! It ain't worth it,' I says, 'no matter how good lookin' you be!'

"She p'ints to a long white shirt the other young woman had left layin' on the chair the night before. 'I'll step out in the hall till you git off them clothes an' git into that gown an' git back in bed, you old fool!' she says. 'Then I'll come in an' take yer temperature, an' bring yer breakfast pretty soon, an' after that the doctor'll see you.'

"So I clumb out of the bunk an' pulled off my clothes, an' got into that long shirt, which I'd saw it layin' there the night before, an' figgered it was that other lady's shirt which she fergot. Then I clumb back in the bunk an' takes another drag at the bottle, an' the young lady comes back in an' makes a pass at my face an' hands with a wet rag, an' sticks a little glass tube in my mouth, an' waits awhile, an' jerks it out an' looks at it, an' sets down a figger on a paper which she slips into a dingus on the foot of the bunk. 'How'm I doin'?' I says. 'I'm 'fraid you'll live,' she snaps, kind of short like. When she's goin' out she says, 'If you want to step to the lavatory it's acrost the hall. I'll be back with yer breakfast in ten minutes.'

"I didn't know what the hell she was talkin' about, but I makes a guess at it—an' I was right. So then I clumb back into bed an' takes a medium drink, an' pretty quick she's back with a kind of a platter. She grabs holt of a crank on the side of the bunk an' gives it a few twists, an' damn if the head end of the bunk didn't begin histin' up till I was damn near settin' up straight. Then she sets the platter on my lap. 'The doctor'll see you in an hour,' she says. 'Here's yer breakfast.' 'Where?' I says. 'Why, right there on the tray,' she says, p'intin' at the platter which all it's got on it is one soft cooked hen's egg, an' a piece of burnt bread about the size of a playin' card an' damn little thicker, an' a little glass with some or'nge juice squoze in it, an' a cup of thin coffee. 'How about a chunk of meat?' I says. 'No meat,' she says. 'I'll take a dozen hen's eggs, then,' I says, 'an' I want 'em fried—one way.' 'No more eggs,' she says. 'You shore as hell feed skimpy,' I tells her. 'I'll be back fer yer tray in twenty minutes,' she says. 'Hell, sister,' I says, 'if this is all I git, you kin come back in twenty seconds!'

"She goes out an' I spikes the or'nge juice an' the coffee with what's left in the bottle an' cleaned up on this breakfast. She comes back after while an' hangs my clothes up in the closet, an' goes off with the platter an' the empty bottle, an' pretty quick a fella comes in all rigged out in a white coat, like a barber. 'Who the hell be you?' I says. 'I'm the doctor,' he says. 'How you feelin'?' 'Damn hungry,' I tells him. He grins an' looks at the paper the lady had wrote the number on, an' sticks a couple of prongs in his ears that's 'tatched with a couple of wires to a little dingus about the size of a half dollar. He holds this here dingus agin my chist an' my back an' tells me to breath deep whilst he listens. 'You must be a hell of a doctor,' I says, 'if you think a man's guts is way up by his neck. I come here fer the bellyache!'

"Well, he grins, an' begun askin' a lot of questions, an' then he puts on a wise look, after I told him where my guts was, an' begun proddin' around my belly with his finger. Part of the time it hurt, but mostly it didn't. He kep' askin' if it's sore here an' does it hurt there? There was a couple of times it hurt like hell where he punched, but I kep' teliin' him no it didn't. I wouldn't give no little white-coated shrimp like him the satisfaction of thinkin' he could hurt me by jabbin' me in the guts with his finger, by a damn sight! After 'while he give it up an' went out an' come back with another doctor all rigged out like he was. An' this last one asks me a lot more questions, an' done some more proddin' around my belly, an' finally he claims I've got a rock in my kidney, an' they better operate. The other one agrees. 'We'll operate at ten o'clock,' he says to me.

"I could tell by the way they talked amongst theirselves that they wasn't so damn shore what ailed me, an' also that they figgered it was quite some operation. An' besides—how the hell could a rock git in a kidney? So I says to 'em, 'How do you boys know I've got a rock in my kidney—could you feel it?' We deduce it from yer symptoms,' the first one says. 'We can't be certain, of course. However we're willin' to take the chanct. After we open the abomnible cavity,' the other one chips in, 'we may find somethin' entirely different. It may possibly be gravel.'

"'Yeah,' I says, sarcastic, 'a pay streak, mebbe! Er it might be you'd run onto an old pick er shovel someone left there by mistake! But the two of you kin go to hell!' I says, gittin' mad, by then. 'Damn if yer goin' to do no rock quarryin', nor neither no gravel sluicin' amongst my guts!' An' what with that I jumps outa the bunk, an' jerks off that shirt, an' gits into my clothes, an' shoves on out past 'em, an' stops in the office an' shakes a couple of ounces out of my poke onto the desk in front of the lady, an' tells her she kin tear up that ticket, an' hits fer the Eldorado an' gits the name of this here medicine off'n that bartender, an' goes to the drug store an' lays me in a dozen bottles, an' then I hunts you up.

"I wisht I'd listened to the bartender in the first place an' I'd saved them two ounces I give the lady. But at that, the bartender claims I was lucky, 'cause if I'd be'n damn fool enough to let 'em cut into my guts they'd of soaked me mebbe fifteen, twenty ounces, an' I'd prob'ly died, to boot.

"But what I claim, two ounces is a hell of a lot to pay fer one soft cooked hen's egg, an' some thin burnt bread without no butter on it, an' a little or'nge juice, an' a cup of weak coffee, an' gittin' yer temperature took, an' a night's lodgin' in a narrow bunk, an' gittin' yer chist heard, an' yet guts prodded! I wisht I'd only gave that lady one ounce. What do you think, John?"

Black John grinned broadly. "W-e-e-l, take it all in all, I guess you got yer money's worth. I'm shore sorry I missed it. I'd figger it was cheap at twice the price. Come on, we'll roll in. We want to be gittin' an early start in the mornin'."

III

SIX DAYS LATER, as they approached the Fish Rapids, One Armed John, who was in the bow, pointed toward a low stretch of shore rip-rapped with coarse gravel. "Look, John! Ain't that a man layin' over there amongst them rocks?"

Black John's eyes followed the pointing finger. "It shore is! Er what's left of one," he added, with a glance at the turbulent rapids.

"I'll bet he's dead!" exclaimed the one armed one. "By God, if he ain't dead er drunk he picked him a hell of a place to lay! Them rocks is hard."

A few minutes later the two landed, drew the canoe from the water, and hastened to the inert form that lay upon its face on the coarse gravel, a few feet back from the edge of the river. The man's clothing was saturated, and Black John pointed to a badly smashed canoe that floated lazily round and round in the huge eddy at the foot of the rapids. "There's his canoe," he said. "The damn fool tried to run the rapids. He wasn't dead when he hit shore, here, because he drug himself clear of the water. An' he may be alive yet. You fetch a blanket to lay him on an' I'll carry him back off these rocks."

The blanket was spread on the ground beyond the gravel, and as the big man lowered his burden onto it, One Armed John cried, "Say—his legs is broke! Look how they wangle. He musta drug hisself out of the water with his hands. An' what's that he's got in his hand, John? My God—it's a—a nugget!"

Both men stared at the large irregular object about which the fingers of the unconscious man had closed in a grip of iron. "It shore looks like it," Black John admitted. "The biggest nugget I ever seen. But to hell with that, now! His legs is busted, all right. You go git another blanket to put over him whilst I git his clothes off an' see how bad he's hurt. If he come down through that last mile of Whitewater it's a wonder there was enough left of him to pick up. I'll bet he's the first one that ever come through alive."

Examination disclosed that the man's body was a mass of bruises. Both legs were broken, and Black John pointed to his chest. "His ribs on the right side is all stove in, an' some of 'em is prob'ly drove into his lung—look at the bloody from there on his lips. Git that bottle of licker out of my pack."

"How about givin' him a dost of my medicine?"

"I don't dare to take a chanct," scowled the big man. "It might cure him so quick he'd run off before we could ask him about that nugget. Git that licker, an' shut up! We'll fetch him to, if we kin—but he ain't goin' to live long."

"What's the use in fetchin' him to, then?" asked One Armed John. "By God, if I was as good as dead, I wouldn't want no one fetchin me to to die all over agin!"

"We've got to fetch him to, if we kin," the big man insisted. "He might have somethin' to tell us—like who he is, er where his folks live, er—"

"Er he might be able to tell us where he got that nugget!" interrupted the other. "By God, John, if we know'd where we could git holt of nuggets like that, we wouldn't never have to bother pannin' no dust no more, would we?"

"Shut up—an' git that licker!" ordered the big man. "An' fetch a cup so we kin dilute it with water."

The man's throat muscles worked feebly as Black John forced the diluted liquor between his lips, and finally his eyelids fluttered open. Wrapped warmly in blankets, he stared up into the bearded face as he continued to swallow sips of liquor. At the end of a half hour he recovered full consciousness.

"It's the nugget," he uttered weakly. "Everyone that's had it is dead. I'm goin' to die, too. I know it. I got smashed in the rapids. I'm all busted up inside. An' I'll die like the Siwash, an' Joe Sims, an' Old Man Long, an' Jules Brule—an' now, it's me."

"Take it easy, pardner," soothed Black John. "Don't try to tell it all to onct."

"I've got to tell it now—er I'll never tell it," moaned the man, his features contorted with pain. "Bury me decent. But don't take the nugget. Leave it in my hand. Jim Hartley's tradin' post burnt on account of it. An' four men have died with it in their hand. An' God knows how many before the Siwash. An' you'll die, too—if you take it. Two hundred an' thirty-two ounces it weighs—an' it's shaped like a heart. It's the devil's heart—er bad luck—er a curse, er somethin'."

Black John fed the man more liquor, and between sips he

told of a succession of deaths, and the burning of a trading post. He grew weaker by the minute, and as he concluded his words were scarcely audible.

"You got any folks?" asked Black John, leaning close to catch the reply.

"No. No folks. Only me."

"What's yer name? So we kin put it on the slab."

"Owen ApRoberts. Born in"—the man uttered an unintelligible name that sounded like 'L'an'fer'—"Wales."

"How do you spell it?" the big man asked.

Feebly, haltingly, the man pronounced letters—double l's, double f's, cw's, and gh's until Black John interrupted him. "That'll do, pardner. We'll let that part go. After all, it's only a slab we're goin' to put up over you—not a warehouse."

The man relapsed into unconsciousness, and an hour later, he died. The big man dug a grave, and with the help of One Armed John, lowered the body into it. As he was about to throw in the dirt, the one armed one glanced into his face.

"Ain't you goin' to take the nugget?" he asked.

"Are you?" countered the big man, eyeing him sternly.

"Hell, no! I wouldn't touch the damn thing anywheres I seen it—let alone take it out of a dead man's hand! But it's the first time I ever seen you pass up any gold. An' besides, you allus claimed you didn't believe in bad luck, an' signs, an' things."

"Signs, an' bad luck is one thing," Black John uttered, impressively. "But a curse is somethin' else agin. 'Specially a curse that's got a record behind it of five deaths an' a fire—an' not a damn miss!"

The grave was filled and the new earth neatly mounded over it. Black John felled a spruce tree, split out a slab, and faced it with his axe. "What the hell was it he claimed his name was? Oh, yeah—Robert Owens." Seating himself on the mound he carved with his belt knife the words:

BOB OWENS
WALES

"There ain't no, use botherin' with the date," he said, sheathing his knife, and driving the slab into the ground at the head of the grave. "If he ain't got no folks, no one would give a damn when he died. An' we've got to be shovin' on."

IV

THE TWO NEGOTIATED the Fish Rapids portage and pushed on upriver. The next day they turned into Halfaday Creek.

"Look, John!" cried the one armed one, as they rounded a sharp bend. "There's smoke comin' out of Olson's old shack. Mebbe someone's moved in."

Black John eyed the thin spiral of smoke issuing lazily from the stovepipe that protruded through the roof of the little cabin. "Yeah," he agreed, "looks like it, don't it?"

"Damn if I'd move into that shack!" One Armed John exclaimed. "Everyone that's ever lived in it has got murdered, er hung, er arrested, er somethin'. It's like that there nugget Bob Owens had. Beats hell how some things is onlucky, don't it, John?"

"Y-e-a-h," drawled the big man, his eyes on the two figures that had emerged from the cabin, and stood waiting at the water's edge, rifles in hand. "An' if them two things—Olson's old shack, an' the nugget—could be sort of combined, a man couldn't practically have no luck at all."

"What? What do you mean, John?"

"The allusion would ondoubtless be too abstruse, in its various intricasies an' implications, fer a mediocre intellect to grasp, on the spur of the moment," replied the big man.

"Oh—like that, eh?" replied the one armed one, perfectly satisfied with the explanation. "I thought you meant somethin' about that there nugget, er Olson's old shack, er somethin'."

"Oh, hell no!" Black John grinned behind the other's back. "An' mind you don't go shootin' off yer mouth about that nugget—here, nor nowheres else. We'll jest step ashore fer a few minutes an' sort of git acquainted with our new neighbors."

As they stepped from the canoe and drew it clear of the water the shorter, stockier of the two men greeted them with a smile that accentuated a deep scar on his right cheek.

"I'd bet a stack of blue ones I'm talkin' to Black John Smith," he said.

"An' I ain't coverin' yer bet," grinned the big man.

"I know'd it! I says to Jeb, here—jest as quick as yer canoe got clost enough to see yer faces—I says, 'By God,' I says, 'if that there big one in the hind end ain't Black John hisself, I'll eat my hat! You look jest like Cuter claimed you did. You know Cuter Malone? Him that runs the Klondike Palace, in Dawson?"

"Yeah, I know him. Can't say he's exactly what you'd call a friend of mine. But I know him, all right. Did Cuter send you up here?"

"Well, he didn't exactly what you might say, send us. He was tellin' us about you all bein' outlaws, up here on Halfaday. An' how, if the police was after him, here's where he'd hit fer, on account the damn police don't dast to bother you, up here."

Black John nodded. "It would be a comfortin' thought, I s'pose, to someone the police was after."

"Yer damn right! An' it's lucky you two wasn't police, er by God, we'd of plugged you before you could draw'd yer guns! What I claim, if the police is scairt to come up here—knockin' off a few more of 'em'll make 'em all the scairter. Am I right— er wrong?"

"Wrong—jest about as wrong as a man could git, an' remain alive. As a matter of fact, Corporal Downey drops in on us, now an' then, when he's huntin' someone. When he shows up, he's neither helped, nor hindered. If any harm should come to a policeman on Halfaday, it would make it mean fer all of us. So you see, if you'd have shot a policeman anywheres along the creek, you'd of be'n hung fer it jest as quick as a miner's meetin' could of be'n got together."

"You mean—Downey comes up here?"

"Yeah—whenever he feels like it—which ain't only about onct a year, on the average. So, if the police are after you, an' you feel like doin' any killin', my advice would be to git a hell of a ways off Halfaday before you do it."

The taller of the two blinked nervously, his left eye twitching as though in a deliberate wink. He seemed about to speak, but the other forstalled him. "Hell, no! The police ain't after us! We jest figgered that if you boys was all outlaws, up here, an' the police was to show up, we'd be doin' you a good turn by knockin' 'em off. Fact is, Corporal Downey did arrest us an' fetch us down to Dawson fer somethin' that happened up the Klondike. But he didn't have a damn thing on us, so he had to turn us loose."

"Yes," agreed the taller man, nervously, "but if he was to dig out some more evidence, he'd arrest us agin—an' mebbe next time we wouldn't be so lucky."

BLACK JOHN grinned. "So you did pull the job up the Klondike, eh?"

"Hell, no!" exclaimed the heavy-set man, scowling at the other. "We didn't know a damn thing about it. Downey nabbed us because we happened to be located on the next claim to this here Green, that got killed. What Walters—er Jeb, I mean—what he meant was that Downey might rig up some evidence to frame us—like police does—an' then he might start huntin' us again."

Black John nodded. "I see. Well, as long as we're goin' to be neighbors, we might's well git acquainted. You guessed my name, an' this here's One Armed John Smith. From what you let drop, I figger yer pardner, there, is Jeb Walters. But you ain't told me yer own name."

The man grinned. "When we come to Halfaday, a few days

back, we went on up to the tradin' post, an' figgerin' our names was our own business, we told Cush—he's the bartender—that our names are John Smith, an' Bill Smith. But he claims there's so many Smiths along the crick that the name ain't allowed here no more. So we draw'd us a couple of names out of a tin can that set there on the bar. He draw'd Jeb Sherman, an' I draw'd William T. Stuart. So we've be'n practicin' callin' one another 'Jeb' an' 'Bill'—but sometimes we fergit.

"We seen how this cabin was empty when we come by, so we asked Cush where you was—Cuter Malone claimin' you was king of the outlaws, up here. We wanted to find out if it would be all right fer us to move in on this location. He claimed you'd went to Dawson, but he says how you wouldn't give a damn if we throw'd our stuff in this cabin. He claimed it was onlucky. But cripes—what I claim, there ain't no sech thing as good luck, an' bad luck."

"I don't know," interrupted the other, his eyes twitching. "We've had good luck, so fer. But I didn't want to move in here. 'Cause if we was to have even medium bad luck, it would be hell."

"Don't pay no mind to him," interrupted the other. "He's worst than some damn woman fer bein' scairt of everything. 'Course, everyone knows a man's luck might run good, er bad fer a spell—like in stud, er faro. But what I mean, there can't no common thing—like a cabin, fetch a man bad luck; not no more'n what a rabbit's foot kin fetch him good luck."

"The hell it can't!" exclaimed One Armed John. "How about Bob Owens an' his nugget?"

"Who's Bob Owens? An' what about his nugget?"

Black John laughed. "Oh, Bob was a fella used to be over on the White. He had a big nugget onct that he claimed fetched him bad luck. But cripes—he'd prob'ly got whatever bad luck he had comin', nugget, er no nugget. Well, so long. We've got to be shovin' on up the crick."

"So long," replied the heavy-set man.

"We'll be seein' you. Cush was tellin' how there's a stud game goin' on up to the fort pretty near every night."

"Yeah, the pastime is favored hereabouts, believin' as we do that it combines the element of chance with jest about the right amount of physical exertion."

"We'll fetch up a poke one of these nights an' prove to you fellas that this shack ain't so damn unlucky, after all," grinned the man.

"Okay," the big man replied. "An' it ain't no more'n fair to warn you that any attempted augmentation of luck by manual manipulation of the cards, comes under the head of skullduggery, an' as sech, is hangable."

"Whatever that means," laughed the man, "I expect yer right. So long. Be seein' you later."

V

AS THE TWO approached Cushing's Fort, the combined trading post and saloon that served the little community of outlawed men that had sprung up on the Yukon-Alaska border, Black John scowled at his companion's back.

"I thought I told you not to say nothin' to no one about Bob Owens an' that nugget," he said. "An' the first thing you do is blab it to a couple of strangers!"

"Yeah—but John, the damn fool claimed that nothin' could fetch a man bad luck—an' we know different! An' besides, I fergot."

"You fergot, did you? Well, jest you try not to fergit this—if you ever open yer head about Bob Owens an' that nugget again, I'll kick the seat of yer pants clean up into yer throat—an' we'll see if that damn medicine of yours'll cure that!"

"You mean you don't want I should say nothin' to no one about it, eh?"

"That," replied the big man dryly, "is the idea I strove to put acrost. So if there's anything about it you don't understand, let's git it cleared up, right here an' now."

"Oh, I know what you mean. You don't need to worry about me. I ain't no hand to go shootin' off my mouth. But that is damn good medicine of mine, ain't it, John? Here I ain't took the first bottle yet—an' my guts ain't hurt in a week."

"They're prob'ly petrified, er atropied, er somethin'."

"Yeah, that's prob'ly it, all right. Cripes, I wisht I know'd all them big words you know, an' there wouldn't nobody know what I was talkin' about."

"It's too bad you don't," grinned Black John, as he swerved the canoe in toward the landing. "An' watch yer step when you git out. You damn near dumped me in the crick, there at Olson's!"

SHOULDERING HIS packsack with the precious medicine bottles in it, One Armed John headed for his own shack as Black John strolled into the saloon.

Old Cush set out a bottle and two glasses. "Back a'ready? I figgered you'd prob'ly wait an' fetch One Arm back."

"He's back. He went on up to his shack."

"Cripes—did he git cured that quick? I figgered he prob'ly had the appendeetis, an' they'd have to cut him open."

"The doctors at the hospital wanted to operate—claimed he had kidney stones, er gravel, er somethin'—but One Arm wouldn't let 'em. He found a bartender that told him about some kind of patent medicine that's guaranteed to cure everything from smallpox to fallen arches. So he laid in a dozen bottles of it."

"Did it cure him?"

"Well—he claims he ain't had the bellyache sence he begun takin' it."

"H-u-m," said Cush, turning to glance into the mirror. "I wonder if it would keep a man's hair from fallin' out? I'm gittin' kinda baldish there on top of my head."

"Hell, a little mange cure'll fix you up."

"Cripes—mange cure's fer dogs! If I figgered this here medicine would keep hair from fallin' out, I'd git a bottle off'n One Arm."

"Oh, shore, it'll do that, all right! An' what's more, it'll fill in that spot where the hair's already gone with as pretty a stand of violets as you ever seen."

"Huh," grunted Cush, sourly, "if your hair was fallin' out you wouldn't be standin' around makin' jokes about it. An' on top of that, a couple of fellas has moved into Olson's old shack."

"Yeah, me an' One Arm stopped there a few minutes, comin' up."

"They ain't no one I would like," opined Cush. "What I figger, Halfaday would be better off without 'em."

"Yeah," agreed Black John, "any crick would. By the way, Cush—you got some of that lead left you laid in to make net sinkers out of?"

"Yeah, I guess so. How much you want?"

"Oh, ten, fifteen pounds."

"What the hell you want of ten, fifteen pound of lead?"

"I crave to indulge in a meticulous, and more or less intricate experimentation regarding the duplication of a certain cardio-form entity, a replica of which I'm anxious to obtain."

"Oh," grunted Cush, "an' if you'd know'd any more big words, I'd of got them throw'd in, too. Well, here's somethin' that makes sense—them last two drinks was on you. An' if you h'ist another whilst I'm out after that lead, you'll git charged with that one, too."

Carrying the lead to his cabin, Black John melted it on his stove, and after considerable experimenting with molds made of clay he carried from the creek, he produced a fairly accurate duplicate of the nugget he and One Armed John had buried with the man at the foot of the Fish Rapids. From a shelf in the cabin he took a tightly corked bottle and a small brush, and for half an hour he busied himself at the table. Then he stepped back and regarded the result of his handiwork critically. "It ain't got the heft of that nugget," he muttered to himself, "but the shape, an' size, an' color is about right. I know'd that bottle of gold paint the Widder Dykes had fer her shoes would come in handy sometime. An' hell—lead's jest as good in the hands of a dead man as gold, any day in the week."

VERY EARLY the next morning he took his rifle and, with the lead replica in his pocket, stepped into his canoe and paddled down the creek.

Passing Olson's old shack before daylight, he slipped on into the White River and dropped down, landing at the head of the Fish Rapids late in the evening.

In the morning he walked down the portage trail to the grave of the man he and One Armed John had buried, and an hour later he returned up the trail. Paddling back upriver, he camped that night on Halfaday, and proceeded on up the creek in the morning. At noon he arrived at Olson's old shack and drew ashore at the clearing where its two occupants were engaged in patching their canoe.

The heavy-set man greeted him with a glance of surprise. "Hello, Smith! How come you was down the crick? We figgered you was up around the fort, somewheres. Figgered on hittin' up that way an' mebbe settin' in a game of stud. But when we shoved the canoe in the water we seen where she was leakin', so we're patchin' her up."

"Oh, I went down early yesterday mornin' to see if I couldn't pick me up some meat. When me an' One Arm come upriver the other day, we seen where a cow moose an' a yearlin' was hangin' out, an' I figgered on knockin' over the yearlin'. But I couldn't locate 'em. It's a damn good thing fer you boys, though, that I was down on the White yesterday."

"How's that?" asked the tall man, his eyes twitching nervously.

"I run acrost Corporal Downey. He was headin' up this way. Claimed he was huntin' a couple of fellas fer murderin' a man named Green on a feeder, up the Klondike. Neff an' Walters, he said their names was—an' he described you two boys to a T. He claimed he'd arrested you onct an' had to turn you loose fer lack of evidence. But he says he's got enough on you now to hang you higher'n hell."

The tall man turned upon the other. "By God, I told you we better not move in here, when Cush told us this cabin was onlucky! There ain't nothin' we kin do now but hit acrost the line into Alasky, an' keep right on a-goin'! Cuter Malone told us the line ain't only a little ways from the fort."

Black John nodded. "Yeah, Cuter's right about that," he said. "But did he tell you what you'd find in Alasky—after you'd crossed the line?"

"No. But hell—Alasky's American territory! The Mounted couldn't foller us in there."

"They wouldn't have to. Because the chances is you wouldn't never come out, nohow. If you was to keep a-goin' after you crossed the line, you'd find yerselves in a two-hundred-mile mess of mountains—an' no trails."

"What the hell's the good of bein' clost to the line, then?" Neff asked.

"We've got a shack about a mile acrost the line. The Alasky Country Club, we call it. We keep it grubbed an' lickered, so when Downey shows up on the crick, the Yukon wanteds slip acrost an hole up there till he goes back to Dawson. Then they come back."

"That's a damn good stunt!" approved Neff.

But the more timid Walters objected. "But s'pose we was snuck up on? Like if Smith, here, hadn't be'n down on the White yesterday when Downey come along? He'd had us before we know'd he was on the crick!"

Black John grinned and winked. "We ain't never be'n snuck

up on yet. Fact is, we've got our own way of knowin' when there's a policeman on the White long before he hits Halfaday. That yearlin' moose wasn't the only reason I happened to be down there yesterday when Downey came along."

"Well—by God! Moccasin telegraft, eh?" Neff cried admiringly. "No wonder you fellas feel safe up here!"

"I don't feel so damn safe, even at that," Walters said, glancing nervously about. "What I claim, if we can't git clean out of this damn country by way of Alasky, we'd ort to hit back down the White an' go out up the Yukon—the way we come in."

Black John shrugged. "You kin try it if you want to. But you wouldn't stand one chanct in a thousan' of gittin' away with it. You see, when Downey described you boys to me, I wanted to steer him off Halfaday, so I told him you'd gone on up the Yukon. I told him me an' One Arm camped alongside of you at the mouth of the White when we was comin' back, the other day—an' how you two kep' on up the big river. So he hit back to notify all the upriver police to be on the lookout fer you. Yer best bet is to stay right here till snow flies. Then if you still want to hit fer the outside, you can slip out over the Dalton Trail with a sled outfit, without goin' anywhere near the Yukon."

"By God, Smith—looks like you figger everythin' out! No wonder yer king of the outlaws. You kin count us in yer gang. An' sence you seen Downey, an' he told you about havin' evidence enough to hang us, we don't mind admittin'—jest between us an' you—we did knock that damn Green off jest as he was about to start fer Dawson to bank a couple of hundred ounces of dust. An' I'm bettin', what with the setup you boys has got up here— the police won't never swing us fer it, neither!"

"It's a thousan' to one they won't," replied Black John, dryly. "Well, I got to be shovin' along. Come on up to the fort when you git yer canoe patched. Chances is there'll be a stud game tonight."

Alone in his cabin, Black John drew a huge nugget from his pocket, placed it on the table, and for a long time stared at it in silence. "Where in hell would a Siwash git a hunk of gold, like that?" he mused. "I never seen its like, anywheres. An' look at its record—at least five men died with it in their hands, an' Jim Hartley's tradin' post burnt. If there's a curse on it, who put it there—an' why? Bob Owens claimed it was onlucky, but hell— Still—five men, an' a burnt tradin' post ain't to be sneezed at. 'Course, they're jest a long string of coincidences—a man's a damn fool to believe that a thing like a nugget could bring bad luck, er carry a curse. Still—he might be a damn sight bigger one if he didn't take common precautions, at that. If a man's goin' to fool with a loaded gun, he better know where the muzzle's at. I don't want nothin' to happen to my cache—so I won't put it there. An' I don't want Cush's fort to burn—so I can't bank it in the safe. An' damned if I'll keep it here in the cabin—I shore as hell don't want no one pryin' it out of my dead hand! It ain't that I'm superstitious. But jest the same, I'm goin' to dig a hole an' cache it by itself back in the brush a ways—jest in case."

VI

AFTER COMPLETING HIS task to his satisfaction, Black John strolled over to the saloon and whiled away the time playing dollar-a-point cribbage with old Cush. At the end of the third game a shadow darkened the doorway and two men stepped into the room.

"Well," exclaimed the big man heartily, "damned if it ain't the boys from Olson's! Let's see—what was them names you claimed you draw'd out of the can? Oh, yes—Sherman an' Stuart. Come on, Cush—git behind the bar there. I'm buyin' a drink an' don't fergit to credit me with forty-eight dollars fer them three games. These is the boys I was tellin' you Downey was inquirin' about yesterday. Only he didn't call 'em Stuart an' Sherman," he added with a grin. "He called 'em"—Walters interrupted by shaking his head fearfully, as he glanced toward

Cush who had turned his back to pass behind the bar. Black John laughed. "Oh, hell —don't mind Cush! I ain't got no secrets from him. He knows as much about the boys here on the crick as I do—mebbe more, fer all you can ever git out of him. He knows about you two knockin' Green off, up the Klondike. He was jest sayin' you was lucky to git away with it."

"It ain't luck; it's figgerin'," said Neff, as he filled his glass from the bottle Cush set before him. "What I claim, if a man uses his head he don't need no luck."

"I don't know about that," Walters said dubiously. "The way I figger it, we was damn lucky Downey didn't have no evidence on us when he arrested us. An' we was lucky agin when Smith, here, turned him back down the White."

"That's where yer wrong!" vociferated Neff. "We got away with that job 'cause I had it all figgered out. An' Downey got turned back down the White 'cause Smith has got things all figgered out, up here. That ain't luck—that's figgerin'. What I claim—any man that believes in good luck an' bad luck is ignerant as hell. A man's luck's what he makes it. Ain't that so, Smith?"

"W-e-e-l, takin' it by an' large, as the fella says, I used to believe about like you do. But that was before I run onto Bob Owens. I ain't so sure—now."

"He's the one that there one armed guy mentioned down to the cabin, that day you come along. Who is this Bob Owens? An' what happened to him?"

"Plenty happened to him. He's layin' there dead at the foot of Fish Rapids. But it goes way back of Bob Owens—this bad luck, er curse, er whatever it is this fifteen-pound nugget carries with it."

"You said a fifteen-pound nugget?" exclaimed Neff, his eyes wide with surprise. "God, I didn't know they come that big!"

"Two hundred an' thirty-two ounces, it weighs—that's damn near fifteen pounds."

"An' you claim he's layin' there dead on account of this nugget? How do you know?"

"Hell—I'd ort to know! One Arm an' I buried him. Here comes One Arm now. You can ask him, if you don't believe me."

"Oh, I believe you all right," the other replied, as One Armed John ranged himself at the bar and filled the glass Cush spun across to him. "But what about this nugget? How could a nugget kill a man?"

"Mebbe it didn't," Black John admitted. "But then agin, mebbe it did."

"You mean, you believe it's onlucky?"

The big man shrugged. "You better jedge fer yerself. The first anyone knows of this nugget, Joe Sims, a prospector, finds a Siwash dead in his blankets with this nugget gripped in his hand. He pries the nugget loose, an' plants the Siwash.

"A few days later, a trapper, name of Old Man Long, finds Sims dyin' in his bunk, after stumblin' an' shootin' himself with his own rifle. He tells Long about how he found the nugget in the dead Siwash's hand, an' reaches under the blanket an' pulls it out, advisin' Long to bury it with him, 'cause he figgers it's onlucky. He dies with it clutched in his hand. But it's a hell of a big nugget, so Old Man Long takes a chanct, an' buries Sims, after takin' the nugget out of his hand.

"He goes on to Jim Hartley's tradin' post, figgerin' to spend the night there on his way to Dawson. The bunkhouse is full of Siwashes that's come there to trade, so Hartley let Long sleep in the tradin' room, along with Bob Owens, an' a breed trapper name of Jules Brule. In the middle of the night Bob Owens wakes up to find the tradin' room all afire. He yells to the others an' grabs up his clothes, an' his rifle, an' blankets, an' makes his way to the door through the smoke. Brule come bustin' out a minute later, an' by that time, what with the draft caused by openin' the door, the room's jest about solid flame— an' out of the flame staggers Old Man Long with his whiskers an' hair all burnt off, an' his shirt afire. He staggers a few steps an' drops dead, havin' prob'ly burnt his lungs out inhalin' them flames.

"It was then that Bob Owens noticed the nugget gripped in the old man's scorched hand. Brule seen it, too—'cause while Bob stood there lookin' down at it, the breed made a dive fer it, snatched it out of the dead man's hand, an' hit fer the brush with it. Not wantin' to see a breed git away with nothin' like that, Bob throws up his rifle an' takes a shot at Brule jest as he got to the edge of the clearin'. His bullet ketched him plumb in the middle of the back, comin' out through his heart, an' Owens runs over an' snatches the nugget out of his hand an' slips it under his shirt.

"Jest then, Jim Hartley comes runnin' around the corner of the burnin' buildin' from his quarters in the back, an' Owens tells him he shot Brule fer settin' fire to the tradin' room—which Hartley believes, because he know'd Brule was sore at him fer turnin' him down when he'd asked fer more credit, the day before.

"In the mornin' Bob Owens slips his canoe into the river an' hits fer Dawson. But he got ketched in the Fish Rapids. His canoe was all smashed to hell, but he managed to drag himself up onto the gravel at the foot of the rapids with the nugget gripped in his hand. Both his legs was broke, an' his chest was all stove in on the right side, his ribs evidently penetratin' his lung. He'd passed out after draggin' himself clear of the water. An' that's where me an' One Arm found him. We fetched him to with licker, an' he told us about the nugget, claimin' there was a curse on it, an' predictin' that we'd shore as hell die, if we took it. So One Arm an' I buried him there."

"An' what become of the nugget?" Neff asked, his eyes bright with avarice.

"He's still got it gripped in his hand."

"You mean it's layin' there—a fifteen-pound nugget—gripped in a dead man's hand! Why in hell didn't you take it? A nugget can't do a dead man no good."

"No," agreed Black John dryly, "but it might do a live one a hell of a lot of harm. Look at its record."

"But—hell—man—luck didn't have nothin' to do with them things! They jest happened."

"Yeah? Well, they didn't happen to me."

"Me neither!" cried One Armed John. "An' by God, they ain't a-goin' to!"

"How long ago did all this happen?" Neff asked, with an obvious attempt to make the question sound casual and impersonal.

"It was when we come upriver the other day. We buried Owens jest the day before we run onto you fellas at Olson's old shack.

"So there he'll lay with that big nugget gripped in his fist, clean on through to the judgment day. I like gold as well as the next man—but damned if I like it enough to monkey with that nugget. Not if it weighed a thousan' ounces! Me an' One Arm buried him decent, right there at the foot of the rapids. An we put a slab over him. BOB OWENS, it says, WALES, on account of him bein' a Welchman."

"But hell, John," Cush said, mopping at the bar with a rag, "you couldn't hardly call him no welcher on account of him knockin' off that breed, which he was tryin' to steal the nugget off'n Old Man Long—an' him dead!"

"No," Black John grinned, "it was on account of somethin' his mother an' father done."

Other men drifted in, and a stud was started that lasted until far into the night. It broke up finally, and the men returned to their claims, leaving only Black John, One Armed John and Cush in the saloon. The somber-faced proprietor stepped behind the bar and set out a bottle and glasses.

"Might's well have a drink 'fore I close up," he said, shoving his steel-framed spectacles from nose to forehead, and eyeing Black John across the bar. "What was this here gag about buryin' a fifteen-pound nugget along with this here Bob Olson you was tellin' about?"

"**BOB OWENS—NOT** Olson," the big man corrected. "You ought to be more accurate in mentionin' names, Cush."

"Huh, what the hell's the difference—when he wasn't no one in the first place?"

"The hell an' he wasn't!" exclaimed One Armed John. "Me an' John buried him—jest like John said. You kin go down there an' look at the grave fer yerself, if you don't believe it!"

"A grave would be easy to make, without buryin' no one in it—let alone a fifteen-pound nugget," retorted Cush skeptically. "John never buried no fifteen-pound nugget in no man's grave! An' even if he did, he wouldn't go shootin' off his mouth about it in front of a couple of coots like Stuart an' Sherman is. Cripes, I'll bet them two is headin' hell bent fer Fish Rapids, right now, to dig up that grave."

"Neff prob'iy is. I'm doubtin' Walters has got the guts to."

"Who's Neff an' Walters?" asked One Armed John.

"That's their real names," Black John replied. "Downey told me about 'em. They pulled off a damn dirty murder somewheres up the Klondike—clubbed a pore devil to death that had the next claim to theirs. Downey knows they done it—but he can't prove it, owin' to certain limitations an' restrictions of the law. An' not only that, but they bragged to me about pullin' off the job. We shore as hell don't want no one like them on Halfaday."

"That's right," Cush admitted, "but there ain't nothin' we kin do about it, till they pull off somethin' up here."

Black John grinned. "Both One Arm an' I can identify that nugget we buried in Bob Owens' hand. Grave robbery comes under the head of skullduggery, an' as sech, is hangable."

"But this here fella is buried down on the White—not on Halfaday," objected Cush. "We don't want to go gittin' loose with our hangin's. We can't hang no one fer somethin' he done somewheres else."

"The p'int ain't well taken," Black John said. "I rec'lect that we held, in the case of Halfaday Crick vs. the U.S. Marshal, that our jurisdiction included, not only Halfaday, but the subtendin' rivers an' cricks, an' all contiguous territory. But even that precedent wouldn't have to be invoked in this instance, because the mere possession of the purloined nugget on the crick, irrespective of where the de facto, er overt malfeasance took place, would make its possessor guilty of skullduggery in the first degree."

"An' besides, Cush," interposed One Armed John, a bit wistfully, "we ain't had a hangin' in a hell of a while."

"Huh," grunted Cush, "if John figgers a man ort to git hung, an' he can't git nothin' else on him, he kin allus think up enough big words to befuddle the boys into actin'."

"Listen, Cush—you jest name one man that we ever hung on Halfaday that didn't have a hangin' comin' to him," challenged Black John. "Jest name one!"

"Oh—they all had it comin', fer as that goes," Cush admitted. "But some of 'em got hung in a kind of a roundabout fashion, at that."

"What difference does that make? As long as they deserved it? It's results that counts—not methods. That's where we've got the law beat all to hell. We know them two birds had ort to be hung fer murderin' Green. The law can't hang 'em fer it, because Downey ain't got no evidence. We can't hang 'em fer it, because the Klondike River ain't quite subtendin' enough, even under a lib'ral construction of the term, to fetch the crime within' our jurisdiction. Therefore, *pro bono publico*, we've got to hang 'em fer somethin' else. Because we shore as hell don't want no sech depraved wretches on Halfaday. That there fifteen-pound nugget is merely bait. If they ain't got larceny in their soul they won't grab it—that's all."

"Yeah, but it's liable to be damn expensive bait," Cush opined.

"S'pose they dig it up an' keep right on a-goin' down to the Yukon? You claim Downey ain't got nothin' on 'em."

"I know he ain't—but they don't. In fact, they seem to think he has. At least, that's the impression they give me when I was talkin' to 'em yesterday. They're scairt to go anywheres near the Yukon. No, sir, if Neff grabs off that nugget, he'll come back to Halfaday with it—an' I aim to be waitin' fer him when he gits here!"

VII

IN THE FORENOON of the second day thereafter, Black John stepped into his canoe and proceeded down the creek to a point half a mile above Olson's old shack where he landed and drew the light craft into the brush. Proceeding on foot, he circled the small clearing that surrounded the cabin, noting that although the canoe was missing, smoke rose from the stovepipe of the cabin. "Jest as I figgered," he muttered. "Walters was afraid to go, so Neff went down alone. He ort to be gittin' back before evenin' if he had good luck."

Slipping back to the foot of the rock wall that formed the valley rim, he moved along its base till he came to a flattish stone that had been fitted neatly over a natural pit in the rocks. "Everyone that's ever moved in here has found that stone layin' here kind of careless like, an' figgered what a hell of a good cache that hole would make with the stone fer a cover," he grinned, as he stooped and removed it. Lifting out two little moosehide sacks, he hefted them in his hands and nodded. "About ninety ounces apiece. Downey claimed they prob'ly got about two hundred ounces off'n Green when they murdered him. They must of squandered twenty ounces. I'll jest take this along—an' if Green had any heirs, I'll turn it over to Downey. If not, I'll put it where the next miscreant that comes along can't git his hands on it."

Replacing the stone, he made his way back to the edge of the clearing and took his position behind a dense thicket of scrub spruce. Toward the middle of the afternoon Walters stepped from the cabin, glanced nervously about him, and proceeded to the spring for a pail of water, pausing to gaze long and earnestly down the creek. Then he returned to the cabin and closed the door behind him.

An hour later a canoe appeared around a bend and beached at the landing. Its single occupant stepped ashore and drew the craft clear of the water. Even before the man turned toward him Black John recognized the thick shoulders and heavy torso of Neff. As the man approached the cabin the door flew open and Walters stepped out, rifle in hand. "Did you git it?" he asked, his eyes darting about the clearing.

"Shore I got it," the other replied, a note of contempt in his voice. "An if you hadn't of been so damn scairt you'd of come along an' got in on it."

"Let's see it."

"Come on over to the cache, an' I'll leave you have a look at it. But you ain't in on a damn ounce of it! By God, I earnt it—paddlin' clean down there all alone, an' diggin' up a dead man, to boot!"

"I don't want in on the damn thing! It's like Smith claimed. It's got a curse on it! It's bad luck—an' I don't want no part of it. Everyone that gits it has got to take it out of a dead man's hand—an' then he's the next dead man! It might be bad luck jest to look at it."

Neff uttered a sneering laugh. "You won't think it's sech bad luck when you see me blowin' in the dough I'll git fer it—better'n three thousan' dollars—more money than you ever seen all to onct!"

As Neff proceeded toward the cache with Walters following, Black John edged through the bush and took up a position behind a nearby jutting rock. Dropping to his knees, Neff reached into his pocket and drew forth a large yellow object, roughly heart-shaped in form. Walters' eyes twitched nervously as he stared at it in rapt fascination. Holding it in one hand, Neff reached down and drew the stone from the mouth of the cache with the other. He peered into the empty hole and, leaping to his feet with a curse, whirled upon the other, who started back in surprise.

"Where's the dust?" Neff demanded. "Where's them two sacks we got off'n Green?"

"Why—they're in the cache. I ain't touched 'em!"

"You lie!"

"I don't lie. Oh, my God! If they're gone, this shack's onlucky—like they claimed." His voice had risen to a shrill falsetto.

"You lie, damn you!" Neff roared. "You figgered it all out. You figgered if I got this nugget, you'd have the dust, an' make me think it was stole. An' then you'd pull out on me. An' if you had, the police would of picked you up, an' you'd of spilt yer guts about Green, an' we'd of both got hung."

"I never took the dust. I ain't be'n near the cache," screamed the man, terror showing in his eyes.

With a bellow of rage Neff leaped to his feet and lunged toward the other, the heavy missile in his upraised hand. Emitting a yowl of terror, Walters swung the rifle muzzle forward and pulled the trigger. There was a loud report, as Neff sprawled full length at his feet with a bullet through his heart, and the yellow lump clutched spasmodically in his hand.

Walters stood as though stunned with horror, his eyes twitching, and his lips muttering over and over again, "Oh, my God! Oh, my God! He's dead! Another dead man—with the nugget gripped in his hand. An' he claimed there ain't no sech thing as luck. Oh, my God! Oh, my God!"

"He was ondoubtless wrong," said Black John, in a calm, stern voice as he stepped from behind the rock with his rifle covering the gibbering man. "The facts don't bear him out."

"Smith!" cried Walters. "Oh, Smith—I—I shot him in self-defense."

"An' him unarmed?" asked the big man, glancing down at the dead man.

"But—he wasn't unarmed. He come at me with that—that *thing!* It's more dangerous than any gun."

"That'll be fer the boys to decide—at the miners' meetin'."

"Miners' meetin'!" shrieked the man, his voice thin with terror. "Oh, my God! Cuter told how you hang folks, up here! You ain't goin' to try me fer—fer—"

"Murder's the word," supplied Black John. "This makes anyway two of 'em you've committed. It's about time you was gittin' ketched up with. Jest hand over that rifle, an' help me git Neff loaded into the canoe, an' we'll be shovin' on up to Cush's."

AT THE miners' meeting in Cushing's barroom, that evening, twenty hard-faced men listened as Black John told of the murder of Green, on the Klondike, and of the fact that Walters and his dead partner had boasted to him of committing it. They listened, also, with bated breath as he recounted the tale of the nugget. All eyes fixed in fascination upon the yellow lump that lay clutched in the hand of the dead man who lay stretched out on the bar—Exhibit A, in the murder for which the craven Walters was now on trial.

"An' in conclusion, I'll say that I was an eyewitness to the shootin' of the *corpus delicti,* here. It was at their cache, which the deceased claimed the defendant had robbed, whilst he was down on the White, robbin' a dead man. Whether the defendant did, or did not rob the cache is a matter of no moment. I looked in it, jest after the shootin'—an' it was, in fact, empty. The thing that does matter is that this defendant did shoot an' kill, to wit, Exhibit A, there on the bar. He will now be given the chanct to lie out of it, if he kin." He turned toward the cowering prisoner. "You got anything to say? Can you think of any reason why we shouldn't hang you?"

"It was in self-defense," faltered the man. "He come at me with that nugget!"

"Is that all?"

"Yes—that's all. I was scairt he'd kill me."

Black John swept the assembly with a glance. "Anyone here of the opinion that the defendant's life was endangered at the time he shot Exhibit A should signify by votin' 'No' to this hangin'—so the rest of us can git a chanct to see what a damn fool looks like. All believin' the defendant guilty will signify by sayin' 'Aye.'" He paused and a chorus of "Ayes" filled the room. Contrary, "No."

A dead silence followed the words—a silence during which the eyes of the men of Halfaday shifted slowly from the dead man to the face of the craven killer—a face from which every drop of blood seemed to have drained, leaving it white as the belly of a dead fish—white and glistening with clammy sweat in the light of the overhead lamp.

Suddenly, with a lightning-like movement, the man's hand shot into the pocket of his shirt and came out clutching a tiny phial. Drawing the cork with his teeth, he swallowed its contents at a gulp.

"If this stuff is quick as they claim, you'll never hang me!" he shrilled, and leaping to the bar he tore the yellow lump from the hand of the corpse. "An' by God—I'll—die—rich!" he uttered, as he collapsed and slithered from the battered brass rail to the floor, the yellow lump gripped in his hand.

Old Cush shoved Exhibit A along, and leaned over the bar to stare down at the dead man on the floor. "Don't it beat hell?" he said, in a voice of awesome solemnity. "There he lays—jest like all them others—dead—with the nugget gripped in his hand. All their life them men wanted gold—er they wouldn't of be'n in the Yukon. An' when they got it—what good did it do 'em?"

The others stood silent, staring down at the yellow lump. Black John's glance swept their faces. "Well," he said at length, "there it is—the nugget that brings bad luck. Does anyone want it? All you've got to do is reach down an' take it."

No man made a move. Presently Pot Gutted John spoke. "How about you?" he asked, glancing into Black John's face. "I thought you didn't believe in curses—an' things like that."

Black John shook his head. "I ain't damn fool enough to fly in the face of facts," he said. "So if no one wants to be the eighth link in a chain of dead men, we'll go ahead an' bury these parties, jest as they are, an' git it over with."

"Whoever it was that put the curse on that nugget, shore raised hell when he done it," Cush said, as he set out bottles and glasses when they had returned from the graveyard. "I'll bet if anyone was to dig that nugget up—even if he didn't die with it in his hand, like the others done, he'd have some kind of bad luck when he come to spend it."

"He shore would," agreed Black John solemnly. "Yes, sir—he shore would."

"I'll bet there don't no one try it!" opined Pot Gutted John. "No, sir—the trail of that nugget is ended. It won't never bring no one no bad luck, no more."

And again Black John nodded solemnly. "I hope yer right, Pot Gut. Yeah—I shore hope yer right."

THUNDER ON HALFADAY

"**THAT'S A HORSE** on you, an' you kin beat them three sixes in one, er else buy a drink," Black John Smith said, as he shoved the leather dice box across the bar toward old Cush, proprietor of Cushing's Fort, the combined trading post and saloon that served the little band of outlawed men that had collected on Halfaday Creek, close against the Yukon-Alaska border.

Cush gathered the dice and, with box poised in hand, glanced toward the open doorway where a man stood peering into the room. He was a wiry little man. His flannel shirt was open at the throat, and the legs of a well-worn pair of overalls were thrust into the tops of his laced pacs. A limp packsack dangled from his shoulders, and as he advanced toward the bar Black John noted that his soft brown eyes held a confiding look—like the eyes of a hound. Rolling the dice onto the bar, Cush glanced at them, returned them to the box, and set out a bottle and three glasses.

"What place is this?" the little man asked, as he paused beside Black John.

"Cushing's Fort, on Halfaday Creek. That's Lyme Cushing himself behind the bar there, an' I'm John Smith—Black John, to be explicit, owin' to my whiskers bein' that color." He nodded toward the bottle. "Fill up. Cush is buyin' a drink."

"Well—I don't know." The little man hesitated, his eyes on the bottle. "It's kind of bad walking, and I am a little tired. I don't think one drink would hurt me any. Do you?"

"I wouldn't go so fer as to say the injury would be irreparable. Why not take a chanct? Steve Brody did."

"Oh, yes—the man who jumped off the Brooklyn Bridge. Yes, it's just like I told Stella. 'Stella,' I said, when she was trying to talk me out of coming up here to the Klondike, 'a man will never get any place if he don't take a chance'."

"That's right," Black John agreed. "But yer quite a ways from the Klondike."

"Oh, back home we call everything up here 'the Klondike'."

"Sort of broad-minded, eh?"

"No. Just ignorant, I guess you'd call it. They don't do a very good job of teaching geography in the schools. Why, I got clear to Dawson before I found out the Klondike wasn't in Alaska— and I went through high school, too. Joe Petty's my name. I'm from Minneapolis."

"Yeah? Well, drink up, Joe. This is Cush's busy day, an' yer interferin' with his routine."

The man filled his glass and glanced about the room. "Kind of a funny place for a saloon," he opined. "I shouldn't think there'd be much trade, way out here. I know a man that runs a saloon in Minneapolis and he's always kicking about not having trade enough. He's on a busy street, too."

"Oh, Cush gits trade enough. Here's lookin' at you."

The little man raised the glass to his lips and took a deep swallow. Tears stood in his eyes as he coughed, and retched, and choked, and gagged. "By Judas!" he exclaimed when he finally recovered his voice. "I didn't know whiskey was that strong. I never drank any before without there was something in it—like seltzer, or something."

"We like ourn neat," Black John grinned. "It's all right after you git used to it."

"I wouldn't want to get used to anything like that. Gosh, it's worse than pepper, the way it burns your throat."

"Fill up agin," invited Black John. "I'm buyin' this one. Mebbe you'll have better luck, next time. Most of that one went on the floor."

"No thanks," the little man said, and turned to Cush. "Have you got any sarsaparilla?"

"Any—which?" asked Cush, eyeing the bung-starter.

Black John laughed. "No, there ain't much call fer pop of no flavor, here on Halfaday. The boys' tastes runs mostly to licker."

"Halfaday," the man repeated. "You've got funny names for

places, up here—like Forty Mile, and Sixtymile, and White-horse."

"I don't know's there any funnier'n some of them Minnesota names. How about Mennehaha, an' Shakopee, an' Sleppy Eye?"

"That's right," Petty agreed. "I guess no name sounds funny

when you get used to it."

"Where you headin'?" Black John asked, eyeing the limp packsack.

"Oh, no place. That is, any place would do. I just kept on walking till I got here. It's like I always say—if you just keep on walking you'll get some place; if you go far enough. You're bound to."

"I think you've got somethin' there," Black John admitted, gravely. But where did you start from?"

"You mean—originally?"

"Well, I wouldn't go back no more'n two, three generations."

"From Minneapolis. I read meters for the gas company."

"Looks like you'd got a mite off yer beat."

"Oh, I quit my job and came to the Klondike to look for gold."

"Find any?"

"Yes, we dug up quite a lot of it on the edge of a lake."

"Who's 'we'?"

"My pardner and I. You see, it was all on account of the Sunday paper—that, and Uncle Josiah. I don't read the Sunday paper much—but Stella does. I've got a workbench down in the basement and I like to go down there Sundays and make things—sleds and kites for the kids, and stuff like that. I made 'em a little wagon, once. And I made Stella a dish cabinet, and when the lady next door seen it she wanted one too. So I made her one and her husband give me seven dollars for it.

"**ONE SUNDAY** Stella called me for dinner and I washed up and come upstairs and she had the Sunday paper all spread out where a lot of pictures was in it of steamboats, and mountains, and Indians, and men in canoes, and some more with packsacks on their back. And she says how I ought to read the piece which told about the Klondike, and how anybody could go up there and stake out a claim and pan out gold. So I read it, and then

I went back to the basement and varnished a couple of chairs for Stella, and didn't think no more about it till one morning along about the middle of the week.

"When I was starting out to read meters, that morning, the trouble wagon was just pulling out to fix a busted main, and I seen that a new man was bossing the crew. So I hollered at the driver and ask him if Jim Foley was sick. Jim, he'd bossed the trouble gang ever since I'd worked for the company. And the driver says Jim had quit his job and went off to the Klondike along with a couple of other fellows to hunt for gold.

"So, all the rest of the week while I was walking from house to house reading meters I'd be thinking about Jim Foley riding on one of them big steamboats, and seeing all them mountains, and paddling along in a canoe, and carrying a pack on his back, and talking to Indians, and digging out gold. The next Sunday there was another piece in the paper about it, and pictures of bears and moose, and some men shoveling gravel into a kind of trough like, and picking out the chunks of gold and putting them in sacks.

"So then I tells Stella about Jim Foley, and I says, 'By gosh, I'd like to go up there and dig up some of that gold, too!' And Stella she jest laughed and tells me to don't be a fool, and where would I ever get the money to go to Alaska? And what would I do when I got there? I says: 'I'd dig up gravel and shovel it in a trough or a pan and pick the gold out of it just like these other men was doing.' And she says, 'Don't be silly, Joe. You ain't got gumption enough to do anything like that—and besides you ain't big enough. You'd look pretty,' she says, 'climbing up one of them mountains with a pack on your back bigger than you are!' 'A small man can carry just as much as a big one,' I told her. 'He's got to make more trips, that's all. Look here, Stella,' I says, 'I might a dang sight better be walking up a mountain or along some crick, if I could find a lot of gold, than to keep on walking from one house to another reading gas meters. Meter reading ain't got no future in it.' 'No,' she says, 'but it's got sixty dollars a month in it.' 'Yes,' I says, 'but what's sixty dollars a month? Look at all the rich folks that's living in big houses and riding around in carriages. Look at Tom Lowery. I read his meter every month and his yard is dang near as big as Loring Park, and he's got so many hired girls and hired men that it would bust a common man jest to feed 'em all—let alone paying them wages. And I'll bet Queen Victoria ain't got a better house than Tom Lowery's. Why, even his barn has got screens on to keep out the flies, and running water in it too. How'd you like to live like that?' I says. 'Well, you ain't never going to on sixty dollars a month. And I don't mind telling you,' I says, 'that I'd just as soon live like Tom Lowery. I'm tired reading meters, anyhow,' I tells her, 'what with women kicking about their meter must be wrong because their bill was bigger than their neighbor's and they didn't use nowheres near as much gas as their neighbor used, and getting all covered with coal dust, and skinning my shins on stuff they leave laying around in them dark basements, and getting bit by dogs, and having women bawl me out for tracking in mud, and claiming I kicked their cat when I only stepped on it in the dark.'

"Well, Stella's all right, far as she goes. 'Sure, Joe, I know,' she says, 'there's a lot better jobs than reading meters—but you haven't got 'em. I wouldn't want to live like Tom Lowery does. And neither would you. You just think you would. What I'd like most in the world,' she says, 'is a nice little place out in the country where we could have our own garden, and maybe a horse and buggy, and some chickens, and a lake nearby where the children could swim and go fishing, and roam around in the woods. But we haven't got it, and there's no chance to get it—so I just don't think about it.' 'But if I was to go to the Klondike and dig up some gold we could have all them things, and more too,' I tells her. 'But it would cost a lot of money to get up there,' she says. 'And what would the children and I do while you was gone? Who would pay the rent? And what would we eat, and wear?'

"Well, she had me there. And then, the very next day, the luckiest thing happened you ever seen—Uncle Josiah got hit by a train. Yes, sir—out by Osseo, it was. He was kind of deef and I guess he didn't hear the train whistle because he drove right onto the track and the limited came around the curve and killed him and his horse both, and smashed his buggy to kindling wood. I was the only relative he had, and named after him, to boot. So after a long rigamarole, the judge ordered the bank to pay me Uncle Josiah's money. After everything was paid up the bank give me six thousand, four hundred and twenty-two dollars and sixty-six cents.

"'And now,' Stella says, 'we can buy that little place in the country. It seems just like providence, or something,' she says, 'because the day after Uncle Josiah's funeral I seen an ad in the papers where a man wants to sell a ten acre lot with a house and barn on it on the edge of a lake right near Sauk Centre, for

six thousand dollars. We'll buy it,' she says, 'and move up there.' 'Yes,' I says, 'and have four hundred and twenty-two dollars and sixty-six cents to live on the rest of our life. There ain't no gas meters to read in Sauk Centre,' I says, 'and ten acres is too big for a garden, and too little for a farm, and besides, I ain't no farmer, anyhow. I'm going to divide Uncle Josiah's money up between us, and you and the kids can stay right here and live off your half until I get back with the gold, because I'm taking my half and hitting for the Klondike.'

"Well, Stella tried to talk me out of it, and when she seen she couldn't, she got mad, and we had it back and forth. Take a woman that ain't never had very much and let her marry into money, that way, it kind of spoils 'em, I guess. Anyhow, I figured she'd have time to cool off before I got back, so I lays three thousand, two hundred and eleven dollars and thirty-three cents on the table and walks out on her. I figured on coming up here and digging out what gold I wanted and getting back by Christmas. But it don't look like it will work out that way, because here it is July already, and I haven't got no gold, and I havn't got no more money, either."

"An' not much else," said Black John, eyeing the limp pack-sack that still dangled from the man's shoulders.

"No, just a piece of canvas, and an extry shirt, and socks, and my spare pants. My pardner took everything else when he skipped out on me."

"Didn't you mention takin' out gold along the edge of some lake?"

"Oh, yes. We dug out quite a lot of it, but my pardner took it all when he went away—stole it, that's what he did. And not only that, he took the blankets and all the grub we had left, and our rifle—after I'd paid for it, back there in Dawson. I not only paid for everything we had, but I loaned him all the money I had left to keep his old mother while we were off on the prospecting trip."

"Where'd you run onto this pardner?" Black John asked. "Who is he?"

"His name is Bill Smith."

"Oh—jest another one of the Smith boys, eh?"

"Do you know him?"

"PROB'LY NOT—THE family bein' more er less prolific in these parts. Where'd you meet up with him?"

"In Dawson. It was a couple of nights after I got there, and I was trying to find Jim Foley. You see, Jim came up here a couple of months before I did, and I knew he'd know all the best places to dig gold. I done him a favor once—so I knew he'd tell me. But everybody I asked didn't know Jim. He was a hard worker, so I figured he'd be out on some crick digging up gold. I knew he wouldn't be very far from town because Jim's got his faults, and one of them is liking to get drunk on Saturday nights.

"I asked where the nearest crick was, but they told me so many I decided the quickest way to find Jim was to wait till Saturday night came and then look for him in the saloons. I went from one saloon to another, but I couldn't find him, nor anyone that knew him, till I came to a place called the Klondike Palace. Gosh, at first, I didn't know what kind of a place I'd got into! There was good looking women in there all painted up and dressed something scandalous, standing up to the bar smoking cigarettes and drinking right along with the men. I was going to duck out before someone seen me in there and told Stella. But I happened to remember that another one of Jim's faults was going to houses of ill fame when he got to drinking. So I began asking about Jim, but no one in there seemed to know him, and I went to the bar and laid down a ten dollar bill and called for a glass of beer, not liking to ask the bartender about Jim without spending some money. And he gave me a small beer and only nine dollars and fifty cents in change, and I kicked about it because in Minneapolis you can get a big schooner of beer for five cents.

"This Bill Smith was standing there at the bar and he explained that beer was fifty cents, in Dawson, and they didn't give out no schooners, on account of the freight, and there not being no brewery in town. We got to talking and I told him about Jim and how I wanted to find him so I could get to work digging out gold. He asked me did I have any money to buy an outfit and I told him I had right around three thousand dollars. So then he told me about Jim and a couple of other fellows going on a prospecting trip to some river a couple of hundred miles away. But he said I didn't need to worry about not finding Jim if all I wanted was to dig gold. He said he had a proposition about a hundred miles back off the river where he could shovel out all the gold we wanted. He said I was lucky to run onto him, because he was looking for a pardner to go back there with him who would furnish the outfit, because he was broke, right now. I ask him how he come to be broke if he had such a good proposition on this crick, and he laughed and said it was easy come, easy go with him. He said he'd been in Dawson a week and had got drunk and gambled away fifty thousand, but he didn't care because he could go back to this crick and take out fifty thousand more in a week's time.

"**HE CLAIMED** he could get lots of pardners but he said most of 'em would prob'ly be crooks and try to beat him out of his claim. He said he could tell an honest man when he seen one—and I looked honest. I told him I'd like to get in on a deal like that because I wanted to get rich by Christmas. He figured that if we worked hard we could take out fifty thousand a week apiece, and in ten weeks we'd have a million to split between us. Or, if we wanted to stretch it to twenty weeks, we could both be a millionaire.

"That suited me all right. But I wasn't going to be played for a sucker, so I asked him if he had any references. 'The best in the world,' he says. 'Cuter Malone, the proprietor of this place, is one of the richest and most influential men in the whole Yukon. Just step back to his private office and he'll tell you if I'm on the level.' So we went back there and he introduced me to Mister Malone, who spoke very highly of Bill Smith, and assured me that I could rely on anything Bill told me. Mister Malone is an important looking man with a big diamond in his tie and another one in his ring, and he verified Bill's state-ment about gambling away the fifty thousand, but said he guessed that didn't bother Bill very much because he had one of the best propositions in the country.

"So the next day we went to the A.C. Store and he picked out what we needed and I paid for it, and just as we were about to start, Bill said, 'Oh, gosh—my mother! The dear old lady has got to eat while I'm gone. Give me what cash you've got left and I'll slip it to her. It will keep her going till we get back even if we decide to stick out there for that million apiece. I'll pay you back and a hundred percent interest on top of it as soon as we get back to the claim.' So I gave him the money, and he was gone for a few minutes, and then he came back and we carried the stuff down to the river and loaded it in our canoe and started out.

"We paddled across the Yukon and up it for a couple of days and then up another river. We kept on going and every crick we'd pass we'd stop and pan out some gravel, but we didn't find anything that Bill said was pay dirt. I asked him why we stopped and fooled with other cricks when we already had a good thing, and he said that a man could never have too much, and if we could make another strike we could sell it for an extra million, or so. We kept on up this river, and one day we came to a falls and portaged around it and camped that night at the top of it. We hauled the canoe out and turned it over on a flat rock and in the night the wind came up and blew it into the river and it went over the falls and got all smashed to pieces on the rocks.

"We each cut a square of canvas out of the tent, and put that, and what grub we could carry, and a blanket apiece in our packsacks, and took the rifle and a shovel and a pan and started to walk. Bill said it was too far to walk back down this river, but we could cut across to the White River and get a canoe from an Indian and go back to Dawson for another outfit. He said it was too far to walk on to his claim with what grub we could carry.

"We found a little crick and followed it up and four or five days later we came to a lake. Bill admitted he was lost. He said he didn't know where the White River was from there, and maybe we better turn back. So we camped there and I got to fooling around with the shovel and pan, and, by gosh, the first pan I panned had a lot of gold in it! Yes, sir—the whole bottom of the pan was yellow with gold. Bill said it wasn't as rich as his other claim, but it wasn't so bad. So we stayed there a week and panned out about fifty pounds of gold—"

"Fifty pounds!" Black John exclaimed. "You mean fifty ounces, don't you?"

"No. Fifty pounds—maybe a few pounds more. I done most of the digging because Bill's shoulder hurt him. It was hard work and sometimes I'd get so tired I'd lay down there on the gravel and take a nap. And one day I woke up and found Bill gone. He'd taken all the grub, and the two blankets, and the rifle, and all the gold. He didn't leave me anything but the pan and the shovel. I was going to hit out and follow him back to that river. But then I got to thinking. You see, I knew Bill was kind of careless or clumsy like, because one day when I was walking ahead of him when he was carrying the rifle, it went off just as my foot tripped on a root and the bullet went right through the side of my shirt. If I hadn't tripped just then it would have gone plumb through me. Bill said he was awful sorry. He said he must have had the safety off and a twig caught in the trigger. After that I always walked behind him when he had the gun. Then another day while we were camped at the lake he did a clumsy thing. The rocks around the lake rise straight out of the water and most places they're a couple of hundred feet high, but right next to where we panned out the gold there is a shoulder of rock only about twenty feet high. The top is nice and flat and that's where we camped.

"**ONE EVENING** I was sitting on the edge of the rock catching some fish for supper when Bill came along with some firewood, and he tripped and fell against me, and knocked me off into the lake. That water is so dang cold that I was numb all over and nearly got drownded before I could swim to the gravel and crawl out. Bill apologized for being so clumsy. He said if it had been him that fell off that rock he'd have drownded sure because he can't swim a lick. But after that I let him catch the fish for supper.

"Right up to the time Bill pulled out on me I thought he was just clumsy or careless. But as I was about to follow him I got to wondering if it was just carelessness? 'Maybe,' I says to myself, 'he tried to kill me.' I hate to think that of him, but by gosh, when he skips out and takes all the grub, and the gold, and blankets, and the rifle, it shows he's a mean man! How did he think I was going to get out of there?"

"He didn't," Black John said.

"Well, that's what I figured. And I figured if that's the way he felt, the less I had to do with him the better. So I didn't follow him because, him having the rifle, he might shoot me. I just took my packsack and the shovel and pan, and kept on going the way we were heading when we found that lake."

"How long ago was it you left this lake?"

"Oh, it must be a couple of weeks."

"How did you make it through? What did you eat?"

"I found some berries. And sometimes I'd kill a bird with a rock. Twice I killed a porcupine with a club. I caught some fish, and some frogs and ate them. I had my pan to cook the things in. But I threw my shovel away, because I knew I couldn't carry very much gold along, even if I found any."

"Could you go back to this lake?" Black John asked.

"I don't know about that. I guess I could, if I wanted to. It's pretty rough walking through those mountains. I wouldn't care to go back there."

"But, man, this strike you made—you shore as hell ain't goin' off an' leave it! Twelve thousan', eight hundred dollars right out of the top gravel in a week!"

"Yes, but that's only six thousand, four hundred apiece—or that's what it would have been if Bill hadn't stole it all. And we could take out fifty thousand a week on Bill's claim. I'm entitled to a half interest in that claim of Bill's. Mister Malone was a witness to our agreement. I'm going back to Dawson and hire some men to go up there with me and work my half of it."

"Listen, Joe," Black John said, "you're damn lucky to be alive! The worst bunch of tin horns an' cheap crooks in the Yukon hangs out around the Klondike Palace, an' this yegg that calls himself Bill Smith is evidently one of 'em. An' as fer Cuter Malone—he's the stinkin'est one of the lot! This Bill Smith never had no more claim than a rabbit. He played you fer a sucker—got you to finance a prospectin' trip—got all the rest of yer money on the pretense of needin' it fer his mother—an' then tried to knock you off."

"But if he hasn't got a claim he's guilty of fraud, or obtaining money under false pretenses, or something. He certainly isn't honest. I'm going straight to Dawson and have him arrested!"

"You'd never find him in Dawson. An' if you did you couldn't prove nothin' on him. It would be his word agin yours—an' Cuter Malone would back him up."

"Well, maybe you're right—if that's the kind of a man Mister Malone is," the little man admitted ruefully. "I guess the only thing for me to do is go back to Dawson and hunt up Jim Foley. The way things turned out, I'll bet Bill lied about Jim going off on that prospecting trip. I'll bet he never knew Jim, at all. Jim will know the best place to dig gold. He's smart, or he'd never got to be boss of the trouble gang. Anyway, I prefer some place right near Dawson. You see, I want to take out quite a lot of gold, and if I dug it down there I wouldn't have so far to carry it to the steamboat. It would save a lot of time and hard work—and I want to get home by Christmas. Stella will be cooled down by then. And I'll buy her and the kids some nice presents."

BLACK JOHN heaved a deep drawn sigh, filled his glass, and emptied it at a gulp. "Joe," he said, "there's quite a lot about this country you don't savvy. In the first place, this Jim Foley is prob'ly a damn good repair boss fer a gas works. He also seems to possess the redeemin' qualities of gittin' drunk Saturday nights, an' frequentin' places of questionable repute. But that don't make him a good prospector. Despite the fact that he's be'n in the country a couple of months, he's jest another damn chechako. He wouldn't know no more about where to make a strike than you do. Besides which, all the good cricks along the Yukon are staked from one end to the other. Most of 'em was staked before the chechakos come flockin' in on us. An' there ain't more'n half a dozen of them claims out of every hundred that's payin' better'n wages—an' wages is sixteen dollars a day. An' here you talk about walkin' off an' leavin' a proposition that pans out better'n two thousan' dollars a day, figgerin' a six day week. An' that right out of the top gravel! How big is this here gravel area you was pannin'?"

"That's the trouble with it, it ain't very big—maybe two or three acres."

"Acres! Cripes, I'd fergot there was sech things as acres! I mean how big is it—how many feet one way, an' the other?"

"Oh, I'd say it's a patch about sixty rod each way, with the crick runnin' right through the middle of it. It's all surrounded by high rocks, and after the crick leaves this gravel bar, it runs over hard rock. You couldn't dig anywheres along the crick—only right there where the gravel is."

"Hum—sixty rod—jest about one good discovery claim. Didn't you sock in no stakes there?"

"Stakes?"

"Shore—to mark the claim. Stakes with the date, an' yer name on 'em."

"No, we didn't do anything like that. But I don't understand. You say most of the claims don't pay better than wages? How about all those men the paper told about that are getting rich digging out gold?"

"The papers prob'ly lied. Most of 'em do. But anyone outside of dredge propositions that's got rich takin' out dust, done so before the chechakos come crowdin' in."

"But why would anyone come clear up here just to make wages? They could stay home and get wages. I could have done that. I could have kept right on reading meters."

"The rest of 'em prob'ly believed the papers, same as you did. Most of 'em know the truth by now. The rest of 'em'll damn soon find it out. But you're lucky. That is, if you kin find yer way back to that lake, you are. Why man—you've got one of the biggest propositions in the country. An' you'd walk off an' leave it!"

"Do you really think so? Well, well, won't Stella be surprised? She said I didn't have any gumption. But I knew I could find gold, if I could get up here. It was lucky Uncle Josiah got hit by that train. Why, just think, only a couple of minutes, one way or the other, and he wouldn't have been on the track—and I'd still be reading meters!"

"Yer luck's too damn good to be true," Black John said dryly. "I'd even bet you kin find yer way back to that lake."

The little man nodded. "Yes, I guess I can. It's quite a ways, though, and the walking's bad. But if you think it's the best thing to do, I'll go back there. I'm kind of tired, but I guess I'd better be starting. I don't want to waste any time, and I'll prob'ly have a hard time finding my shovel. You see, I carried it a couple of days before I threw it away, and I haven't got any money to buy a new one, or a blanket, either." He turned from the bar, and was halfway to the door when Black John stopped him.

"Hey—hold on! You don't mean yer hittin' out to find that lake right now—jest as you are?"

"Why, sure. There's no use wasting time."

"But—what are you goin' to eat?"

"Oh, fish, and frogs, and porcupines, and birds, and berries— the same as I did before."

"Well—I'll be damned! I don't know what this here gumption is that yer wife claims you ain't got. But if it's guts she means, you kin tell her fer me that she's out of her head! What do you figger on doin' when you git to the location—if you do git there?"

"Why—dig out a lot of gold, if I can find my shovel. I've still got my pan."

"Yeah—an' what'll you do when Bill Smith comes back?"

"Oh, I don't think he'll go back there. He didn't like to dig much on account of he claimed his shoulder hurt him. I guess that's why he pulled out."

"Look here, Joe—don't be a damn sucker all yer life. What he pulled out fer is to git back to Dawson as quick as God will let him an' record that location. An' he'll record it in his own name—figgerin' that you're bushed. An' there wouldn't be a damn thing you could do about it."

"Well, then—what's the use of me going back there?"

"Yer goin' back, all right—an' I'm goin' with you. An' by God, we're takin' blankets, an' plenty of grub along. Damned if I'm goin' to sleep cold, an' eat frogs!"

"Oh, will you go back with me? That will be fine. We'll go in pardnership. But—what if Bill Smith does come back?"

"That'll be his hard luck," Black John said. "An' it ain't that I'm tryin' to horn in on that location, neither. Fact is I've kinda took a likin' to you, Joe. I'd hate to see you git holt of the wrong end of the stick."

II

THAT EVENING AT Black John's table the little man ate ravenously. "It's nice to have salt on your meat," he said, "and some tea to drink. And," he added, with a glance toward the extra bunk, "it's sure going to be nice to sleep in a bunk with blankets over you. A little square of canvas don't keep the cold out nights, and if it rains and you have it over you the water runs under it and gets you wet anyhow."

"Yeah, you shore must of had a miserable trip gittin' here from that lake. Could you draw a sort of rough map to show which way you come?"

"Oh, no. I couldn't draw a map. You see, the country was all about the same. I had to climb over mountains, and go around 'em, and follow up some cricks, and down some other ones. But if I had some boards I could make you a nice dish cabinet to put there on the wall."

"To hell with a dish cabinet! What we got to do is figger how to git back to this lake. Don't you know what direction it would be from here?"

"Well, Bill Smith figured that the White River would be south of where we were. But then Bill admitted he was lost when we found the lake. You see, I kept on coming the way we were headed when we found it, and it must have been kind of southish, because the sun would be on my left hand in the mornings and my right hand in the evenings, except sometimes it would be the other way—and on cloudy days I didn't know where it was."

"Didn't you have no compass?"

"Yes, but it wasn't any good, so I threw it away. It's just like the man at the store told me—it kept pointing north, and I didn't want to go that way."

"That's so," grinned the big man. "I never thought of that. But if you headed south, the lake must be somewheres north of here. We've got that much to go on—I hope. An' you say you went up some cricks an' down others. That shows you must of crossed anyways one divide. You was in at least two different watersheds."

"Watersheds? No, I wasn't in any building at all. I didn't even see any buildings. You mean what we call water closets, I guess."

"That's a damn pore guess—even fer a chechako," grinned Black John. "I've got a feelin' that if we find this lake, it's goin' to be by the grace of God, er because yer luck holds out, rather than anything we kin do about it. You better roll in an' git a good night's sleep, an' I'll slip over an' throw our trail outfit together."

Old Cush eyed Black John somberly as the big man stowed the supplies into two packsacks. "I've know'd you to do a lot of fool things, John, take it first an' last—but never nothin' so foolish as hittin' out to foller a two-weeks' back trail of some damn chechako which he didn't know where he was goin' when he started; nor where he's be'n when he got here. They hadn't ort to let fellas like him into the country. Cripes—he'd be lost if he got two streets off'n his gas meter route!"

"It's his luck I'm bankin' on—not his woodcraft," grinned the big man. "Why, he even throw'd away his compass because it p'inted north when he wanted to go south. But—remember Uncle Josiah an' that train of cars!"

"Yeah—but from this here Josier's angle, it was damn pore luck."

"Shore. But me an' Joe ain't tacklin' this proposition from Uncle Josiah's angle. Therefore the luck's clearly on our side. Not only that, but apparently it's a phenominal streak of luck. What with a damn crook like this so-called Bill Smith takin' shots at Joe's back, an' shovin' him off rock ledges, an' skippin' out an' leavin' him to git bushed, Joe ain't got no right to be alive—an' he wouldn't be, if his luck wasn't runnin'."

"Every streak of luck's got to break sometime," Cush warned lugubriously. "You'll be in a hell of a fix if you got way out in the mountains somewheres an' yer grub runs out."

"Oh, I don't know. If Joe Petty could make it through without even a rifle to git meat with, an' no blanket, I guess we'll manage to get through all right."

"Yeah—but he et frogs."

"Well—what of it? Go back to the Good Book. John the Baptist went him one better—he et locusts an' wild honey."

"Yeah—but you ain't no John the Baptist, by a damn sight. You ain't even a 'Piscopalian! An' what's more, they ain't no locusses in them mountains."

"Ignorin' the theological angle, I'm still bankin' on Joe's luck holdin' till we find that lake."

"Huh—they ain't but damn few lakes in the country. How do you know he ain't lyin'? I wouldn't believe no chechako which one drink of licker would gag him. An' which he ain't got no more sense that to holler fer sass-prilly pop, on Halfaday!"

"He wasn't lyin'," Black John replied with conviction. "That lake's in there, somewheres. I'd bet on that. The thing is to find it."

"'You claim he wasn't lyin'—how about him tellin' about takin' out better'n fifty pound of dust in a week's time, workin' only one shovel an' pan? I s'pose that ain't lyin'?"

"I don't think so. They done better than that on some of them early claims on Bonanza."

"Yeah, but it was sourdoughs done it—not some damn chechako which would throw away a compass 'cause it p'inted north!"

"A chechako could take out jest as much dust as a sourdough, onct he's blundered onto a rich pay streak."

"Yeah—but whoever heard of makin' a strike on a lake? Strikes is made on cricks—not lakes."

"Gold's where you find it," Black John reminded him. "A hell of a lot of sourdoughs passed up that moose pasture on Bonanza where Carmack made his big strike. An' Carmack might as well have be'n a chechako, as fer as makin' a strike goes. He was a moose hunter; not a prospector."

"Huh—s'pose there is a lake, an' s'pose you could find it, an' s'pose there is a rich proposition on it—what's it gittin' you? You claimed you didn't want to horn in on it."

"No—an' I don't. It's jest like I said—I've kind of took a likin' to Joe. He's sech an honest, earnest little man. He's the most trustful human I ever seen. He ain't got no right in the world to be alive, after what he's be'n through. An' the hell of it is, he don't even realize it. Then, there's Stella, an' them children, an' that little place out in the country with the horse an' buggy, an' the chickens an' all. Mebbe I'm thinkin' about them." Black John paused and his voice became suddenly hard. "But mostly I'm thinkin' about that coot that calls himself Bill Smith. I want to find that lake before he gits back to it. There's too damn many fellas like him besmirchin' the name of Smith in this country, as it is."

"Well—takin' it first an' last, John—you ain't sech a hell of a credit to the name, at that. Trouble is with you, a man can't figger you out. Let some pore woman, er some damn fool like this here Joe come along, an' anyone would think you was the softest hearted man in the country, the way you help 'em out. An' then agin, let some damn crook come along, you git so tough with 'em you take everything they've got an' mebbe hang 'em, to boot. An' all the time, by God, yer the biggest crook of 'em all!"

"Why—you damn old badger! Callin' me a crook right to my face. Ask Corporal Downey—he'll tell you if I'm a crook, er not."

"Yeah—an' Downey would tell it with his tongue stuck so fer in his cheek it would look like he had the mumps. You ain't foolin' Downey, none. It's jest that yer smart enough to not git nothin' on you this side the line."

"My old pal," grinned the big man. "I never thought I'd live to see the day you'd go back on me, Cush."

"I ain't gone back on you. I ain't told you a damn thing you don't know. I jest claimed no one could figger you out. Cripes, John—Halfaday would be a hell of a place if you wasn't here! I jest wisht I was as smart as you be—that's all."

III

FOR THREE DAYS Black John and Joe Petty traversed the foot-hills heading for a huge snow-capped mountain around the base of which Petty insisted he had come. On the morning of the fourth day, with the peak behind them, the two stood at the fork of a creek that wound its way between high mountains.

"Now listen, Joe," the big man said, "you came down this crick, didn't you?"

"Sure I did."

"Well then, you must of come down one of these two forks. Try an' think which one it was. It'll make a hell of a lot of difference because they flare wide apart."

"That's right. But I don't remember any fork. You see, there was a lot of forks on a lot of cricks. I wouldn't of known I come down this crick at all if we hadn't found my tracks in the mud back there where I caught them frogs."

"Yeah, but we ain't goin' to find no more tracks. From here on up these cricks run over solid rock."

"I guess that's right. Well then, the only way to find the right crick is to do like we used to when we was kids and would lose a ball in the weeds. We'd spit in our hand an' say, 'Spit, find that ball!' Then we'd hit the spit with our finger and whichever way it splattered the most, we'd hunt—an' we'd find the ball dang near every time." Gravely the little man spat into his left palm and brought a finger of his right hand down sharply upon it with the result that most of the spittle flew toward the left. Without hesitation he pointed to the left hand creek. "That's the one I came down," he announced. "Spit don't lie."

"My God!" breathed Black John, eyeing the little man in awe. "There seems to be more to gittin' around through this country than I ever knew. Come on—but if that luck of yourn ever breaks, we're goin' to be in a hell of a fix—jest like Cush said."

"Listen, Joe," Black John said, "you ain't got to worry about how many million you'll quit on till we find that lake. Look up there about a quarter of a mile ahead—see where them two big slabs of rock has broke loose an' toppled together formin' a sort of arch over the crickbed. Did you come down through that arch; er didn't you?"

"Why, sure I did! That's the only way I could have got down

the crick. You can see for yourself that no one could get around it."

"But don't you remember comin' down through there? Hell, no one could pass a formation like that an' not notice it!"

"No, I don't remember it. You see, there's a lot of rocks, and they're all different. A man couldn't remember 'em all."

"You never come down this fork," the big man exclaimed testily. "Even you would remember that landmark!"

"Spit said I came this way—and spit don't lie," insisted the little man stoutly.

They went on, and well toward evening his faith was justified. As they came upon the charred remnants of a fire he reached down and picked up a discarded sock. "Look," he said, "here's the sock I throw'd away because the heel wore out and hurt my foot. I've got the mate to it in my pack."

BLACK JOHN heaved a long sigh of relief, and the following day they topped a divide from the summit of which they gazed out over a wooded basin of vast extent beyond which lay a range of mountains.

"Now look this over careful," Black John said. "You must of crossed this divide right where we're at, er you couldn't of come down that crick. Is yer lake in this basin; er did you cross a divide on the other side of it?"

"Oh, yes, the lake is in the mountains—there's mountains all around it. I guess I must have come across this valley, because I remember of going on and on through the woods for about a week, I guess. That was the week it was cloudy most of the time, and even when it wasn't I couldn't hardly ever see the sun for the trees."

"An' you didn't have yer compass then?"

"No, I'd throw'd it away. But I wish we had it now. It would come handy, seeing that we're trying to go north. But the last time I was here I wanted to go south."

"Oh, shore—I'd fergot that. But the sun—them few times

you could see it—was it always on yer left in the forenoons, an' yer right in the evenin'?"

"No—that's the funny thing about it—sometimes it would be just the opposite. That's why I ain't so sure it's safe to go by the sun. It might fool you."

"Didn't you never hear of the north star?"

"Oh, sure. But there's lots of other stars, and I don't know which one it is. And besides—it wouldn't have done me any good, that trip, because I wanted to go south."

"Oh, yeah. I keep fergittin'," the big man grinned. "Lookin' from here at them mountains I'd say that there was two passes that would let a man out of this valley—that notch you kin see way over there to the left—an' the deep one off to the right. You must of come down through one of them passes. Stop an' think—don't you remember which one it was?"

"No," replied the little man cheerfully, "I'm sure I don't remember. But it won't take us long to find out!" He paused, spat into his hand and repeated the performance by which he had selected the left hand fork of the creek. This time the spittle flew to the right and he pointed unhesitatingly to the right hand notch. "That's the one I came through," he announced, with conviction. "It's like I told you—spit don't lie. Come on, let's go. We can't waste much time if I'm goin' to get home by Christmas."

Midway of the valley they came to a considerable stream. "You don't, perchanct, rec'lect crossin' this river, I s'pose?" Black John asked.

"Well, I don't know. I crossed some river, and this might be the one. I crossed it quite a few times. Or maybe there was quite a bunch of rivers."

"Most likely only the one," Black John observed. "The fact is, you was lost in here fer a week. It looks to me like we're goin' to save about five, six days time crossin' this valley. That is," he added, "if yer spit picked out the right notch. If not, we'll be some thirty, forty miles off our course."

"Oh, sure I was lost. I was lost all the time. Even when Bill and I were at that lake we were lost."

"Jest spit yer way clean through to Cush's, eh?"

The other laughed. "Oh, no—I couldn't do that! You see, I didn't know there was any such place as Cush's. Spit can't tell you which way to go, if you don't know where you're going."

"Oh," replied Black John gravely, "there seems to be certain technicalities in connection with the spit method of orientation that I ain't be'n able to grasp yet. But I'll bet I'll know more about it by the time I git back! Come on—let's pull our pants off an' git acrost this river."

Late the following afternoon they came to the mountain range that bounded the valley on the north, and began the ascent of a deep gulch that led upward to the divide. The going was extremely rough. Huge rock fragments blocked the narrow canyon, necessitating much climbing. And brush grew thick along the banks of the tiny stream that trickled among the rocks. They camped that night on a tiny flat, and pushed on at daylight the following morning. At mid-day Black John swung the pack from his back, built a small fire, and hung the tea pail to boil.

"I don't believe you ever come down through this gulch," he said, "er you'd shore as hell remember it. It must of be'n the other one."

"No. This is the one, all right," the little man insisted stubbornly. "Spit don't lie. And I had so much rough walking that I couldn't have remembered this place, even if I'd never been here before."

"Oh," Black John said, "well, in that case, s'pose you rustle a little more dry wood while I slice up this pork."

The little man stepped into the spruce thicket to return a moment later smiling. "See," he said, tossing an object to the ground beside the fire, "I knew I was right. Here's my shovel that I threw away."

"Well I'll be damned!" exclaimed Black John. "That goes to show, Joe, that a man never ort to lose confidence in his guide. An' didn't you say that you only carried the shovel a couple of days before you throw'd it away? In that case, this lake can't be no hell of a ways from here."

"No. We can see it when we get to the top. It took me about a day and a half to climb up there, and when I got to the top I looked back and there was the little lake shining like a looking glass. Why it looked almost like I could jump to it—and here it had took me a day and a half to get up there!"

That evening they topped the divide and, sure enough, there lay the little lake shimmering in the last rays of the setting sun.

"Yer luck shore held, Joe," Black John said, his eyes on the sparkling water. "We'd ort to make it by noon tomorrow. But tellin' you the truth, when we started out I figgered our chances of ever findin' this lake was damn slim."

"Oh, I knew we'd find it," smiled the little man. "It had to be right where I left it. It was just a question of coming back here—that's all."

"Yeah, I think you've got somethin' there. I guess you could go anywheres, Joe—if yer spit held out."

"Oh, sure—so could you, if you just remember how to do it!"

"I ain't so shore," grinned the big man. "There ain't no railroads in this country. An' even if there was, I ain't got no Uncle Josiah to start a streak of luck with. But don't never go explorin' no desert, Joe—you'd never in God's world git back!"

IV

THE GRAVEL BAR that the little creek traversed at the outlet of the lake showed that during the week the two men had spent there they had scarcely scratched the surface, and that in only two or three spots. Black John filled and washed pan after pan, staring down wide eyed at the gold that lay, butter yellow, in the bottom of each pan. He scowled at the two stakes set, one at either end of the bar. He read the inscription: "Wilhelm Schmidt. June 20, 1901." The stakes conformed with regulation, and were duly designated as Numbers 1, and 2.

"Who in thunder's Wilhelm Schmidt?" Joe Petty asked, squinting to read the words. "Gosh, someone must have come here after I left!"

"He's ondoubtless yer pardner, Bill Smith."

"But we didn't put up these posts. And he left here before I did."

"Yeah—but he know'd you couldn't stay here without no grub. So he hung around till he seen you go. Then he socked in his stakes."

"Oh, then maybe he just went down to Dawson to record the claim. Maybe I misjudged him, after all."

"Yeah? Well you notice, I s'pose, that your name don't show on the stakes—jest his?"

"That's so. Then he did steal the claim!"

"Well, he's took a preliminary step."

"But half of it's mine—even if he didn't put my name on the posts. So we'll just go ahead and dig out what gold we want."

Black John grinned. "We can't do that," he explained. "In the first place we ain't got enough grub along to do no extensive diggin' on. An' in the second place we've got to take certain steps to establish yer rights to this property."

"How do you mean?"

"Well, we'll sock in yer stakes right beside his, puttin' yer name an' the date on 'em. Then we'll hit fer Dawson to find out if this here Schmidt has recorded the claim."

"But if he has," Joe objected, "I wouldn't have any rights here at all, would I? Because his posts are dated first."

"Well—that's the way it generally works out. Sometimes, though, there's exceptions."

"I think the best thing to do is just to pull his posts out and throw them away. Then mine would be the only ones here."

"Cripes, Joe," the big man exclaimed, "that would be an illegal act! I'm shore you wouldn't want to do nothin' illegal, no more'n I would. It would savor of dishonesty. Ain't you got no ethics?"

"I don't think so," replied the little man doubtfully. "You put the stuff in the packsacks, back there at Cush's. I ain't be'n to the bottom of mine yet. What do they look like? I'll go and see."

"Don't bother," Black John replied. "A man wouldn't hardly need 'em in a case of this kind. I most likely fergot to fetch 'em along."

"But if he's recorded this claim for himself, I'm just out of luck, eh?"

"I wouldn't go so fer as to say that—considerin' Uncle Josiah, an' what's transpired sence his demise. No, I'd say yer luck's still runnin'. I kin tell better when we git to Dawson. Come on, we'll git them stakes planted, an' pull out. You said that this crick runs into that river you come up from the Yukon on, didn't you? Er have you got to spit to locate the Yukon from here?"

"Yes, we followed this crick right up from that river. We were hitting for the White River when we found this lake. But we haven't got any canoe, and it's a long ways to Dawson."

"Hell—we've got an ax! We'll build a raft an' float down."

"Why sure! It's funny Bill didn't think of that when we lost our canoe. He said we'd have to hit over to the White River and find some Indians."

"He never intended fer you to git back to Dawson."

"But what if he is coming back here, and we should meet him on the river? He might try to kill me, so I couldn't tell the police what happened."

"Ondoubtless the effort would fall short of success," Black John said. "If we do meet him, you better let me do most of the talkin'."

THREE DAYS down the river they sighted two canoes drawn up on the bank where their occupants had evidently stopped to prepare a mid-day meal. Working the raft toward the spot, they landed, and Joe Petty stepped ashore to greet a large man who sat beside a fire with three Indians.

"Hello, Bill! Why did you pull out and take all the gold and the grub? And why didn't you put my name on those posts, too?"

"How the hell did you git here?" snarled the man.

"He come acrost to Cushin's Fort on Halfaday Crick," Black John answered.

"How the hell could he git there without no grub an' no blankets?" the man demanded.

"Et slim, an' slep' cold."

"Well—seein' he got there, what good did it do him?"

"That's what we want to find out. He claims he was a pardner of yourn."

"He's a damn liar! How's he goin' to prove it?"

"I'll prove it by Mister Malone!" the little man piped. "He was a witness to our agreement—right there in his office."

"Haw, haw, haw! Say, that's a good one! Go ahead an' prove it by Cuter."

"Joe, here, claims that not only he paid fer the outfit you fellas had, but he loaned you all the rest of his cash to keep yer old mother whilst you was gone. He says you offered him a half interest in a rich proposition, somewheres upriver."

"He's a damn liar. Hell, I don't even know if my mother's livin' yet! An' I never had no rich proposition up no river at that time. But I've got one now all right! Nothin' like it sence Bonanza! An' only the one discovery claim on the crick."

"If it's as good as you say," Black John answered mildly, "it looks like there'd be plenty in it fer the two of you. You look to me like a man that would want to do the right thing. I believe Joe here when he says you an' him was pardners. Why not deed him over half the claim?"

"What the hell do you take me fer? A damn fool? That location's all recorded in my name—an' him nor no one else gits a damn cent of it—only me! What if he was my pardner? How's he goin' to prove it? Cuter Malone'll claim he never seen him before. I tended to that."

"But this man's got a wife an' some kids back there in Minneapolis. They're pore folks—never had nothin' much. Think of them—back there, waitin' fer him to come back, hopin' he'll fetch some gold so they kin take things a little easier. Joe, he thinks a heap of his wife an' them kids."

"Why the hell didn't he stay home with 'em, then? Saps like him hadn't ort to be turned loose, nohow. The fool would believe anything a man would tell him."

"Yeah—trouble with fellas like him, they think everyone else is honest as they are. That's why the cheap crooks kin take advantage of him."

"Hey, who the hell you callin' a cheap crook?" The man leaped to his feet, then stood peering sharply into the other's face. "S-a-a-y—ain't you Black John Smith?"

"So called."

"Say, I know'd it—soon's I got a good look at you. The smoke kep' you half hid, me, settin' back of the fire there. So that's the way of it, eh? He gits through to Halfaday an' tells you about this proposition, an' you come back with him, figgerin' to horn in on it. Well, yer out of luck, this time. I don't give a damn how smart folks claim you be. I've got that location all staked out proper, an' recorded—an' there ain't no way you kin horn in on it. Not you, nor that fool Joe, nor the police, nor not even the commissioner hisself! You're a fine guy to go callin' other folks crooks. You better go back to Halfaday amongst them other outlaws."

"Well—mebbe yer right," Black John admitted mildly. "I guess we might's well be shovin' along, if that's the way you feel about it. I jest figgered that mebbe you'd like to do the right thing when you know'd all the facts. But it seems I was wrong."

"Listen, Bud," the man snarled, emboldened by Black John's attitude, "the right thing fer me, is to git holt of every damn thing I kin—an' then hang onto it. Savvy?"

"Yeah—I grasp yer p'int. Gittin' holt of a thing's fairly easy, sometimes. Hangin' onto it's the hard part. So long."

"Didn't I tell you he's a mean man?" Joe said when they were once more on the river. "It looks like if Mister Malone would tell a lie, I haven't got a chance."

"Cuter Malone'll lie all right," Black John said. "But that part don't make no difference. His word ain't worth a damn, nohow."

"I haven't got any money at all now," Joe said. "I'll have to get a job when we hit Dawson. I don't suppose there'll be any meters to read. But I'm kind of handy at carpentering, and I noticed there's quite a lot of buildings going up."

"That's right," the big man replied. "I expect you better hook up with a job of some kind. I've got a little dust on me. I'll pay yer bill fer a week at the hotel. That'll give you a chanct to look around."

"Oh, thank you! I tell you, you're a fine man, Mister Smith. I was sure lucky to run onto a man like you—after the experience I had with Bill. Are you going back to Halfaday Crick? Where will I send the money to?"

"What money?"

"Why, the money to pay you back for my board bill at the hotel. I'll send it to you as soon as I get a job."

"Oh, yeah. Well, jest let that ride fer the present. Fact is, I might hang around the big river fer a spell. I've got a little business over on the Alaska side. Might drop down an' 'tend to it. I'll be seein' you on my way back."

V

ONE EVENING, A week later Black John stepped into the office of the hotel to find Joe Petty seated at a table laboriously penning a letter.

"I'm writing to Stella," he explained. "I got a job day before yesterday, working on that new warehouse the A.C. Company's putting up. Sixteen dollars a day. She'll be glad to hear that. I didn't write to her before because there wasn't nothing but bad news to write about."

"If all you've got to write about is this here job you better tear it up," Black John grinned. "Because me an' you are hitting out fer that lake in the mornin'."

"Oh, no, I couldn't do that. Why, I haven't even made enough to pay you back for my board bill yet. And besides, it wouldn't do any good to go back there. You see, I went to Mister Malone and asked him if he didn't remember the pardnership agreement I had with Bill Smith, and he told me to get to hell out of there, that he'd never seen me before. So I went to the police and told them all about it, and a nice policeman named Corporal Downey went down to the recorder's with me. He looked up the records and found that this Wilhelm Schmidt had recorded the claim and had been issued a grant for it. Corporal Downey said he was sorry—but there isn't anything I can do about it. He said it was too bad that a damn crook could get away with a thing like that. But as long as I had no proof, I was out of luck."

"Out of luck, eh? Ondoubtless you fergot to tell Downey about Uncle Josiah."

"No, I didn't say nothing about him. I just told Corporal Downey about what happened after I got here. But I did tell him that miserable Bill Smith called you an outlaw, right to your face."

The grin behind the black beard widened. "An' what did Downey say about that?"

"Well, you see, I hadn't told him what your name was before that. I just didn't bother to tell him about going clear over to Halfaday Crick. I just said I'd run onto a man that went back to that lake with me and found those posts in on the claim. Well, when he found out who it was I'd run onto, he said that if you were my friend maybe my case wasn't quite as hopeless as it looked. He said you've got ways of getting at things that the police haven't got. But I told him that Bill was an awful tough talking man, and that we came away from there because you seemed kind of scairt of him. And when I said that Corporal Downey kind of choked like he'd swallowed part of his cigar. 'Even so,' he said, when he could talk again, 'if I was you, I'd sort of trail along with Black John.'"

"All right. That's jest what I'm askin' you to do. So now you've got Downey's word fer it, are you willin' to start back up there with me in the mornin'?"

"Why—sure—if you think it will do any good. But Mister Malone acting like he did, and the recorder claiming the location was recorded in Schmidt's name, and the police not being able to do anything, I'm afraid we'll just be wasting our time. And I'll prob'ly lose my job, to boot."

"I'll promise to git you another job, if you want one. Better roll in now, an' git a good night's sleep. We'll be pullin' out early in the mornin'.

VI

IT WAS EARLY one evening nearly a week later when Black John and Joe Petty walked across the gravel bar at the outlet of the little lake and climbed the steep slope that led to the flat-topped rock-shoulder, Schmidt and his Indians were at supper.

"What the hell you doin' back here?" the man demanded truculently, reaching swiftly for the rifle that rested against a rock at arm's reach.

"Better jest leave it there," Black John suggested smoothly. And the man's face paled slightly as he stared into the muzzle of the .45 that had suddenly appeared in the big man's hand.

"What the hell's this," he growled. "A hold-up?"

"No. Me an' Joe wouldn't stoop to nothin' like that. Fact is, we come here to sort of give you one more chanct to do the right thing by Joe. You know damn well what's right, an' what's wrong in this matter. You know Joe's entitled to a half interest in this location. I'm appealin' to yer better nature. Will you deed his half interest over to him?"

"Not by a damn sight—yer crazy!" The man rose to his feet and stood glaring at Black John as the big man slipped the revolver into the front of his shirt.

"But—how about his wife an' kids?"

"To hell with his wife an' kids! He's the one that's got to think of them—not me. They could starve, fer all I give a damn—an' him along with 'em."

"All right. Have it yer own way. You've spoke yer piece—an' we've listened. But there's one thing I'd like to call yer attention to. Someone has removed Joe's stakes. We set 'em up right beside yourn. You got any idea who done it?"

"I did. An' what's more, I had a right to. Them stakes was set in after mine. The claim was already staked when you come along here."

"That's so. But I've jest be'n down an' I recorded this location in Joe's name. An' he's s'posed to have his legal stakes in place."

"There ain't no legal stakes on this claim except mine. How the hell could you record this claim? It was recorded already. I paid my money, an' I've got my grant—an' I've got the papers to prove it." Reaching into his pocket he withdrew a paper which he held out for Black John's inspection. "Read the date on that grant. It's a good two weeks ahead of the date on them stakes you put in."

"Damn if it ain't," Black John agreed, scrutinizing the paper the man held tightly in his hand. "But there's more to a grant than jest the date on it."

"What do you mean—more?"

"Well—I notice that this here grant of yourn was issued in Dawson fer one thing."

"Where the hell would it be issued? That's where the recorder's at, ain't it?"

"Fer the Yukon—yes. But there's one thing you overlooked. Er mebbe you jest ignored it. A slight technicality, you might call it. But it seems to have a bearin' on this case."

"What's that? What the hell you talkin' about?"

"Merely callin' yer attention to the fact that this here location lays in Alaska—not in the Yukon. It's a matter of eight miles west of the boundary."

"You lie!" The man's face flushed suddenly, and his voice rose to a shrill falsetto.

"No I don't. The line's marked with monuments at reg'lar intervals. You either didn't notice 'em, er you didn't heed 'em. I don't know which. An' it don't make no difference. I dropped downriver an' recorded this claim at Eagle—"

With a choking sound like the snarl of a wild beast, the man launched himself straight at Black John who stood scarce six feet away, and close to the edge of the rockwall. The big man side-stepped swiftly as the other shot past—straight out over the edge of the rock. A shrill shriek of terror was followed by a loud splash as the man's body struck the water.

Joe Petty ran helplessly up and down the edge of the rock, his eyes wide with horror, as the man reappeared and wildly thrashed the surface with his arms. "Oh—do something," he cried. "Get a rope, quick! He can't swim a lick. He told me so, himself."

"There ain't no rope handy," Black John replied. "An' we wouldn't need one, even if there was. It looks like the lake's goin' to cheat us out of a hangin'."

"Oh—I can't see him any more. He's sunk," cried Petty, wringing his hands.

"That's good. Ondoubtless the weight of his sins drug him

down," the big man said, and turned to the Indians. "You fellas show us where his cache is, an' then git to hell out of here!" he ordered.

"No savvy cache," one replied.

"Okay. You don't git paid, then. We'll give you each an ounce a day fer the time you've put in, if you'll show us where the dust is."

WITHOUT A word one of the Indians indicated a fissure in the rock, a short distance away, and a few minutes later the three took their departure, each clutching his little poke of dust.

As they passed out of sight the little man turned to Black John: "And you mean—all this is mine? All the gold, and everything?"

"Shore as hell."

"And—it's all legal, and everything?"

Black John shot the little man a reproachful glance. "Why, Joe—shorely you wouldn't think I'd stoop to an illegal act."

"No, no! I didn't mean that. Of course you wouldn't. I—I just can't hardly believe it—that's all. But—half of it's yours," he cried impulsively. "I'd never had any of it if it hadn't been for you. I'll deed you half of it, right now."

"No," the big man replied, "there's certain technicalities that makes it onwise fer me to hold property in Alaska. I won't bother you with the details, other than to say it runs back to a matter concernin' the army. Of course if you feel like takin' me into pardnership in this proposition, I'll be damn glad to comply. I ain't fool enough to turn down an interest in the best strike that's be'n made sence Bonanza. I'd rather remain as a sort of silent pardner, though. I don't need the scratch of a pen from you to know I'll git my share of the dust. I know an honest man when I see one. So now you kin send fer yer wife an' family, an' build you a big house here—big as that man's in Minneapolis you was talkin' about. An' yer yard will be bigger'n any damn park you ever heard of. An' the kids kin swim an' ketch fish in the lake, an' roam in the woods like yer wife wanted they should."

The little man shook his head. "No, I don't think Stella would like it here. It's too far away. There ain't no school for the children. And there's no one to talk to."

"Hell—they could go to school in Dawson! An' as fer talkin', she could talk to you."

"That's the trouble. Stella does quite a lot of talking. It's all right if it's spread around among a lot of people. But I wouldn't want it all bunched on me. I guess we better get that little place out in the country, like she wanted."

"But—who'll run this layout here?"

"Why, I figured maybe you would."

"W-e-e-l-l, it's a leetle further into Alaska than I'd prefer, if I was to pick my location. But I guess mebbe I could work it. I could put on a gang an' cut a trail from here to Cush's that a man could travel in a couple of days of lively goin'. That is," he added with a grin," providin' I don't run out of spit findin' my way back here agin. An' I could put on a crew to git out the dust. Besides which, I kin put you on a steamboat fer the outside, with cash enough in yer pockets to see you back home, an' a draft on Minneapolis to take care of them Christmas presents, an' that there place in the country."

"You mean—you'll lend me all that money, on top of that board bill in Dawson—so I can get back home by Christmas!"

"It ain't a loan—merely an advance. But with you way off there in Minnesota—how the hell will you know yer gittin' yer proper cut?"

"Ha, ha, ha! You're a droll fellow, Mister Smith. Look what you've done for me, already! Why—just looking at you anyone would know that you would never cheat anybody. Listen—what's that rumbling kind of a sound? It sounds like thunder—way off there toward Halfaday."

"It might be, at that," grinned the big man. "More likely, though—it's a couple hundred fellas turnin' over in their graves."

BLACK JOHN SOLVES A CRIME

TWILIGHT WAS DEEPENING into dusk as Black John Smith rounded a point in his descent of the Yukon and allowed his paddle to trail, rudderwise, as he caught the flicker of a tiny fire on the river bank a quarter of a mile below. Slanting toward it, he landed and drew his canoe clear of the water, to be greeted by a young man in the uniform of the Northwest Mounted Police.

The big man smiled. "'Bout time to camp fer the night, an' seein' yer fire, I swung in. Kinda lonesome fer a man campin' all by himself."

"Lonesome's right!" exclaimed the policeman. "My name's Buck—Rollo Buck. And I've been stuck here for a week!"

"Hum. Canoe get away on you?"

"No, Corporal Downey left me here and went off up some damn crick to investigate a murder. What's your name?"

"Smith."

"Smith, eh?" the younger man smiled. "Not Black John Smith, I hope—the notorious king of the outlaw gang up on Halfaday Crick, that I heard about in Whitehorse."

"Well, hopin' don't cost nothin'," the big man replied. "I've got the same name as him, anyhow—John Smith. But how come Downey didn't take you along on this here murder case?"

"He claimed there wasn't room in the canoe. But just between you and me, I've got a hunch that he wanted to hog all the credit for solving that murder. He didn't want any other police-man along."

"You pretty good at murder-solvin'?"

"That's just the trouble—they won't give me the chance," the officer replied, in an aggrieved tone. "First it was Saskatchewan, where the prairie's so damn flat there ain't any landmarks, and on a cloudy day a man can't tell one direction from another. I got lost hunting some cattle rustlers, and the inspector raised hell about it. Soon afterward I got orders to report at Tagish. And there the country's so damn mountainous a man can't see more'n a couple of miles in any direction. The sergeant in command there sent me out to investigate a complaint about a crazy man raising hell on some crick—but I couldn't even find the crick. How do they expect a man to investigate a place he can't even find? The sergeant drew a map, but I couldn't make head nor tail to it. So when he heard they were short-handed at Whitehorse he sent me down there."

"Hum. An' wasn't the country around Whitehorse built to suit you?"

"It wasn't so bad around Whitehorse. The country was all right. But the fact is, I never had much experience with a canoe, and the inspector sent me downriver a ways to arrange for next winter's firewood, and I tipped over and lost my outfit, and then broke both my paddles, and I'd have been floating down the damn river yet if a steamboat hadn't picked me up and taken me back. That was last month, and here a couple of weeks ago, when Corporal Downey was in Whitehorse, he happened to tell the inspector that he was short-handed at Dawson, and the inspector said he had a man he could spare, and ordered me to go back with Downey. Why he did that is more than I can see—because, God knows, he's short-handed at Whitehorse himself."

Black John grinned. "Jest the old police game of passin' the buck, eh? But you'll prob'ly get along all right with Downey."

"I don't know about that," the other said. "I'm afraid he's jealous of me already. Take this case here—the first time I could show what I can do, and I don't get the chance. This guy's standing there on the point waving his shirt when we came along, and we go ashore and he tells us about this dead man he finds in a shack up a crick a little ways above here. I started right in asking him questions, but Downey butted in, and the upshot of it was that he dropped down to this camping place where there's a good spring. He left me the tent and half the grub, and he and this guy went off in the canoe. He told me to wait here till he got back—said it might be a couple of weeks. He left the rifle and told me I wouldn't have any trouble killing some ducks or a moose. But getting a moose isn't as easy as he seems to think. I've seen three of 'em, but the damn things run away before I get a chance to shoot 'em."

"Yeah. That's a habit they've got. A man can't blame 'em none, when you come to think about it." As Black John listened, he

had hung his tea pail over the fire, and removing a chunk of meat from his pack, cut a liberal slice and placed it in his frying pan."

"Gosh! Beefsteak!" the policeman exclaimed. "It's a long time since I've seen any of that!"

"Be'n short of meat, eh? I'll cut off another slab an' you can fill up. Only this is moose—not beef."

"Did you kill a moose?" the other asked, a note of respect in his voice.

"I found a dead one up the river a ways."

"But how do you know it isn't spoiled?"

"It hadn't be'n dead very long when I found it."

"But it might not be fit to eat! Maybe it died of some disease."

"'Tain't likely. There was a bullet hole in him jest behind the shoulder. It looked to me like he died of that. I seen somethin' movin' in the bush an' took a shot at it, an' when I went over there I found this moose."

"I never have any luck. I shot at all three of the ones I saw. But I didn't kill any.

"The only meat I've had since I used up the bacon Downey left me is a duck I shot in a little lake back over the hill—and it wasn't very good. It was tough as leather, and tasted like rotten fish."

"The flavor wouldn't be appetizin'," Black John agreed. "What kind of a duck was it?"

"It was a big one. There's his head laying over there. I had a chance to shoot a lot of little ones, but when this big one came swimming along I got him. That was three or four days ago. I've had chances to get the smaller ones a dozen times since, but after finding what they taste like, I passed 'em up."

BLACK JOHN glanced at the head. "Them smaller ones would have tasted different," he said. "That was a loon you shot. No wonder he tasted fishy. Looks to me like you've got a hell of a lot to learn."

"Oh, sure—there's prob'ly a lot of unimportant little things. But I'll pick those up easy enough. What I want is the chance to show what I can do."

"Well, you've be'n showin' it, ain't you?"

"I mean something big. I didn't join the Mounted to fool around with such piffling matters as cattle rustling, and crazy men, and firewood. I want to work on murders and things like that. I want to carry on scientific investigations—use my powers of observation and deduction. Like—well, like Sherlock Holmes."

"Quite a fella—Sherlock. Did you fetch along a needle?"

The other laughed. "A man doesn't need to be a dope addict to be a scientific detective. I want to make a name for myself. I want to get ahead."

"Yeah. It would be a good thing to git—if you could."

"What?"

"Why—a head. A man finds frequent use fer one."

"I mean, I want to go on up. I want stripes."

"Stripes, eh? Well—quite a few folks is wearin' 'em. Personally, they're somethin' I've never strove fer. Fact is, there's be'n times when I've be'n put to quite a bit of trouble to keep from havin' 'em forced on me."

"Are you in the police?"

"No. But I've had more er less to do with police matters."

"Oh—I thought, from what you said, that maybe you were working in plainclothes. What is your business?"

"I'm a prospector."

"Did you ever make a strike?"

"Well, now an' then I've struck it kind of lucky—nothin' to brag about."

"This is a big country. There's a lot of police work to be done up here. Take that Halfaday Crick gang. From what I heard in Whitehorse, they're a regular bunch of outlaws."

"Yeah, I've heard that rumor myself."

"They say this Black John Smith is smart as hell. They claim he won't allow any crime on the crick, so the police won't have any excuse for going up there."

"Yeah, that's the talk, all right."

"This Halfaday Crick is in Downey's district—and he don't seem to do anything about it. By gosh, I don't know what he's thinking about!"

"There's be'n times when I'd liked to know'd that, myself. Downey's a good man, though—takin' him by an' large, as the Good Book says."

"I don't see how you figure he's such a good man—letting a gang of outlaws hang out in his district and not doing anything about it, just because they don't pull off any crimes on their own crick. I hope he gives me the chance to clean up on 'em. I'd like to match my wits against this Black John."

"Well, you might get the chanct—who knows?"

"Downey don't rank me so much. He's only a corporal. It won't be long before I rank him. Then I'll be in command of this district. And you bet, the first thing I'll do will be to clean up on that Halfaday Crick outfit! I'll show Downey whether he can leave me sitting here beside the river doing nothing while he takes all the credit for solving a murder. He can't make a damn fool out of me!"

"That's right, Rollo," Black John agreed gravely. "It looks to me like God saved him the trouble."

II

SHORTLY AFTER DAYLIGHT the following morning, as Black John kindled the fire and sliced a couple of steaks into the pan, Buck stepped to the spring close to the river's edge for a pail of water. A loud hail greeted him and a canoe bearing two Indians slanted shoreward. Giving them no heed, Buck carried the water to the fire, filled the tea pail, and suspended it over the blaze.

The canoe landed and the Indians stepped ashore—a girl of eighteen or twenty, and a young man. "We got de good luck," he said as the two stepped to the fire. "We go Dawson for fin' p'lice. But p'lice ees here."

Buck scowled. "Well—what about it?"

"Ma trap git stole—wan hundre an' twenty trap—all gone."

"Who stole 'em?" Buck asked.

"We ain't know who stole 'em. Git p'lice fin' out."

"Listen here," the officer said, "don't you suppose the police have got something else to do besides chase around through the brush every time some damn Injun loses a trap? You must have some idea who stole 'em. Go find your own traps. And next time, don't bother the police unless it's something important."

Black John turned a steak in the pan. "How many traps you got left?" he asked.

"We got no mor' trap," the young woman answered, tears showing on her eyelashes.

The big man turned to Buck. "The loss of all their traps is damned important to these folks," he said. "It might mean the difference between eatin' an' starvin' this winter."

"Well, why the hell don't they take care of their traps, then—if they're so damn important?" the officer growled, and turned to the Indians. "Where did you have these traps? Where were they stolen from?"

"Trap in cabin. We go Selkirk git debt. Breeng back de grub, de blanket, de shell for de gon. W'en we com' to cabin—trap ees all gone."

"Where is your cabin?"

The man pointed upriver. "Oop crick, fi', seex mile."

"Where is this crick?"

"Com' een de riv' 'bout two, t'ree mile from here."

"You mean your traps were in the cabin when you went to Selkirk for supplies, and when you got back, they were gone?"

"Yes. Trap all grease wit' bear fat, an' hang oop een cabin. W'en we com' back, trap all gone. We got no trap. No git no fur, no git no debt no mor'."

"Was the cabin locked?"

"No. Got no lock."

"How the hell do you expect to keep anything if you don't lock it up?" Buck asked testily.

Black John grinned. "It ain't customary to lock cabins in this country," he said. "I've be'n livin' here an' there along the river fer quite a while, an' I never locked a cabin yet—an' never seen one that was locked."

"It's a damn fool way to do—anyway you look at it."

"Yeah? Well, look at it this way—the strong cold is on—some pore devil has had bad luck on the trail. He's about all in when he staggers onto a cabin. There's no one there. He shoves the door open with mebbe the last ounce of strength he's got left, lights a fire in the stove, cooks himself a good hot meal, an' goes to bed in a warm bunk. If the door had be'n locked, he'd have died."

"That wouldn't happen once in a hundred times."

"It wouldn't have to happen only the once—to that particular fella," the big man replied.

Buck turned to the Indians. "Well, you are out of luck. You claim it's eight or ten miles to your cabin. How the hell do you expect me to get there—walk?"

"We got canoe."

"You wouldn't get me in that damn thing!" Buck exclaimed, with a glance at the light craft. "I tipped over in a bigger one than that. I couldn't go up there, even if I wanted to. I've got no canoe, and besides I'm under orders to stay here till Corporal Downey gets back. You better get yourselves another bunch of traps, and forget about it."

"No kin git mor' trap," the young woman said in a voice that trembled slightly. "No kin git no debt for buy trap."

"You see, they used up all their credit buyin' them supplies," Black John explained. "I'm on my way to Dawson, but I ain't in so much of a hurry I couldn't spare a day er so to help these folks out. S'pose we take my canoe an' go on up there with 'em, an' sort of look the ground over? It might be that you'd git the chanct to show Downey what you kin do—might get a chanct to use them powers of observation an' deduction you claimed you had."

Buck snorted. "Do you expect me to waste my time trying to find out who stole a bunch of stinking traps?"

"The Mounted don't call it wastin' time when a native appeals to 'em fer help. Not in this country, they don't. I've know'd Downey to travel hundreds of miles on a case a damn sight less important than this one."

"He's a damn fool, then."

"Well—mebbe. That ain't exactly the reputation he's earnt along the river. But possibly us folks has misjedged him."

"Speaking of Downey, he told me to stay here till he got back. S'pose he'd come along and find me gone. What would he say, then?"

"If you leave a note pinned to the tent flap, teilin' him where you went, an' why, he'll say you done right. This here loon killin' assignment you've got don't seem of much importance, nohow— bein' as they ain't no good when you kill 'em. But if he comes along an' finds out you refused to investigate this complaint, what he'll say couldn't never be printed in no Sunday School book—you can bet yer life on that."

"He'd never know about it," Buck growled.

"That's what you think. But s'pose I was to git drunk in Dawson an' go shootin' off my mouth where Downey could hear me? An' I wouldn't put it beyond me to do jest that."

"Why the hell can't people mind their own business!" Buck snapped.

"Yeah. That's what I was wonderin'. Your business is policin'."

"Oh, well—we might as well go on up there and get it over with," the officer said testily. "It's piffling business for a policeman to be wasting his time on. I feel like a damn fool."

"Oh, shore. But if you was to locate them traps, mebbe Downey wouldn't find it out."

III

THE CREEK UP which they paddled was a slackwater stream that wound and twisted through rush beds with scarcely a perceptible current. Ducks rose in clouds from the marsh, thickly studded with small rocky islands. And it was on one of these islands that the Indian beached his canoe in front of a little pole and mud cabin set close to the water's edge just beyond the natural rip-rapping of stones whose surfaces were polished smooth by countless years of ice grind.

Black John beached his canoe beside the other and the two stepped out, the officer following the two natives to the cabin, where he stood in the doorway peering into the dark interior.

"Get a light in there," he ordered. "I'm no damned owl. I can't see in the dark."

The young woman lighted a tin bracket lamp, and the man pointed to a piece of wire that dangled from the ridgepole. "Trap hang dere," he said. "Som'wan cut de wire—steal de trap."

Stepping inside, Buck examined the wire, and looked around the tiny room, as Black John strolled up and leaned against the doorjamb. Buck reached down and picked something from the door. "A-ha—a pair of gloves!" he exclaimed.

The big man grinned. "Well, damn if it ain't! Them powers of observation an' deduction of yours is shore marvelous."

The officer frowned, and there was a patronizing note in his voice as he said: "To your mind, I suppose, these are just a pair of gloves."

"Well, barrin' the slight grammatical error, I'm inclined to agree with you. There ain't nothin' about 'em to suggest that they're a pair of pants, er a drink of licker."

Buck turned to the native. "How many people live here?"

The Indian pointed to the woman. "Me an' her. We marry."

"Had any visitors lately?"

"No."

"Okay." The officer turned to Black John, holding out the gloves for inspection. "You see—there's only one other person been here, and that's the thief. When we find the man that owns these gloves, we've got the man that stole the traps."

"Simple as all that, eh?"

"It is—to a man who is trained to use his faculties. To you, they're just a pair of four-bit canvas gloves. But I saw at a glance that they couldn't have belonged to either of these people. Their hands are small, while these gloves are of large size."

"The haberdashin' industry shore lost a genius when they tried to make a policeman out of you, Rollo."

The young woman picked up one of the gloves which Buck tossed onto the table, and examined it. "Dem Joe Blackbird glove," she said.

"Who's Joe Blackbird?" the officer demanded.

"My papa."

BUCK SCOWLED and turned to the man. "I thought you told me you hadn't had any visitors."

"No. Joe Blackbird no com' here. He mad on me for marry he's girl. He want she marry Paul Peshawba. Paul, she say she geev heem fifty trap, an' wan canoe, an' four dog eef Annie marry heem. But Annie no like Paul Peshawba. She ron 'way an' go wit' me to pries' an' we git marry."

"So, that's it, eh? You skipped off with Blackbird's daughter and made him sore because he lost the chance to sell her to this other Injun, an' he gets even by slipping up here and stealing your traps while you're off after supplies."

The young Indian shook his head. "No. Joe Blackbird no steal trap. He good mans."

"Hell—any Injun'll steal! Especially if he's sore at someone. Anyhow, he prob'ly figured he had that much coming to him. Or else he figured that if he stole all your traps and put you out of business, the girl would have to come back, and he could sell her to this Paul What's-his-name. Where does Blackbird live?"

"Live Ogilvie."

"Where the hell's Ogilvie?"

"It's downriver a piece," Black John explained. "It's a tradin' post acrost from the mouth of Sixtymile. We'll pass there on the way down to Dawson."

Buck turned to the Indians. "I s'pose this Blackbird has a lot of traps of his own. How can I tell yours when I arrest him, if he's got 'em all mixed in with his?"

"I got ma mark—tree li'l notch file on de pan."

"What do you mean—pan?"

"The trigger pan," Black John explained. "It's the dingus that springs the trap when an animal steps on it."

"All right," the officer said, addressing the natives, "I'll go down to Ogilvie and arrest this Joe Blackbird and get your traps back. You can pick 'em up at the trading post. Better hold off about a week, though, because I've got to wait for Downey, and it might be a few days before he shows up."

He turned to Black John. "We might as well go on back. I'm taking these gloves along for evidence. Wonder what Downey'll say when he finds out I slipped up here and solved this case while I was laying around waiting for him. I'll bet he didn't clear up that murder as easy as that!"

"Prob'ly not," Black John agreed. "But mebbe the fella that done it didn't leave no gloves layin' around." He turned to the young Indian. "Does Joe Blackbird travel around in a rowboat or a canoe?" he asked casually.

"Joe got canoe. Got no boat."

"What difference would that make?" Buck asked, shooting Black John a glance.

"Oh, difference of a mile an hour, mebbe. Canoes handle easier'n what boats do."

THE TWO returned to the camp beside the river, and that evening after supper, Buck glanced across the little fire as Black John filled his pipe. "You see, now, what I mean by a man using his powers of observation and deduction in solving a crime. The instant I saw those gloves, I knew I'd get my man."

"Yeah. But you've got to admit, Rollo, that if them gloves belongs to the man that stole them traps, it was a damn dumb trick for him to leave 'em layin' around."

"All criminals are dumb. They all make mistakes."

"They do, eh? I always figured it was only the ones that got caught that made the mistakes."

"They all make some mistake or other—every damn one of 'em. All there is to this police business is being smart enough to take advantage of these mistakes."

"That's all, eh? By Cripes, I'll remember that—in case I should ever take a notion to infringe a mite on the law."

"Better not try it," advised the officer. "There's smarter men than you doing time because they thought they could beat the law. Just remember—there's no such thing as the perfect crime."

"Ain't, eh? Well then, there must be a hell of a lot of folks gettin' away with imperfect ones."

"That's because there was no competent policeman on the job. I wish Downey would show up. I'm anxious to get down to Dawson and get to work on some important cases."

"We could pull out in the mornin'," Black John suggested, "an' slip down to Ogilvie. We could take the outfit along an' leave a note in a split stick by the spring where Downey couldn't help seein' it. Then, by the time he got to Ogilvie, you'd have this case all cleared up. You see, if you wait here fer Downey, he might butt in an' make the arrest himself—so's to get the credit. That would be kind of too bad—seein' how you done all the observin' an' deductin'."

"By gosh, you're right!" Buck agreed. "We'll roll in, now, and get an early start in the morning."

IV

AT OGILVIE, OFFICER Buck strode into the trading post followed by Black John. Gorman, the trader, shifted his glance from the new policeman to the face of the big man.

"Hello, John!" he greeted. "Which one of you fellas has got the other in tow?"

Black John laughed. "Oh, I picked him up fer loiterin' on the river bank, an' shootin' loons out of season. Meet Constable Rollo Buck, of the Mounted." He turned to the other. "Rollo, this here is Tom Gorman. He's be'n in the country ever sence the Yukon was jest a little crick. You might say he's grow'd up with the river."

"Glad to know you, Gorman," the officer said. "Do you know an Injun by the name of Joe Blackbird?"

"Shore I do."

"Where will I find him?"

"Why, at home, I s'pose."

"Where does he live?"

"About a mile down the river. Got a shack at the foot of the big eddy. Good foot trail all the way. You can't miss it. What do you want of Joe?"

"I'm going to arrest him for the theft of some traps."

"Guess you'll find yer sort of barkin' up the wrong tree, young feller," Gorman said. "Joe never stole no traps—nor nothin' else. He's be'n tradin' with me for twenty year. There ain't an honester Siwash in the hull damn Yukon. I'd trust him with anything I've got."

"I'm not interested in his previous record, nor in any advice you may have to offer in the matter of policing," Buck snapped. "As a matter of fact, Blackbird did steal over a hundred traps from his son-in-law."

"You mean from Johnny Seven-up?"

"I don't know what his name is, and it don't make any difference. He and his wife live on an island in a big slough a few miles upriver."

"Does Johnny claim Joe stole his traps?"

"No. He don't believe he did. But that don't alter the facts."

Black John explained. "You see, Tom, Rollo, here, went up an' investigated the case. He done some observin' an' deductin'."

"Oh."

"Yeah. By the way, Tom—anyone bought any red paint off'n you this summer?"

"Red paint? Let's see—yeah, Bill Emory bought a couple of gallons to paint the *Mary Ellen*. An' that damn Paul Peshawba bought a quart, 'long in the spring."

"What has red paint got to do with it?" Buck asked testily.

"It's a different color from blue," Black John explained, "so I figgered mebbe someone might of bought some."

Buck frowned. "You always manage to horn in with some damn fool question, don't you? Like asking this Johnny Seven-up whether Blackbird traveled around in a rowboat or a canoe— as if it made any difference!"

"Well, a man kinda likes to know about them things," Black John said. "An' if he ain't had no trainin' in observin' an' deductin', he's got to ask questions. It's the only way he can find things out."

"You wait here till I come back," Buck ordered, a note of impatience in his tone. "I'm going down and arrest Blackbird. I'll bring him back here shortly, along with those stolen traps. If Downey shows up before I get back, tell him where I've gone."

As the officer stepped from the room Gorman eyed Black John, a slow grin widening his lips. "Where in hell did you git him?" he asked.

"Found him up the river a ways gnawin' a loon which he claimed was a duck. Downey left him there while he went upriver to investigate a murder. From what I gather, Rollo has be'n passed on from one detachment to another clean from Saskatchewan. He's gettin' damn clost to the end of his rope, though. Downey'll prob'ly pass him on to Forty Mile, an' when they pass him on, he'll be in Alaska. He'd ort to make a damn good U. S. marshal."

"You ort to know," Gorman retorted. "Here comes Downey, now."

Black John greeted the officer who stepped through the doorway. "Hello, Downey! Lookin' fer somethin' important?"

Downey grinned. "Not very, I'm afraid. Seems like I've mislaid a rooky somewheres along the river. Ain't seen nothin' of him, I s'pose?"

"Yeah, quite a bit. I seen how he wasn't doin' no good where he was at, bein' as he'd missed three moose, an' shot a loon. So I fetched him down here. A Siwash an' his wife got all their traps stole an' reported the loss to Rollo. First off, he wasn't goin' to do nothin' about it, claimin' it to be too pifflin' a business fer the Mounted. But when I p'inted out that it was damned important, from their angle, an' that you might raise hell with him if he didn't look into it, he allowed he'd investigate. So I took him up where these folks live, an' he done some observin' an' deductin'. He told us to tell you to wait here till he come back. He's gone down to Joe Blackbird's. Aims to arrest Joe, an' fetch back them stolen traps."

"Joe Blackbird!" Downey exclaimed. "Why, the damn fool! Joe's one of the best Siwashes in the country. I'd trust him with a million dollars."

"Yer kinda lib'ral with yer trusts," Black John remarked. "But you ain't far off on Rollo. He's ambitious, though—Rollo is. You know the first thing he's goin' to do when he gets in command of the Dawson detachment?"

"No," Downey chuckled, "what's he goin' to do—dredge

through the mountains so the Yukon'll run the other way, an' the damn chechakos will have to paddle uphill to get here?"

"Nothin' as easy as that. He's goin' up to Halfaday Crick an' wipe out a gang of outlaws that's rumored to hang out there."

Gorman joined Downey in a roar of laughter. "He don't know who you are, eh?"

"I told him the name was John Smith. But his powers of observation an' deduction wasn't keen enough to notice that my whiskers is black, an' to kinda put two an' two together."

"Inspector Cartwright wished him off onto me, up to White-horse," Downey said ruefully. "I'll pass him on to Forty Mile, first chance I get, an' let Sam Steele worry about him. Damn if I can figure how he ever got into the service, in the first place."

"You fellas won't be bothered with him fer long," Gorman opined. "That's one good thing about the Mounted—it's hard to git into; but damn easy to git out of."

Downey turned to Black John. "You say you went along with Buck to investigate that trap stealin'?"

"Yeah. He didn't have no canoe, so I took him up there."

"Got any idea who stole the traps?"

"Oh shore, I know who done it."

"Who?"

"Paul Peshawba."

"I wouldn't be surprised," Downey said. "He's given us trouble before."

"He prob'ly done it, all right," Gorman agreed. "I wouldn't trust him fer as I kin spit. Besides that, he's sore at Johnny Seven-up on account he married Annie Blackbird. He offered Joe some traps, an' a canoe, an' some dogs fer Annie, an' when Annie found it out, she skipped out with Johnny, an' they went down to the mission an' got married."

"It's a wonder Joe would want his daughter to marry Pe-shawba," Downey said. "He knows what kind of a fellow he is."

Gorman grinned. "Old Joe's no damn fool. He know'd Annie

wouldn't marry Peshawba, no matter what he offered. He don't trust Peshawba, no more'n what I do. But he didn't dast to turn down his offer, fer fear Peshawba would lay fer a chanct to git even—like knockin' him off some night, er stealin' him blind, er somethin'. Peshawba lives too damn clost fer him to take a chanct on makin' an enemy of him. So, when he told Annie about Peshawba's offer, he know'd she'd do jest what she done—skip off with Johnny Seven-up. An' Joe's pretendin' to be sore at Johnny, jest to make the play look good."

"Hum," Black John mused, "them Siwashes is shore masters of duplicity, ain't they, Downey?"

Gorman's wife announced dinner, and as the meal was concluded, Buck appeared, hustling the manacled and bewildered Indian ahead of him.

"I got my man," he announced proudly, as he came to a stand before Corporal Downey, who, with the other two, had just seated himself on the bench in front of the trading room.

"Get the traps?" Downey asked.

"No. I hunted all through Blackbird's traps—figured he'd prob'ly mixed the stolen ones in with his own—but I couldn't find any with notches filed in the pans. Then I tore up every damn thing around the place trying to find where he'd hidden 'em. But I didn't have any luck."

"Didn't, eh?" Downey's voice sounded ominously low, and level, as he pointed at the prisoner. "I notice that Joe's eye looks kind of puffed up. An' his lips looks swollen, too. Know anything about that?"

Buck shifted his feet uneasily. "Why—yes. I—I hit him a couple of licks."

"Hit him, eh? Was he resistin' arrest?"

"Well, not exactly. It was after I arrested him. He refused to tell me where he'd hid the traps. He admitted that the gloves I picked up at the scene of the crime were his. But he claimed he didn't know how they got there. Claimed he'd lost 'em a week or so ago. He kept on denying he stole the traps. But with all the evidence against him, I knew he was lying, so I hit him a couple of belts to make him talk."

"You mean, you hit him after you had him handcuffed?"

"Why sure! You've got to make 'em talk."

Downey's lips tightened. "Did they teach you that down at Regina?"

The constable flushed. "No. But a policeman's got to use his head, hasn't he?"

"That's right. His head; not his fists. Take them cuffs off that man!"

"What?"

"You heard me."

"But—"

"That's an order!" Downey's words cut sharply on the protest, as the constable surlily complied. As the man was released, Downey continued. "You claimed you tore up everything around the place, down to Joe's. Here's another order—go back down there an' put everything back where it was when you found it—every damn thing, jest like it was."

Buck's face was flaming. "You mean—"

"You heard me. I mean jest what I said." Downey turned to the Indian. "I'm sorry this happened, Joe. This man's new. He's got a lot to learn. You go back with him, and see that he leaves all your stuff jest like he found it. When he gets through you come back an' tell me if he done a good job. If anything's broke er damaged, tell me about that, too, an' I'll see that you get paid for it."

The old Indian's puffed lips twisted into a grin. "You good mans," he said, and pointed to Buck. "Heem no good."

When the two had returned, a couple of hours later, and Blackbird reported the damage, Downey turned to Buck. "Come on along now, an' we'll pick up the thief, an' fetch back them traps of Johnny Seven-up's. John says you promised to leave 'em here at the post for him."

"What do you mean—pick up the thief?" Buck asked surlily. "I had the thief, and you made me turn him loose."

"That's what you think. But yer wrong. John, here, figured out who stole the traps."

The three proceeded to the cabin of Paul Peshawba, located at the mouth of a creek, half a mile above the post. The Indian greeted them with a smile.

"Ah, Co'p'l Downey! Glad to see ma fran'. W'at kin I do for help de p'lice?"

"You can stick out yer hands so I can slip these cuffs on you. An' then you can tell us what you done with Johnny Seven-up's traps."

"Me—I ain' got Johnny Seven-up trap! Got ma own trap. No see Johnny Seven-up, long tam."

"It's better not to see a man when you go to steal his traps," Downey replied dryly. "Come on—where's yer traps? We want to run through 'em — jest in case you've got Johnny's mixed in with 'em."

Still smiling, the man pointed to a small storeroom, half dugout, half poles, that protruded from the side of a cutbank. Black John jerked the door open, and hauled out several bunches of traps. Running swiftly through them, he began tossing out traps until he had gone through the entire lot. Then he counted those he had tossed aside. "Hundred an' twenty," he announced. "Johnny was right on his count."

Peshawba's smile changed to a scowl. "Dem my trap!" he snarled. "You no kin prove!"

Constable Buck stepped forward and, stooping over the pile of traps Black John had thrown out, examined the pan of each, as the others looked on. When he had finished, he turned to Downey. "This man is right," he said. "There isn't a damn bit of evidence to show that those traps ever belonged to Johnny Seven-up! He told me, himself, that all of his traps were marked with three notches filed in the pans. And not a single one of these traps is so marked!" Gaining confidence from the sound of his own voice, he continued, pointing at Black John. "And as for Smith there, he's nothing but a big four-flusher—pretending to know who the thief was, and then picking out the traps. He stood around all during my investigation, like the dumb yokel he is, not paying any attention to anything. Why, he didn't even attach any significance to those gloves of Blackbird's that I found on the floor of Seven-up's cabin. They didn't seem of any importance to him. And then, just to make an impression, I suppose, he did ask Seven-up one question—whether Joe Blackbird traveled around in a rowboat or a canoe—as if that made any difference. And again, down at the trading post, he asked Gorman whether anyone had bought any red paint, this summer. And when I asked him what red paint had to do with the case, he told me it was a different color from blue!"

Downey grinned. "Well, it is; ain't it?"

"Of course it is! Any damn fool would know that. But—"

"Then, he was right, wasn't he?"

"Why—sure. But—"

"I've found that when it comes to dopin' out the ways of crooks, big er little, Black John is generally right."

A QUEER, gurgling sound issued from Constable Buck's throat. "Black John!" he gasped.

"Yeah. Black John Smith, of Halfaday Crick. I thought you two was acquainted, er I'd introduced you before."

The big man grinned. "So you see, Rollo, when you rank Downey, an' get in command of the Dawson post, you'll know what the king looks like, when you hit out fer Halfaday to clean us outlaws up."

Buck stood, wide-eyed, his face flaming, as Downey turned to the big man. "Now that we've got the thief an' the traps, you might go ahead an' tell us how you worked it out, John. I ain't quite clear on it, myself—from what Buck's told me."

"Well, you got to remember, Downey, I ain't had the advantage of no reg'lar course of study in observin' an' deductin', like Rollo has. I've sort of picked it up the hard way. An' there's be'n times when it would of made quite a difference if I'd be'n wrong. But, from what I seen up there to Johnny Seven-up's place, there didn't nothin' seem to be of no importance except a smooch of red paint on one of them rocks in front of the shack."

"There was no red paint on any of those rocks!" Buck exclaimed. "I personally examined those stones, and I can positively state that there was no paint of any kind on any of them."

"In this here personal examination you give them rocks, I don't s'pose you noticed that the surface of one of 'em was rough while the others was all smooth, did you?"

"Sure I did. But I attached no importance to it."

"That shows, Rollo, that yer powers of observation are runnin' way ahead of yer powers of deduction. You'd ort to deduced, like I did, that someone must have turned that rock over fer a purpose. An' when I picked it up an' looked at the other side, I seen why—it was because it had a smooch of red paint on it—like someone had landed a rowboat with a red bottom there. A man wouldn't jamb a canoe up onto them rocks hard enough to take the paint off. So I figured that the one that went to all that trouble to cover up his tracks was the thief—someone with a rowboat with a red bottom. That's why I asked Gorman about the red paint.

"Now, about them traps that you claim ain't Johnny Seven-up's—when you personally examined 'em a few minutes ago you didn't find no notches filed in the pans, so you claimed there ain't no evidence to show they was Johnny's. Yer powers of observation ort to showed you that them pans was all a mite flatter on one side than the other, an' then yer powers of deduction would have told you that them notches had be'n filed off." He turned to Peshawba. "You filed off Johnny's marks, all right, Paul, an' you even wet the filed edges so they'd rust up. But you made one big mistake, jest like Rollo, here, claims all crooks makes—you fergot to notice that Johnny's traps was greased with bear fat, whilst yours is greased with steamboat oil. You can see there's a mite of difference in the color. I notice you've got a rowboat pulled up over there. We'll jest step acrost an' tip it over—an' if it's got a red bottom, yer shore as hell out of luck."

The Indian gave a shrug of resignation. "A'ri'—I steal Johnny trap. I'm mad on heem for mar' Annie Blackbird. I'm steal heem trap—mebbe-so no kin git no fur—Annie got to go home—I git her."

Black John slowly shook his head. "It's sad to contemplate, Paul—but yer nothin' but a damn thief. Seems like some folks never can learn that honesty is the best policy. Ain't that so, Downey?"

"That's right," Downey agreed, and turned to Buck. "An' by the way, you'd better turn over them handcuffs an' yer service revolver."

"What! What do you mean?"

"You're under arrest for abusin' a prisoner, an' destruction of property. Joe Blackbird reported that you smashed his bunk lookin' under it, besides rippin' some boards off'n his woodshed. When we get to Dawson I'm sendin' you on to Forty Mile, preferrin' charges against you. Inspector Steele will act on your case."

Black John grinned. "An' it ain't goin' to tax even your powers of deduction, Rollo, to figure out what Sam Steele is goin' to do when he reads them charges. Sam, he's figured to be one of the toughest cops in the Yukon—an' one of the squarest. But you'll get along all right. Jest hit one of the stores fer a haberdashin' job. You can fit gloves real nice."

BONUS MATERIAL

LOST!

THE TRUE STORY OF THE
FIFE LAKE TRAGEDY

This story is not fiction. Every word of it is true, just as it was told to Mr. Hendryx by Charles LaBar, who found the bodies of John and Willie Gilde, by several others of the searchers, and by the mother and older brother of the boys themselves. For, upon hearing of this tragedy, *The American Boy*, realizing that something had gone wrong, sent Mr. Hendryx to Fife Lake to find out what that something was; sent Mr. Hendryx because most of his time in the last thirty years has been spent in the wilderness.

Mr. Hendryx did find out. In a letter accompanying the manuscript he writes: "I have told about it in this story, and I hope that every boy who goes hunting, or who expects that he will ever go out into wild, unfamiliar country, will read it. It isn't any sermon, as you will see; I couldn't preach a sermon if I wanted to. But it does point out the mistakes these two boys made—the mistakes that cost them their lives—and tells how other boys can avoid them."—*The Editors.*

ON A CERTAIN Monday morning, the 19th of December, 1921, to be exact, the little village of Fife Lake, in Grand Traverse County, Michigan, awoke to dig itself out of a foot and a half of drifted snow. Shovelers called cheerily across the snow-choked street to other shovelers. Pedestrians laughingly wallowed knee-deep upon their early morning errands—for Fife Lake laughs at snow. Then suddenly the shoveling ceased. Quick, hoarse words passed from man to man. The shovels were hurriedly thrust into the drifts and abandoned. The pedestrians halted and, their errands forgotten, turned and plunged back to their homes. For word had come from a little farmhouse four miles to the northward that two boys were lost in the snow!

Like magic the news traveled from lip to lip. And Fife Lake answered the call! Grim-faced now were the shovelers and pedestrians, as they hurriedly dressed for the snow trail, and wide-eyed and silent were the women as with trembling fingers they prepared lunches. Five minutes later the street was filled with men, shifting their guns from hand to hand as they donned mackinaws and mittens, sinking to their knees in the soft snow as they crowded paper wrapped lunches into wide pockets. Teams hitched to bobsleds appeared and into the sleds swarmed the men. The horses were headed northward to a point some five miles distant where a little traveled road crosses a great cedar swamp. For the word had passed that the boys were lost in this swamp.

And at the same moment other teams carrying sledloads of men were converging upon the swamp from the northeastward, for the men of South Boardman, eight or ten miles away, were also answering the call, as were all the farmers between.

THE SEARCH AND ITS END

IT WAS SLOW and heavy going, this breaking trail through the soft, new-fallen snow—slow and heavy for the first three miles and worse for the remainder of the distance, for the little-used road through the swamp holds to the north, while the main road with its hard-packed bottom under the new snow turned to the east.

At last the swamp was reached, the horses blanketed and made fast to trees, and the men, agreeing upon the signal of a shot when the boys were found, began a systematic search of the swamp.

Only those who have traversed a cedar swamp in winter can have any idea of the grueling work such a search entails. Snowshoes were of no use whatever because the ground was a tangle of fallen logs and saplings that lay buried under the snow, or protruded from it to lean against the standing timber at every conceivable angle. And between these logs the feet of the searchers sank every now and then into spring holes whose ice-encrusted water was concealed by the new-fallen snow. Add to this the circumstance of every twig and limb of the dense evergreen thicket being bent low with a burden of snow which, like a heavy white screen, shut off the view beyond a very few feet, and at each step brought down a deluge of snow upon the heads and shoulders of the searchers. Nor was this all, for word had passed that the boys had been missing since Saturday afternoon, and not a man in the party who did not shudderingly hesitate to set his foot down upon one of these ominous looking white mounds that covered the logs on the ground.

The morning passed. Slowly, methodically, with the utmost care, the men explored a section of the swamp, while other men scoured the desolate and uninhabited pine plains that stretch to the northward.

Noon. Two of the searchers, Charles LaBar and Arthur Hodges, pause at the foot of a tree that has somehow escaped axman and fire to rear its noble head high above the snow-buried plain thickly dotted with fire-blackened stumps that once were Norway pines. Thrusting his gun, butt downward, into the snow, LaBar climbs the tree. For a moment nothing is visible but the desolate waste of white. Then, beneath a bush of scrub wild cherry not far distant, he detects a blur of movement. He looks closer and beside the bush stands a gaunt and shivering hound. As they approach, another hound staggers from beneath the bush. They bark, and as the two men approach still closer the barks change to growls—ominous, threatening growls that mean business. What is that? There—protruding from the surface of the drift upon the south side of the bush? A dark patch—the crown and part of the visor of a small cap. Hodges stoops—only to draw quickly back. With a growl of fury the older of the two hounds, Fannie, sinks her teeth into his thigh. Luckily, Hodges is heavily clothed and the fangs but graze his flesh.

Hodges draws back, and pulling the untasted lunch from his pocket, unwraps the paper and feeds it to the starving dogs. And then, with tight-pressed lips, LaBar raises the muzzle of his gun into the air and fires. Dark figures dot the snow. The men of Fife Lake are coming out of the swamp and hurrying across the bleak pine plain. They have heard the shot. The search is ended.

A mile to the northward of the farm of Cornelius Gilde a long narrow cedar swamp stretches for fifteen miles east and west, with a north and south reach of a half-mile to a mile. In this swamp John Gilde, aged thirteen, and his brother, Willie, aged eight, had set a line of traps. Between the Gilde farm and the swamp a succession of cleared fields alternate with patches of hardwood timber. To the northward of the swamp, the devastated pine plains stretch in endless fire-swept desolation, a mute but eloquent relic to the greed of the lumbermen and the indifference and negligence of a state department.

Shortly after noon on Saturday, the seventeenth of December, Mrs. Gilde, with her oldest son, Ed, and the youngest, a fair-haired little boy of three, started for town, leaving John and Willie at home. There were purchases to be made, and Christmas presents to buy, and these things the mother must attend to, for during the winter months the father is employed in a Grand Rapids factory.

"Better not go look at the traps today," warned the mother as she stepped into the sleigh and cast a weather-wise eye at the dull leaden clouds that sent forth a cold drizzling rain, interspersed with squalls of snow that drove viciously before a fitful east wind. Then the horses started, and the sleigh slipped silently away over the sodden snow.

WENT TO INSPECT THEIR TRAPS

FOR SOME TIME John and Willie busied themselves about the farm. Then drawing on their rubber boots, they took the shotgun from its place, unchained the two hounds, Fannie and Trip, and started for the cedar swamp.

A neighbor saw them cross the field, as he remembers it, at about half past two o'clock. The rain continued to fall, and with their backs to the wind, the boys headed westward, crossed the road a mile away that later the searchers from Fife Lake were to traverse, and entered the swamp at a point nearly a half mile beyond. Two wood choppers returning from a pulp-wood camp located several miles away say they saw the boys enter the swamp just before dusk. If so, they were the last persons to see the boys alive.

It was long after dark when the Gildes returned from town to find that the two boys had gone. In the meantime, the wind had swung into the north. The weather had turned colder, and the rain of the afternoon had become a blinding, driving snow-storm. So fierce was the storm, in fact, that many farmers who had tarried late that evening in town, stayed there all night rather than attempt to reach their homes in the blizzard.

Believing that the boys had sought shelter in some neighboring farmhouse, Mrs. Gilde did not worry much until the following morning. On Sunday the older brother, Ed, and several of the neighbors searched all day. The weather had cleared, but the north wind blew cold, whirling the snow into huge drifts. All Sunday night the search was kept up, but not until Monday morning was a general alarm sounded and the organized search begun that ended at the foot of the cherry bush on the stump-dotted pine plains.

From the time the boys entered the swamp until their bodies were found by LaBar and Hodges, their movements are, of course, a matter of conjecture. But, after thoroughly going over the ground myself in company with one of the searchers, I know as well what happened as though I had been with them to the end. A few tracks were still discernible under the snow in the swamp— that is, under the new snow. They were recorded in the old snow where, here and there, the boys in their pitiful wandering through the blackness of the swamp had stepped upon a log in crossing it. Manifestly no tracing out of their course was possible, but from the widely separated points at which the tracks were found, it is pretty certain that they wandered about in the swamp for a good part of Saturday night. Then at last they gained the open, emerging from the north side of the swamp onto the pine plains.

They had left home with the wind in their backs, so they headed into the wind and struggled on. The little fellow was worn out so his brother carried him, or at least helped him along. This is the general belief of the searchers who uncovered the bodies, as the older boy lay on his back with an arm about the body of the younger, who lay on top of him.

By the time they reached the bush where their bodies were found it is probable that they knew they were headed wrong. For they knew the country, having trapped the swamp in winter and herded cattle on the pine plains in summer. Only to the inky darkness of the night and to the driving snow can be as-cribed their failure to realize their false direction sooner, for there are no stumps or bushes to the southward of the swamp and they must have stumbled against many in the half mile they traveled after gaining the open. But it was too late.

Chilled to the bone, exhausted, they stuck the gun butt downward into the snow and lay down in the miserable shelter of the straggling bush and there the wind-driven snow covered the tortured little bodies. And there also lay down the two faithful hounds upon the opposite side of the bush, where the trackless snow showed that they had not stirred from the place until the searchers arrived, and scorning hunger and cold, faith-fully guarded the bodies of the friends and masters they loved.

Had they forsaken their post the bodies would have remained snow-buried until spring. Even after the bodies were loaded onto a sleigh and taken home, the dogs remained at the spot, and later had to be forcibly removed.

WHY WERE THEY LOST?
WHY DID THEY DIE?

WHAT WENT WRONG? Why did these boys get lost? And having become lost, why did they die? These are questions that are of the utmost importance to every boy, and man, too, who ventures off the beaten paths. For it is not only boys who succumb to the savage relentlessness of the wilds, as you shall see. The questions are of importance because in knowing their answers, and in taking the commonest precautions to prevent these same mistakes and similar ones, lies just the difference between survival and death. Had John and Willie Gilde known the answers, they would have been alive today. For they were both normal, healthy, husky boys. What happened to them might as easily have happened to you.

Had they gone about it rightly there is no reason why they should not have weathered that storm, which was of less than twenty-four hours duration, in comparative comfort, especially as the thermometer did not register lower than fifteen degrees above zero, and probably did not average as low as twenty. No one I asked seemed to know the exact temperature, and I recorded guesses that ranged from fifteen to thirty above zero. I do know that at my home, thirty miles northwest of Fife Lake, where I keep an accurate weather chart, the thermometer readings were: Dec. 17th, +33. Dec. 18th, +28. Dec. 19th, +24.

But the exact temperature cuts no figure, anyway. Had these boys taken proper precautions, and by proper precautions I do not mean extraordinary precautions, they should have comfortably weathered the storm, even at a much colder temperature.

FINDING ONE'S WAY HOME

LET US FIRST consider the getting lost. When we speak of a person being "lost" what do we mean? I should say that for practical purposes a person is "lost" when he does not know the position of the point he occupies relative to some known, or fixed point, from which point the location of his starting point or his objective may be ascertained.

There is no question in my mind that many animals possess a sixth sense, or an instinct of direction, at least a "homing" instinct. I have seen many instances of the working of this instinct, the most striking being the return of horses in Montana to their home range from points hundreds of miles distant, when the circumstances absolutely precluded any possibility of their back-tracking. Also the case of a hound which was shipped by his master from his home in Elizabethtown, Ohio, to Seymour, Indiana, by express, a distance of probably seventy-five miles, and the second day thereafter he showed up, tired and hungry, at his master's door.

Certain people also are credited with this "homing instinct," and I am inclined to believe, rightly so. I know of numerous instances in which little Indian boys between the ages of five and ten, who had been removed from their homes on the Fort Belknap Reservation by train to the Fort Peck Reservation in Montana for schooling, returned on foot to their homes, a distance of considerably more than a hundred miles across what was at that time open cattle range.

Old hunters, trappers and woodsmen, are often credited with this sixth sense, or instinct, but for this there is no foundation. The reason these men are rarely lost is not because of any "sense" or instinct that you or I have not got, but because they have learned by experience to make use of the five senses which they have, obviously far and away the most important of which is the sense of sight. By force of long habit these men subconsciously note the "lay of the land." This includes the position of the natural landmarks, such as lakes, swamps, hills, ridges, distinctive trees or clumps of trees, the location and direction of creeks and rivers, and, in fact, anything whatever that would serve to aid them in shaping a course, or in identifying a location. Also they take unconscious note of the turnings and twistings in circumventing natural obstructions. Upon entering large black spruce swamps where the terrain is nearly always flat, and the trees so thick that one place looks exactly like another, they mark their trail by now and then breaking a branch or blazing a trunk.

The best advice I can give anybody upon the general subject of how to avoid getting lost, is to form the habit of studying the "lay of the land." You don't need to go into the wilderness to do this. Do it now. Do it in the city. Take long walks in unfrequented parts of your city, and then back-track, or make short cuts using your landmarks as guides—don't read street signs, and ask policemen—there are no street signs and policemen in the wild country. Do it on your tramps into the country. Keep on doing it. Do it some more. After a while you will find that you do it naturally, subconsciously—and when you find that out, you can credit yourself with as much "sixth sense" or "instinct" as any white man has.

But there are certain conditions under which anyone may become lost, even among comparatively familiar surroundings. These conditions are, however, temporary conditions, due to darkness, storm, or fog.

WHEN LOST—CAMP!

LET US SUPPOSE that you are lost, or for any reason are unable to continue to your objective. What is the first thing to do? Obviously, the thing to do is to CAMP. If the reason for the interruption of your journey be other than the fact that you are lost, if you are temporarily disabled by a twisted ankle, or a broken snowshoe, it requires no effort of will to decide to camp. But if you are lost, it is a far different matter. The state of being lost seems to create a condition of unreasonableness of mind. Either the lost person stubbornly refuses to admit to himself that he is lost, or he becomes panic-stricken and incapable of rational reasoning. In either case the last thing he wishes to do is just the very thing he must do, and that is to CAMP. In the first instance his impulse is to continue stubbornly on in the direction he believes to be the right one, every step carrying him farther and farther out of his course, and farther and farther from the chance of being found by a searching party. In the second case, in the frenzy of fear and panic, he charges sense-lessly about, first in one direction, then in another, until he drops from exhaustion.

Consider first the temporary conditions of darkness, storm, or fog. You will have to camp for only a matter of hours until the condition is relieved. The first and absolute essential (I refer particularly to winter conditions) is a fire. To build a fire you must have matches and the matches must be dry! A belt ax, or at least a heavy knife, is another essential.

Select a wind-sheltered spot, build your fire, rig some sort of reflector of boughs, or brush, or a blanket, place yourself between it and your fire, and you can pass twelve, twenty-four, or even thirty-six hours in comparative comfort, even without food. But don't dry your moccasins or snowshoes close to the fire. I have trapped and hunted and fished since I was eleven years old, much of the time alone, and have spent many nights in the open, sometimes with the temperature far below zero, and I have never yet experienced more serious mishap than a little temporary discomfort.

To go back to the matches, the absolute essential. Have plenty of them and have them dry. Yes, I know I said that before, and I may say it again before I get through. If I could have said it to John and Willie Gilde that Saturday they would be alive today.

To keep the matches dry a waterproof container is essential. There is an absolutely reliable metal match box on the market which may be purchased at reasonable cost. Personally, I have never used anything but certain thick, wide-mouthed glass bottles whose corks are pounded in very tight. Several of these are always in my outfit, and at least one in the pocket of my clothing. I have been told that the objection to bottles is that they will break. Maybe they will; however, I have yet to break the first one in thirty years of camping. And my outfit has been consigned to the mercy of every conceivable means of conveyance on land and on water from a dog sled to a transcontinental flyer.

If you are on a trip where there is even a remote possibility of spending a night or two in the open, food will of course add greatly to your comfort, as will a blanket or sleeping robe. If you are trailing through sparsely settled, or non-inhabited regions, food, a good bed and a complete change of clothing are likewise essential.

As I said, if you are actually lost it is going to take a firm effort of will to force yourself to camp. But remember this: You will camp—sooner or later! Or God Almighty will camp you! It is up to you. Either camp the moment you believe that you are lost, and save yourself and the searching party hours of grueling toil, or push blindly on until you fall into the snow, too tired to care—too weak to help yourself if you did care— bushed. The snow will cover you up. It will be your last camp. I have seen several such last camps. They are not pretty to see.

A word here in regard to helping the searching party. In the outlands simply apply the rule of three. By night, three fires lighted in a row on some ridge or hill means help. By day, three smokes similarly placed means help. Night or day, or during a storm or fog, three shots in rapid succession, then a long interval and three more, means help. At night, though, one shot is as effective as three, as no stray hunter is apt to be firing his gun by night.

Suppose now that the darkness has passed, or the storm or fog has cleared, and you are still lost. By day your knowledge of the relative position of the sun in the different seasons will put you right, so on a clear night will the north star guide you. If you don't know the north star, it is time to make his acquaintance—he is always ready to help you on your way. If clouds obscure the heavens there are still ways to set yourself right. In cedar swamps and heavy timber the moss forms more thickly low down on the tree trunks on their north side. Don't trust to examination of one trunk, though. Examine many and the preponderance of moss will be to the northward. Also on many soft wood and some hardwood trees, in localities having winter severe enough to freeze the sap, weather scars will be found on the southwest side of many exposed trees. Do not look for weather cracks or scars in the thick woods. You won't find them. The position of the tree must be such that the afternoon sun can strike the southwest side of its trunk, and thaw the sap. It is this thawing and freezing that cracks the bark, and makes the weather scar. In this connection, however, you must beware of fire scars, which in some instances are hard to distinguish from weather scars. A fire scar generally shows dead wood beneath it, a weather scar rarely does, as the bark is generally grown completely together.

Another guide in winter is the position of snowdrifts. But here extreme care and an absolute knowledge of conditions are necessary. You must know to a certainty that a particular wind, whose direction you remember drifted that particular snow. Older snow, or newer snow drifted by a wind that perhaps you do not remember, will set you all wrong. Best acquire much experience in snow before attempting to use the drifts as a guide.

The direction of the flow of streams will often set you right, though always remember that in a hilly country you may have crossed one or several more ridges than you think you have, and thus come out onto an entirely different watershed.

IF YOU CARRY A COMPASS, CARRY TWO

LASTLY, THERE IS the compass. However indispensable this instrument may be to navigators upon the waters, it is decidedly nonessential upon land. I have noticed a peculiarity about the compass. The sourdough, the only man who is fit to carry one, rarely does so. The chechako or tenderfoot is almost sure to have one, and he might better carry a billiken. If you are addicted to its use either throw it away, or get another. Because the first time you will really need it will be the first time you get lost, and then you won't believe it. You will level a space, set it down, and gravely consult it. But you will know so much better than the little needle does which way is north that you will decide it is wrong. Something has got the matter with the tarnal thing! You will shake it a little up and down and sidewise, and although the needle is oscillating freely upon its pivot, you know it is pointing wrong. So you stick it in your pocket in disgust, and follow your own north, which is probably southeast, or due west.

However, it is a curious psychological fact that while a tenderfoot will rarely believe his compass if it indicates north in a different direction from his notion of it, yet rarely will that same tenderfoot doubt two compasses placed side by side, both their needles pointing in the same direction. He cannot conceive of two instruments going wrong in precisely the same way. Your sourdough knows that so long as his needle is balanced his compass is right. Therefore, if you must be guided by compass, carry two.

MEN FROZEN TO DEATH ON THE TRAIL

A NOTED EXPLORER once said that accidents in the wilds can always be traced to one of two things: Either ignorance of local conditions, or incompetence. And he spoke a true word. Let us consider a few actual instances of men who came to their death by way of adventure in the cold. I could cite many, but three or four will do.

I recall the case of a wood chopper on the Koyukuk River in northern Alaska who was found frozen to death on the trail. The "strong cold" was on—more than fifty below zero. His grub ran low, and instead of starting for Bettles, the nearest supply base, while still enough grub remained to feed him on the hundred mile trail, he waited too long, and when found with only twenty-five miles of the distance covered, his only remaining bit of food was a half chewed piece of raw bacon. A glaring case of incompetence. The man was not competent to do the thing he started out to do.

Another case is that of two chechakos who were frozen to death while attempting to cross the Yukon Flats with a sled outfit. Now, the sled is not used on the Yukon Flats. There was a good toboggan trail, and under ordinary circumstances no trouble would have been experienced had these men undertaken the two hundred and fifty mile traverse of the Flats with a toboggan. But they were ignorant of local conditions, so they started across that wind-swept barren with the sled, the runners of which were twenty inches apart. The toboggan trail was a sixteen inch trail, so one runner of the sled was continually dragging in the deep snow. Their dogs and themselves were soon worn out. They were bushed.

So much for the chechakos, and of course it is the chechakos or tenderfeet that furnish most of the casualties in the big country. But not always. Take the case of Inspector Fitzgerald of the Royal Northwest Mounted Police, one of the best men the North ever had. Ignorant of local conditions he certainly was not, and no man living should charge Fitzgerald with incompetence. Yet he and his patrol of three constables were frozen to death while attempting to carry the mail from Fort McPherson to Dawson in the winter of 1910-11. The reason? He wanted to make a record trip over the five hundred mile trail, so he cut the Arctic standard ration to two and one quarter pounds of food per man per day. He allowed no safety factor. Storms assailed him, the strong cold came on—fifty—sixty below zero. The Dawson trail was obliterated. The patrol was lost. Even then they could have saved themselves had they not waited too long before hitting the back trail. The grub gave out. They ate the dogs, even boiled the harness, but it was no use. Fitzgerald was the last to die. He was found within ten miles of Fort McPherson. He almost made it back—but not quite. Fitzgerald made two mistakes on that trip, and the mistakes were fatal. The first was in cutting down the Arctic standard of grub, and the second was in not turning back to Fort McPherson while he still had grub enough to take him there. If the making of mistakes spells incompetence—but I am not the one to impute incompetence to a man like Fitzgerald.

THE MISTAKES THE GILDE BOYS MADE

TO RETURN NOW to the Fife Lake tragedy. There would have been no Fife Lake tragedy had John and Willie Gilde known how to avoid making the mistakes they made, and had realized the importance of not making them.

The first mistake was, obviously, in disregarding the advice of their mother, who was wiser in weather lore than they.

Second: They started out in a cold drizzling rain without waterproof clothing. A word here regarding winter undercloth-ing. Wool is far superior to cotton. Even though you are able to keep dry, even a medium heavy wool undergarment is better than a heavy cotton one, for if you have a hard trail you are going to perspire, and the wool quickly absorbs this body moisture, and thus reduces the possibility of a chill when you sit down to rest. Furthermore, upon any venture into the woods in winter there is the possibility of getting thoroughly soaked to the skin. You may break through thin ice, or a sudden rise in temperature may bring down a torrent of rain. It is possible to remain reasonably warm and comfortable in wet woolens at temperatures even below zero, while cotton garments cling to your skin with a cold clammy chill that is deadly.

Third: They carried no matches! In point of importance this mistake easily takes first place. And right here let me say that even though their pockets had been full of matches, unless at least a part of those matches had been carried in a waterproof container, they would have been absolutely useless. For when found the two bodies were soaking wet to the skin, and the water from their saturated clothing had run down into their rubber boots. No matter how hard the wind blew, or how thick the snow fell, had the boys had the means of making a fire they would have experienced no danger. For in the cedar swamp there was an abundance of dry fuel, birch bark, dead cedar limbs, dead balsam, etc., that could have been gathered in a few moments and awaited only the touch of a match to spring into life-giving fire. The boys had a knife with them, but in this instance they could have built a fire and maintained it indefinitely by breaking dead branches with their hands. If when darkness overtook them in the swamp, they could have camped and dried their clothing beside a fire, all would have been well with them.

Fourth: When finally they emerged from the swamp they headed into the wind. Reasoning that as they had reached the swamp by traveling with their backs to the wind, they would reach home by heading into it. The wind had changed—but of this they knew nothing. And such a wind! Full-freighted with its heavy burden of snow, it drove out of the north, howling its unobstructed way across those stump-studded pine plains. In the pitch blackness of the night the wind was their only guide, and the wind proved false. In this particular instance, however, this last mistake was of no consequence. For, after struggling for hours through that dense swamp, chilled to the bone with the deadly chill of their wet clothing, at the point of physical exhaustion from toiling over logs and crashing through thick brush, utter body-weariness had already claimed them. The wonder is that they ever emerged from the swamp. But still game, still fighting the relentless storm, they pushed on into the very teeth of that snow-laden wind. Even had they come out on the south side of the swamp and headed directly for home, some two miles distant, their exhausted little bodies would never have made it.

On and on they pushed upwind, falling, struggling to their feet and wallowing a few rods further through the ever deepening snow, that clutched at their legs dragging them down. The older boy helping his little brother, until the time came when they fell to rise no more. But they were game to the last. Of such stuff are heroes made.

My hat is off to you, John and Willie Gilde!

As I stood beside that drear cherry bush, holding in my hand an empty shotgun shell that I had kicked out from under the deep snow—the shell that told the men of Fife Lake that the search was ended—I gazed for a long time over the half mile of bleak waste that lay between that bush and the swamp, and step by step I pictured that last brave struggle of those two little boys as they fought the darkness and the storm. And then my thoughts turned to a single newly dug grave, in the little cemetery at Fife Lake, at the bottom of which lie two small caskets side by side, and from that grave to the lonely farmhouse scarce three miles from where I stood, where certain Christmas presents have never been opened, and where a heartbroken mother sobbed out her story, and a little boy of three asks every day, "Where is Willie, Mama? Will Willie come home today?"

The tears froze on my glasses—and the pine plains blurred.

THE
HALFADAY
CREEK
LIBRARY

JAMES B. HENDRYX

James B. Hendryx's classic series returns to print! The author of more than 50 novels and anthologies, he's best known for his characters set around the outlaw community of Halfaday Creek in the Yukon. Set during the Gold Rush of the late 1890s, Hendryx penned over a hundred stories featuring these characters over the span of 25 years for a variety of pulp magazines.

Now, Altus Press has committed to return these to print. Using the original pulp magazines as the source material, along with the illustrations from their original pulp magazine appearances, these uniform edition books will be augmented with rare material taken from the James B. Hendryx archives held by the Leelanau Historical Society in Leland, MI.

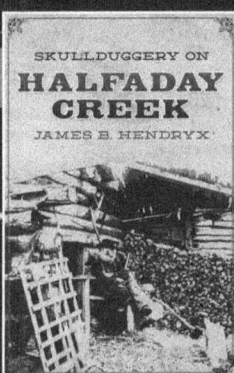

Leelanau Historical Society

Celebrating 150 Years of Leelanau History

Leelanau County was officially established in 1863 when the State of Michigan was a young 26 years old. People were attracted to the natural resources from the beginning—first as a way to earn a living and build a home, and later to enjoy recreation away from the cities. Early settlers arrived on the islands beginning in 1839, while Native Americans populated the Leelanau peninsula until pioneers began exploring the area in 1847. For the next 45 years, the villages known today—and some that are abandoned—were settled. North and South Manitou Islands and the Fox Islands officially joined the county in 1895.

The Leelanau Historical Society was launched in 1957 by a group of residents dedicated to collecting and preserving Leelanau's history. Leland, first established in 1853 and later the county seat, seemed the natural location for the Society. When the old county jail became available in 1959, the museum found its first home. Through generous donations and grants, a new museum was built in 1985 and later expanded.

Today, the collections and archives contain more than 11,000 items. Visitors to the museum learn about Leelanau life and maritime history from exhibits, educational programs and publications. The Society continues to collect, document and preserve items relating to Leelanau history.

203 East Cedar Street, Leland, MI 49654

Tel. (231) 256-7475

info@LeelanauHistory.org

http://www.leelanauhistory.org/

www.ingramcontent.com/pod-product-compliance
Lightning Source LLC
Chambersburg PA
CBHW071833020726
47502CB00004B/1341